D1230573

BONTSHE THE SILENT

I. L. PERETZ

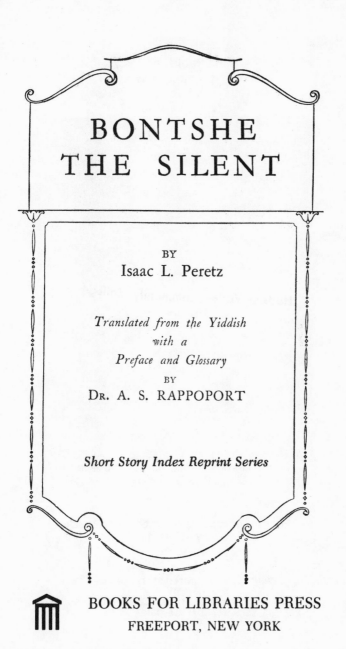

BONTSHE
THE SILENT

BY
Isaac L. Peretz

*Translated from the Yiddish
with a
Preface and Glossary*
BY
DR. A. S. RAPPOPORT

Short Story Index Reprint Series

BOOKS FOR LIBRARIES PRESS
FREEPORT, NEW YORK

First Published 1927
Reprinted 1971

INTERNATIONAL STANDARD BOOK NUMBER:
0-8369-4055-5

LIBRARY OF CONGRESS CATALOG CARD NUMBER:
77-178454

PRINTED IN THE UNITED STATES OF AMERICA
BY
NEW WORLD BOOK MANUFACTURING CO., INC.
HALLANDALE, FLORIDA 33009

PREFACE

ISAAC LOEB PERETZ was born at Samosj,
in the government of Lublin, on the 25th of May,
1851, and died at Warsaw in March, 1915. He
wrote first in Hebrew, but he is best known as an author
in Yiddish or Judæo-German, the dialect of the Jews
in Russia and Poland.

He is one of the most modern, the most powerful and
most European of Yiddish authors. In his stories
and sketches the influence of European literature is
more noticeable than in the work of other Yiddish
authors. Russian realism, the irony of Anatole
France, the symbolism of Maeterlinck and Ibsen, the
characteristics of the decadence school have in turn
exercised their influence upon Peretz, who was well
acquainted with general European literature. In
spite, however, of his capacity to assimilate, Peretz
always remains original. He assimilates but he does
not imitate. He has the advantage over other Yiddish
writers that his stories and sketches lose but little of
their comprehensibleness when translated into any
European language. Although the situations he
creates are drawn from Jewish life, Peretz does not
deal with specifically racial characteristics but with
their universal import. In his work local life does
not occupy the most prominent place as it does in the

work of other Yiddish writers. Like other Yiddish authors, Peretz, too, aims at the education of his people, but his sympathies are with humanity at large. Not only the Jews, but all those who suffer and are oppressed, who are groaning under social slavery, who have lost the power of thinking, knowing only the power of suffering, are the heroes in whom Peretz is interested. His stories, in spite of the symbolism underlying some of them, offer consolation, not only to the few, but to all the submerged and downtrodden who have an opportunity to read them. Peretz was the first to introduce in the Yiddish literature the human, all-too-human, element, and he has opened to the Yiddish reader new and vast horizons, for in his Yiddish types he really describes human types. Peretz's heroes are Jews, it is true, but they can just as well be French, British or American by the psychology and humanity which characterize them. And yet, Peretz rarely attempts to portray modern men and women, or to describe modern situations. His characters and themes are as a rule taken from the life of a bygone age.

Peretz is not a humorist, for his humour is always forced and never flows evenly, but he excels in his delineation of character and especially in his descriptions of psychological states of mind. In his stories and sketches where he describes pathological phases he reveals the master ; witness the story, " During the Epidemic," where the hero is led to suicide on account of an unsatisfied sexual desire. In " The Crazy

Beggar-Student " the hero, a sort of would-be Hamlet,
a Russian Raskolnikoff, is tortured by the question
" Who am I ? "   His thoughts are the tangled and
confused thoughts of a half-madman, and the author
reveals a wonderful psychological insight, describing
with the master hand of a Maupassant a play of
emotion, a human drama played within.   Frequently
suffering the pangs of hunger, despising and even hating
himself for his inactivity, this Hamlet of the Ghetto
is burning with a desire to be up and doing something.
But, alas, suffering and hunger have confused his
brain, and analysis has killed his will-power.   His
dreams of deeds are the dreams of a half-madman.

Peretz may be said to have really created the type
of the " batlen," whom he often describes with a rare
psychological insight.   The " batlen " is not only a
beggar-student, but generally a man who has no situation in life.   He shuns the struggle for life and is incapable of earning his living, compelled to live on the
charity of his co-religionists.   Peretz has treated the
type of the " batlen" not as a social, but as a psychological problem. He has described the soul of the " batlen," his inner struggles and agitations, the play of his
emotions, the drama that is often going on within him.
The author has shown the gigantic fight some of these
inactive beings have to wage against their instincts of
life, the passions and desires which they are never able
to gratify.

Although a realist, depicting life as it is, Peretz

also criticizes both the customs of the Ghetto and the social order. He often pleads for his heroes, but there is always an undercurrent of irony in his stories. His irony extends to superstitious religion and philosophy alike. He has a deep contempt for the conventional lies of religion and for intelligence devoid of love. His irony, however, extends to the false religious humility of both Jews and Christians. He is at once an artist and a novelist, both ethics and æsthetics having inspired his work.

Peretz has often been called an aristocrat in his tendencies. This is to a certain extent true, but he is an intellectual aristocrat who loves democracy. He is an aristocrat by temperament, but his sympathies are with the humble and oppressed, and he delights in describing their life. With a master hand he depicts the moral beauty, the heroism and the noble sentiments which dwell in the hearts of his heroes. Witness the stories : " The Messenger," " Domestic Peace," where even the working men and artisans, ignorant of the Holy Law, are treated with an exquisite sympathy.

What distinguishes Peretz in the history of Yiddish literature is the fact that he was the first to open new horizons. Whilst his predecessors and contemporaries only depicted the local customs and characteristic traits of the Ghetto, he drew from general sources of thought and inspiration and thus brought Yiddish literature nearer to modern European literature. Although addressing himself to a Jewish audience, his voice goes

*beyond the narrow racial circle, for he speaks to
humanity at large. He describes Jewish poverty, but
it is a poverty that appeals to human pity in general.
Tender and pathetic, analytical and psychological,
Peretz describes saintly love, marital affection, gentleness and unselfishness, and many other virtues. All
these virtues, brought out by suffering, are met with
in the humble Jewish families, but they are also common among the men and women of other nations, among
those who dwell on the lower scales of humanity.
Peretz's tender and sweet stories from the lives of
lonely Jews will therefore appeal to Jews and Gentiles
alike.*

ANGELO S. RAPPOPORT.

NOTE —*Hebrew and Yiddish words in italics are explained
in the glossary; the superior numbers refer to the notes.*

CONTENTS

		PAGE
I.	BONTSHE THE SILENT - - -	13
II.	WHAT IS THE SOUL? - - -	23
III.	THE MESSENGER - - - -	37
IV.	MARRIED - - - - -	49
V.	THE REPUDIATED DAUGHTER -	73
VI.	DOMESTIC PEACE - - -	77
VII.	IN THE BASEMENT - - -	83
VIII.	THE POOR BOY - - -- -	93
IX.	FOUR GENERATIONS—FOUR WILLS	105
X.	THE DEVOUT CAT - - -	111
XI.	THE CABBALISTS - - - -	115
XII.	HE WHO GIVES LIFE - - -	121
XIII.	MOONPEARLS AND OLD WARES -	145
XIV.	DEVIATING FROM THE RIGHT PATH	151
XV.	JOCHANAN THE GABBAY - -	155
XVI.	YENKEL THE PESSIMIST - -	159
XVII.	ORMUZD AND AHRIMAN - -	163
XVIII.	IF NOT HIGHER - - -	169
XIX.	THE CRAZY BEGGAR-STUDENT -	175
XX.	DURING THE EPIDEMIC - -	187
XXI.	THE MIRACLE OF HANOUKA -	219
XXII.	THE SICK BOY - - - -	227
XXIII.	THE STAGNANT POOL - - --	233
XIV.	VENUS AND THE SHULAMITE -	237
XXV.	SHAMMAI RATMAN - - -	245

I

BONTSHE THE SILENT

HERE, in this world below, the death of Bontshe produced no impression whatever. In vain you will ask : " Who was Bontshe ? How did he live ? What did he die of ? Was it his heart that burst, his strength that gave out, or his dorsal spine that broke under a burden too heavy for his shoulders ? " No one knows. Maybe it was hunger that killed him.

Had a bus horse fallen down in the street, people would have displayed much more interest than they did in this case of a poor man. The newspapers would have reported the incident, and hundreds of us would have hurried to the spot from every street to look at the poor carcass and examine the place where the accident had occurred. But were there as many horses as there are men—a thousand millions—then even a horse would not have received such distinction.

Bontshe had lived quietly, and quietly died ; like a shadow he passed over the face of the earth. At the ceremony of his circumcision no wine was drunk and no clinking of glasses was heard. When he celebrated his confirmation he made no brilliant speech. He lived like some dull grain of sand on the sea shore, disappearing among the millions of its kind. And when the wind at last carried him off to the other side, no one noticed it. In his life-time the soil of the roads never kept the impression of his footsteps, and after his death the wind swept away the small board over his grave. The grave-digger's wife found it at some distance from the grave and made a fire with it to boil a pot of potatoes. Three days only have passed since Bontshe's death, but you would ask the grave-digger in vain to show you the spot where he had buried him.

Had there been a tombstone over Bontshe's grave, a learned archæologist might have discovered it after a century, and once more the name of Bontshe would have been heard among us. He was only a shadow. No head or heart preserved his image, and no trace remained of his memory.

He left behind neither child nor property. He had lived miserably, and miserably he died. Had it not been for the noise of the crowd, someone might, by accident, have heard how Bontshe's vertebral column was snapping under a too heavy burden. Had the world had more time, someone might have noticed that during his life Bontshe's eyes were already dim and his cheeks terribly hollow. He might have noticed that even when he was not carrying loads on his shoulders his head was always bent to the ground, as if he were looking for his grave. Had there been as few poor people as there are horses in street buses someone might, perhaps, have asked : " What has become of Bontshe ? "

When they took him to the hospital, Bontshe's corner in the basement did not for long remain unoccupied ; ten people of his kind were already waiting for it, and they knocked it down among themselves to the highest bidder. When they carried him from his hospital bed to the mortuary chamber, twenty poor patients were already waiting for the place vacated. And scarcely had Bontshe left the morgue, when twenty corpses extricated from underneath the ruins of a house that had fallen down were brought in.

Who knows how long he will remain undisturbed in his grave ? Who knows how many corpses are already waiting for the piece of ground he is buried in ? Born quietly, he lived in silence, died in silence, and was buried in an even greater silence.

But it was not thus that things happened in the other world. There, the death of Bontshe produced a deep impression, a veritable sensation. The bugle-call of the Messiah, the sound of the ram's horn, was heard throughout the seven heavens : " Bontshe the Silent has died." Broad-winged archangels were flying about, announcing to each other that Bontshe had been summoned to appear before the Supreme Judgment Seat. In Paradise there was a noise, an excitement, and one could hear the joyful shout : " Bontshe the Silent ! Just think of it ! Bontshe the Silent ! "

Very young angels, with eyes of diamond, gold-threaded wings, wearing silver slippers, were rushing out, full of joy, to meet Bontshe. The buzzing of their wings, the clatter of their small slippers, and the merry laughter of those dainty, fresh, and rosy little mouths, filled the heavens and reached the throne of the Most High. God Himself knew that Bontshe was coming—

The Patriarch Abraham stationed himself at the gate of heaven, stretching out his right hand to Bontshe in cordial welcome : " Peace be with you," a sweet smile illuminating his delighted old countenance.

What means this rumbling and rolling here in heaven ? Two angels were rolling an armchair of pure gold for Bontshe. Whence this luminous flash of light ? It was a golden crown, set in with the most precious stones, that they were carrying—for Bontshe.

" But the Supreme Court has not yet pronounced judgment ? " ask the astonished saints, not without a tinge of jealousy."

" Bah ! " reply the angels, " that will only be a formality. Against Bontshe, even the attorney for the prosecution himself will not find a word to say. The case will not last five minutes. Don't you know who Bontshe is ? He is of some importance, this Bontshe."

When the little angels seized Bontshe in mid-air and played a sweet tune to him ; when the Patriarch Abraham

shook hands with him as if he had been an old comrade ;
when he learned that his chair was ready for him in
Paradise and that a crown was waiting for his head, that
before the celestial tribunal not one superfluous word
would be spoken in his case, Bontshe, as once upon earth,
was frightened into silence.   He was sure that it could
only be a dream from which he would soon awake, or
simply a mistake.

He was used to both.   More than once, when he was
still on earth, he had dreamed of picking up money from
the floor.   Veritable treasures were lying there !—and yet
—when he awoke in the morning, he was more miserable
and poorer than ever.   More than once it had happened
to him that someone in the street had smiled at him and
spoken a kind word to him.   But when he found out his
mistake, the stranger turned and spat out in disgust, full of
contempt.   " Just my luck," thought Bontshe, scarcely
daring to raise his eyes, afraid lest the dream should
disappear.   He is trembling at the thought of suddenly
waking up in some horrible cavern full of serpents and
lizards.   He is careful not to let the slightest sound escape
his mouth, to stir or move a limb for fear of being recognized and hurled into the abyss.   He trembles violently,
and does not hear the compliments paid to him by the
angels, nor does he notice how they are dancing around
him.   He pays no heed to the Patriarch's cordial " Peace
be with you," nor does he even wish good-morning to the
celestial court when he is at last brought in.   He is simply
beside himself with fear.

His fear increased greatly when his eyes involuntarily
fell upon the flooring of the Supreme Court of Justice.
It was of pure alabaster, inset with diamonds.   " And my
feet," thought Bontshe, " are treading such a floor ! "   He
grew quite stiff.   " Who knows," he thought, " what
rich man, what Rabbi, what saint they are expecting ?   He
will soon arrive and mine will be a sad end ! "

Terror-stricken, he did not even hear the President of
the Court call out in a loud voice :   " The case of Bontshe
the Silent ! "   He did not hear how, handing over a

dossier to the counsel for the defence, he commanded :
" Read, but briefly." All around Bontshe the whole hall
seemed to be turning. A muffled noise reached his ears,
but in the midst of the din he began to distinguish more
clearly and sharply the voice of the angelic advocate—a
voice as sweet as a violin :

" His name," the voice was saying, " suited him even
as a gown made by an artist's hand suits a graceful body."

" What is he talking about ? " Bontshe asks himself.
And then he heard an impatient voice interrupting the
speaker :

" No metaphors, please."

" Never," continues the advocate, " never has he
uttered a complaint against God or men. Never has a
spark of hatred flamed up in his eyes, never has he lifted
his eyes with pretensions to heaven."

Again Bontshe fails to understand what it is all about,
but once more the harsh voice interrupts the speaker :

" No rhetoric, please."

" Job succumbed, but Bontshe has suffered more than
Job."

" Facts, dry facts, please," the President emphatically
calls again.

" He was circumcised on the eighth day."

" Yes, yes, but no realism, please."

" The clumsy barber-surgeon could not stanch the
blood—— "

" Go on, go on."

" He was always silent," the advocate proceeds, " even
when his mother died and at the age of thirteen there came
a stepmother, a serpent, a wicked woman."

" Perhaps after all he means me," thinks Bontshe to
himself.

" No insinuations, please, against third persons," angrily
says the President.

" She used to begrudge him a piece of bread ; throw
him a few musty crusts three days old and a mouthful of
tendons for meat, whilst she herself drank coffee with
cream."   2

" Come to business ! " cries the President.

" She never spared him her finger nails, blows, or cuffs, and through the holes of his miserable musty rags there peeped out the blue and black body of the child.   Barefooted he used to chop wood for her in winter, in the biting frost.   His hands were too young and too weak to wield the dull axe, and the blocks were too big.   More than once did he sprain his wrists, more than once were his feet frozen, but he remained silent.   He was silent even before his father——— "

" Oh, yes, the drunkard," laughs the accusing attorney, and Bontshe feels cold all over.

" Even to his father he never complained," the advocate concludes.

" He was always miserable and alone, had no friends, no schooling, no religious instruction, no decent clothes and not a minute of respite."

" Facts, facts," the President once more interrupts.

" He was silent even later, when his own father, the worse for drink, seized him by the hair and threw him out of the house on a bitterly cold and snowy winter night.   He picked himself up from the snow, without weeping, and ran whither his eyes carried him.   He was silent during his lonely walk, and when the pangs of hunger began to torture him, he begged only with his eyes.

" On a wet and foggy spring night he reached a large town.   He entered it like some drop of water that is falling into the ocean, but he nevertheless passed his first night in the police jail.   He was silent, without asking the why or wherefore.   Set free, he started to look for work, for the hardest work possible ; but he was silent.   What was even harder than work itself, was the finding of it, and he was silent.   He was always silent.   Splashed by the mud thrown at him by strangers, spat upon by strangers, driven with his heavy load from the sidewalk into the midst of the road, among cabs, cars, coaches, and vehicles of every sort—at every instant looking death in the face, he remained silent.   Bathed in a cold sweat, crushed under the heavy loads he was carrying, his stomach empty and tortured, he was silent.

" He never calculated how many pounds he was carrying for a farthing, how often he stumbled for a penny and how many errands he had to run, how many times he almost breathed his last when going to collect his pay. He was always silent. He never dared to raise his voice when asking for his pay, but like a beggar or a dog he stood at the door and his dumb and humble request could only be read in his eyes. ' Come later,' he was told, and he disappeared like a shadow until later, when he would ask even more quietly, nay beg for his due. He was silent even when people haggled for his pay, knocked off something from it, or slipped a counterfeit coin into his hand. He was always silent ! "

" Then after all it is me that they mean," Bontshe consoles himself.

" One wonderful day Bontshe's fortune changed," proceeded the advocate, after taking a drink of water. " Two spirited, frightened, runaway horses were rushing by, dragging a rich coach with rubber wheels. With a broken skull the driver lay way back on the pavement. Foam was spurting from the mouths of the animals, sparks flew from their hoofs, and their eyes shone like glowing coals on a dark night. In the coach, there sat a man, more dead than alive. Bontshe stopped the runaway horses. The man whose life he had thus saved was a Jew ; he proved to be of a charitable disposition and was grateful to Bontshe. He handed over to him the whip of his dead coachman, and Bontshe became a driver. The charitable man even found him a wife. He did more : he provided Bontshe with a child. And Bontshe always kept silent."

" They mean me ; they mean me," thought Bontshe, strengthening himself in his belief ; but nevertheless he dared not raise his eyes on the august tribunal. Still he listened to his angelic advocate.

" Bontshe was silent," continued the latter, " even when his benefactor became bankrupt and neglected to pay Bontshe his wages. He was silent when his wife ran away

from him, leaving him alone with an infant in arms.   He
was silent even fifteen years later, when the same child
grew up till he was strong enough to throw the father out
of his own house."

"They mean me ; they mean me," Bontshe thinks
joyfully.

"He was silent," continued the defending angel, as his
voice grew still softer and more sad, "when his former
benefactor paid all his creditors except Bontshe, to whom
he did not give a penny.   And when, riding again in his
coach with rubber tyres and with horses like lions, the
benefactor one day ran him over, Bontshe still kept silent.
He did not even tell the police.   Even in the hospital
where one is allowed to cry, he kept silent !   He was silent
even when the house physician refused to approach his
bed unless he had paid him fifteen coppers, or when the
attendant refused to change his bed linen unless he gave
him five coppers.

"He was silent in his death agony, he was silent in his
last hour.   Never did he utter a word against God, never
a word against man.   I have spoken."

Bontshe began to tremble in his whole body.   He knew
that after the speech for the defence it was the turn of the
prosecution.   "What will the prosecuting counsel say
now ? "   Bontshe did not remember his life.   Down
below he used to forget everything the moment it occurred.
The angel advocate had recalled to his mind all his past.
Who knows what the prosecuting angel will recall to his
memory ?

"Gentlemen judges," begins a strident, incisive, and
stinging voice—but stops short.

"Gentlemen," he begins again, this time more softly,
but once more he interrupts himself.

And at last, very soft, a voice issues from the throat of
the accuser :

"Gentlemen judges !   He was silent !   I shall be silent
too."

Profound silence fell over the assembly.   Then from
above a new soft, sweet, and trembling voice is heard :

"Bontshe, my child, Bontshe," said the voice, and it sounded like a harp; "Bontshe, my well-beloved child."

And Bontshe's heart begins to weep for joy. He would like to raise his eyes, but they are dimmed by tears. Never in his life had he felt such joy in weeping.

"My child, my well-beloved!" Since his mother's death he had never heard such a voice or such words.

"My child," continues the President of the Celestial Tribunal, "you have suffered everything in silence. There is not a limb in your body that is whole, not a bone that is intact, not a corner in your soul that is not bleeding—and you have always kept silent.

"Down below upon earth they never understood such things. You yourself were not aware of your power; you did not know that you could cry and that your cries would have caused the very walls of Jericho to tremble and tumble down. You yourself did not know what strength lay hidden in you. Down below your silence was not rewarded, but down below is the world of falsehood; whilst here in heaven in the world of truth, here you will reap your reward.

"The Supreme Tribunal will never pass sentence against you; it will never judge and condemn you, nor will it mete out to you such and such a reward. Everything here belongs to you; take whatever your heart desires."

For the first time Bontshe ventures to lift his eyes. He is dazzled by so much light and splendour. Everything is sparkling, everything around him is flashing, beams are issuing from all sides, and he droops his weary eyes once more.

"Really?" he asks, still doubting and embarrassed.

"Yes, really," replies the President of the Celestial Tribunal; "verily I tell you that it is so indeed, and that everything here is yours; everything in heaven belongs to you. All the brightness and the splendour you perceive is only the reflection of your own silent goodness of heart, the reflection of your own pure soul. You will only be drawing from your own source."

"Really?" Bontshe asks again, but this time his voice sounds more firm and assured.

"Certainly, certainly, certainly," he is assured on all sides.

"Then, if such is the case," says Bontshe with a happy smile, "I should like to have every morning a hot roll with fresh butter."

Abashed, angels and judges drooped their heads; whilst the accuser burst out into loud laughter.

II

WHAT IS THE SOUL?

———

I RECOLLECT as if in a dream a short little Jew with a thin pointed beard, who used to walk about in our house, and who from time to time caught me up in his arms, covering me with kisses. Afterwards, I again remember the same little Jew lying ill in bed and groaning; whilst my mother, standing at the bedside, was beating her head with her fist.

One night I suddenly woke up and saw our house full of Jews; whilst heartrending cries and lamentations reached my ears. Growing frightened, I began to howl. One of the Jews came up to me, dressed me, and taking me by the hand, brought me to the house of a neighbour, where I passed the night. When I returned the following morning I scarcely recognized my home. Straw lay strewn all over the floor, the big mirror had been turned to the wall, the chandelier covered with a tablecloth; whilst my mother, without shoes and in stockinged feet, was sitting on a low footstool on the floor.[1] Catching sight of me, she burst out into weeping, sobbing aloud: " The orphan, the orphan." On the window-sill I noticed a burning night-lamp by the side of which stood a glass of water covered with a rag.[2]

They told me that my father was dead, and that his soul was purifying itself in the water and drying itself with the rag. If I earnestly and conscientiously recited the *Kaddish*, then my dead father's soul would soar up straight to heaven. And I imagined the soul to be a bird.

One day, when my schoolmaster's assistant was taking me home, I saw not far from our house a few birds flying very low. "Little souls are flying," I exclaimed.

The assistant looked round and said: "Go on, you silly fool, they are only birds, ordinary birds."

I asked my mother about it: "Mother, how can one tell the difference between a soul and an ordinary bird?"

When I had attained the age of fourteen I was already studying the *Talmud* with the commentaries of *Rashi*, the *Tosafot*, and *Maharsha*, with my master, Zorah Pinch. Even to-day I know not whether Pinch was really his surname, or merely a nickname given to him by his pupils on account of his habit of pinching them mercilessly. He never waited until we had really deserved punishment, but would generously pay in advance. "Remind me of it," he would say to the victim, "and I will deduct it next time." As he was also the operator in the rite of circumcision he had a very sharp nail[1] so that every pinch of his cut us in the flesh, taking away our breath. And he used to taunt us, saying:

"Why art thou crying? Don't cry for nothing. I am only pinching thy *body*; what harm can it do unto thee? Why shouldst thou care if the worms in the grave have less to eat?

"The body," he went on, "is only dust and mud. Do you want a proof of it? Rub your hands one against the other and you will see."

We applied the test, and convinced ourselves that indeed the body was only mud and dust.

"And what is the soul?" I asked.

"The soul is spirit," replied the master.

Zorah Pinch hated his wife like poison; but for all that he cherished his daughter, Shprinze, like the apple of his eye. We, on the contrary, hated Shprinze because she used to denounce us to her father, whilst we loved the *Rebbetzin* because she sold broad beans and peas on credit,

and more than once she had saved us from the hands of
the master.

It was I who stood highest in the favour of the *Rebbetzin*.
I used to get the biggest overmeasure, and when the
master was about to lay hands on me, she would exclaim :
" Murderer, what dost thou want of the poor orphan ?
His father's soul will surely take vengeance on thee."

He would let me go ; but it was his wife who got my
share of pinches, cuffs, and blows.

I remember how one winter night I came home from
school, my flesh so pinched and numbed by the bitter
frost that I was aching in every limb. Lifting up my
eyes to heaven, I sobbed bitterly and thus I prayed :
" Father, dear, revenge me on Zorah Pinch ! Master of
the Universe ! " I cried, " what does he want of my soul ? "
I had entirely forgotten that he was only pinching my
body, but " man is not master over his sufferings."

On certain holidays, however, Zorah would close the
big folio of the *Talmud* and tell us stories. He then
became quite another man. He would take off his cap
and remain with his head covered with feathers under
which his velvet skull-cap was scarcely visible. He would
unbutton his coat, a smile would hover round his lips,
and his very voice would change.

When he was teaching us he used his loud, angry voice,
the voice in which he spoke to his wife ; but he told us
stories in the gentle, soft voice which he assumed when
talking to Shprinze, his " dear soul."

We were always begging him, like one who endeavours
to raise the pity of a brigand, to tell us a story. We did
not know then that Zorah knew only one chapter of the
tractate, *Baba Mezia*, with which he began and finished
the school term. He was thus compelled to fill out the
time with stories, especially during the long winter term,
when there were no festivals. And we fools, ignorant of
this fact, used to pay heavily in broad beans and peas for
such stories. One day we even raised money among
ourselves to buy Shprinze a red spencer. For this gift
Zorah Pinch told us how the Lord was choosing souls

from his treasure store and blowing them into bodies. And I used to imagine that the souls were stored up in the treasure house of the Lord like the goods in my mother's shop—in all sorts of cardboard boxes, red, green, and white, tied up with a piece of string.

" And when the Lord," so the master told us, " chooses a soul and commands her to descend upon earth, she trembles and weeps. Later on an angel visits the soul in the mother's womb and teaches her the entire *Torah*. As the moment of birth approaches, the angel gives the child a tap on the nose, and the soul immediately forgets all that she has learned. That is the reason," explained our teacher, " all Jewish boys have a sort of furrow in their upper lips."

Towards the evening of the same day we went out of town to skate, and there we met some Christian boys of our acquaintance. To my great surprise, I noticed that Yantek, Voytek, and Yashek also had a furrow on their upper lips, just as we Jewish boys had.

" Yashek," I asked one of them, risking my life in doing so, " Yashek, hast thou, too, a soul ? "

" And what the devil has that to do with thee, thou soul of a dog ? " was his sweet and clear reply.

In addition to my studies with the Talmud teacher, I had also another teacher to instruct me in the art of penmanship. He had the reputation in the town of being a great heretic, and none of his neighbours would ever dream of borrowing from him, or lending him any kitchen utensils.[1]   He was a widower, and no one in the town believed that his daughter, Gittelé, a girl of my own age, was capable of making meat strictly *kosher*. This master, however, was very accomplished, and my mother was anxious that her only son should learn to write.

" I beg you, Mr. teacher," she said, " not to teach the child any heretic subjects. Do not read the *Books of the Prophets* or the *Hagiographs*, with him, but simply teach him how to write an ordinary letter, a letter beginning with ' My dear friend '."

And yet I am not sure that my master kept his word.

When I told him the story of the furrowed upper lips, he flew into a violent rage, jumped up from his seat and, pushing back the chair with his foot, began to pace up and down the room, shouting : " Ignoramuses, assassins, bats ! " Gradually, however, he grew calmer, sat down again, polished his glasses, and drawing me towards himself, said :

" Don't believe all this nonsense, my child. You have seen the Gentile boys on the ice ? You have observed them ? What are their names ? "

I told him their names.

" Well," said he, " has any of these boys other eyes than yourself, other hands, other legs, or is there any part of their body that is differently shaped from yours ? Don't they laugh just like you, and when they are crying do their tears differ in any way from the tears you yourself are shedding ? Why, then, should they not have a soul even as you have ? No, my child, men are all the same, are all equally the cherished children of the same God, who is their common father, and the same earth is their country !

" It is true," continued my master, " that to-day the nations hate each other, every one imaging that it is *the* nation, the chosen one, the crown of all nations, the favourite of the Lord. We hope, however, that better times will dawn for humanity—days when the nations will all recognize one God, and obey *one* law ; days when the words of our prophets will come true. Then wars will cease, envy and hatred will disappear, and all will serve and worship one Creator, and the words of our Prophet will come true—' For from Zion will come forth the Law.' "

The words of the Prophet were familiar to me, as I was in the habit of reciting them in my morning prayers.

My master continued to talk for a long time, although I understood but little of his fine words. I found it difficult to believe in the equality of all men, or that a Gentile was also possessed of intelligence. I knew that my master was a heretic, an unbeliever, that he did not even believe in the transmigration of the soul. And yet, did I not see with my own eyes how after the death of Fradel the fast woman, a black dog was walking about on the top of the roof of the house she had occupied ? Then again my master of penmanship never cut his nails according to the prescribed ritual ; that is to say, only cutting every other nail and burning them with a piece of wood. He used simply to throw the pieces out of the window.[1] More than once I made up my mind to run away from my master ; to tell my mother that he was blaspheming God and His Messiah. I would have run away from him, had it not been for . . . but, no doubt, you have already guessed whom I have in mind.

Some of my master's words, however, stayed in my mind and produced an impression upon me. I firmly believed that soon the time would come when all the nations would learn wisdom from Israel. In our small town all were firmly persuaded that the days of Israel's redemption, and the arrival of the Messiah, were near at hand. People found this prophecy in the book of *Daniel*, in passages from the *Zohar*, and in an apocryphal *Midrash*. It was whispered that the Rabbi of Kosenitz had given up reciting the confession of sins in his daily prayers, which is only done on high festivals and half-holidays. News had also come from Palestine that no fox had appeared in the course of the year on the Wall of Lamentation, which is supposed to be a sure omen that the Messiah is on the point of appearing.

All the inhabitants were preparing for the advent of the Messiah, and the community did its best to delay the paying of rates and taxes. " Soon," they said, " the Messiah will be here, and then the local authorities will never dream of claiming the arrears from the Jews." As for myself, I was firmly convinced that in a very short time that self-same Yashek, my Gentile playmate, who had stretched out his leg whilst I was skating on the ice and performing a " cobbler " so that I nearly broke my neck ; that Voytek and Yantek, who caused me much misery, would all humbly approach me and ask me for the solution of a

question of ritual law. I, of course, being a merciful son
of Israel, would not harbour in my heart any feeling of
revenge against them, but would readily forgive and
instruct them in the Law. I would reveal unto them the
secret of the paper and the iron bridges. (It is well known
that at the advent of the Messiah the wicked will pass over
an iron bridge and be drowned, whilst the just will safely
pass over a cardboard bridge.) I would tell my Gentile
playmates not to dare cross the iron bridge. The best
thing, however, I thought, would be for them to keep
away from both bridges, and thus save their souls.

On New Year's eve I completed my course of instruction
in one chapter of the Talmud, and felt as happy as the Jews
must have felt when they were redeemed from Egyptian
bondage. I was told that my new teacher, Rabbi Yosel,
never pinched his pupils nor did he beat them without
cause. I had frequently seen Rabbi Yosel in the Synagogue and knew him well. He was a tall Jew with very
thick eyebrows and long lashes, so that you could scarcely
perceive his eyes. He frequently wore his coat unbut-
toned, and from beneath the two points of his long white
beard there peeped out his *talith katan*. Rabbi Yosel
was in the habit of treading softly and talking in a subdued
voice, as if everything he did was fraught with mystery.
He used to nod his head mysteriously, raise his eyebrows,
wrinkle his forehead, purse up his lips, thrusting both his
hands into his girdle. I had the impression that every
word he uttered was full of exceptional meaning and
significance, and that he was really soaring to dizzy
heights.

Formerly Rabbi Yosel had been a *delegate* of one of the
Rabbis of the *Hassidim*, and even now he used to sell
various objects on the Rabbi's behalf, such as blessed oil,
coins, amulets, and talismans. He was the foremost
expert in our town at reciting a formula against an evil
eye, and whenever the local Rabbi happened to be unwell,
it was Rabbi Yosel who preached in his stead the sermon
on the *Great Sabbath* and on New Year's day, or pronounced a funeral oration. The local Rabbi, being a

man of advanced age, weak, and feeble, it was generally expected the Rabbi Yosel would succeed him, after " a hundred and twenty years."[1]   Rabbi Yosel was also a wonderful *Baal Tekiah* (blower of the ram's horn), and when he recited the blessing before blowing the ram's horn, all the worshippers literally trembled like fish in water.

I was very proud of becoming a pupil of Rabbi Yosel. Even before the Day of Atonement, I found an opportunity to talk with him about the soul.   The soul had indeed become a sort of *idée fixe* with me, haunting my thoughts and giving me no respite.

First of all, Rabbi Yosel did his best to cure me of all that nonsense about the fraternity of nations, and to inspire me with the ambitious idea of a " chosen race."

" It is not without good reason," said he, " that we are in exile, subject to all sorts of humiliations and plagues not even mentioned in Holy Scripture.   Had we been like the other nations, then we, too, should have had our share of joy and pleasure in this world below.   The child whom the father loveth he punisheth, to induce him to study the Law and reach all the gates of intelligence."

" And yet," continued Rabbi Yosel, " even among us Jews not all souls are equal.   There are vulgar, common souls ; souls, for instance, like that of your teacher, Zorah Pinch, whilst your master of penmanship has a soul similar to that of Korah.   There are, on the other hand, high souls, very high souls, some of them come straight from the channel underneath the throne of glory.[2]   There are also superior souls which have the quality of fine flour."

I confess that I understood but little of these qualities and distinctions among the souls, and especially of that channel underneath the throne of glory.   I understood, however, what was meant by fine flour, and I imagined the difference between the various souls to be somewhat similar to the difference existing between barley, rye, or wheat flour, and that particularly fine flour employed for the *halah*, which is baked for the Sabbath.   The most superior souls, I imagined, must be made with *saffron* and raisins.

"The principal thing, however," said Rabbi Yosel, "is suffering. No soul is ever lost, for all must return to the degree they had occupied before they descended into this world below. And the souls are purified by means of suffering. The Creator of the Universe, in His great mercy, sends us suffering, to remind us that we are only flesh and blood, a broken shell; that we are nothing. He only has to cast one glance upon us, and we dissolve into dust. In the next world, too, the souls are being purified by suffering."

Thereupon Rabbi Yosel told me all about the poor souls, and what suffering they had to undergo in the seven spheres of hell.

At the approach of the Feast of Tabernacles, being still free from school, I had leisure to watch what was going on in our household. It happened to be a washing day —and during the night I dreamed that I was in the next world. I saw angels extending their hands from heaven to seize the little souls returning from the earth. A choice was made among these souls and only the pure souls, white like driven snow, soared up like doves, flying straight into Paradise, whilst the polluted sinful souls were thrown into a big heap and hurled into the icy ocean. There, black angels were standing and snatching up the poor souls to wash them thoroughly. Thereupon the souls were placed in big black pots and boiled in the fire of hell. And when this soiled washing was being pressed so as to squeeze out the dirt, the groans and lamentations of the poor souls were heard from one end of the world to the other.

In that piled-up heap of soiled linen, I recognized the soul of my teacher of penmanship. I saw his long nose, his hollow cheeks, and his pointed little beard; and he was wearing his blue glasses. The more his soul was being washed, the blacker it grew.

Thereupon an angel called out: "This is the soul of the teacher, the heretic"; and turning to me, he continued in an angry voice : " If you walk in his ways, your soul, too, will become as soiled as his, and nightly will it be washed until it is doomed to eternal perdition."

" No, no," I cried in my sleep, " I will not walk in his ways." My mother woke me up, removing my hand from my chest.

" What is the matter with you, my pet ? " she asked in a frightened voice, " you are perspiring and wet all over. *Pfu, pfu, pfu*," she spat, and blew over me.

" Mother," I said, " I have been in the next world."

On the following morning my mother asked me quite seriously whether I had come across my father during my visit to the next world.

" No," I replied.

" That is a great pity," she answered, " for I am sure that he would have sent some message for me."

But what was the good of all this when my teacher of penmanship merely laughed at me and my dreams ? I was anxious to save his soul and told him my dream, but he only replied that dreams were nonsense and that he cared nothing for them. He tried to convince me by quoting passages from the Bible and the *Talmud*, where it is said that dreams were rubbish ; but I stopped my ears, refusing to listen to him.

I now saw clearly that his soul was doomed to perdition, that his end would be a terrible one, and that it was my duty to avoid him as if he were a harmful beast ; for he wanted to kill my soul, my young soul.

But what was the good ? A hundred times had I promised myself to tell my mother everything, but I never kept my word. A hundred times I had come to her to unburden my heart, but every time methought that I saw Gittelé standing behind my mother, spreading out her tiny hands, beckoning to me and imploring me with her big eyes not to say anything. And the silent prayer of her eyes proved stronger than my piety. I felt that for her I would do anything, not only throw myself into water or fire, but even allow my soul to be damned and go down to perdition.

Alas! It was a great pity, though. My mother, my teachers, and the talmudical scholars in our town, firmly believed that I was destined to become a great man one day. Although I had now escaped from the terrible nail of Zorah Pinch, I was not much happier in the hands of Rabbi Yosel.

I had already attained the ripe age of sixteen, and my mother was being besieged by our marriage-brokers and match-makers. And yet my conduct and behaviour were still very childish. On the evening following the Day of Atonement I was still in the habit, like the other boys, of collecting the pieces of wax that trickled from the wax candles. Even during my studies I used to hide my hands under the table and knead the wax into all sorts of shapes and forms. I incurred the enmity of the beadle of our synagogue, who hated me like poison, and I had also to suffer much misery at school.

"Where are you now?" Reb Yosel asked me suddenly one day. Plunged in my meditations, I was taken unawares, and quickly withdrawing my hand from under the table, I pointed out the passage of the *Talmud* with my wax-covered fingers.

Reb Yosel grew pale with fury. Quietly, without uttering a word, he opened a drawer, took out a thin string with which he tied up my two thumbs. He squeezed them so hard that I nearly fainted. But that was not all. My master rose, fetched the broom, quietly selected a very thin, flexible rod and then began to belabour my two tied-up hands. How long did it last? It seemed to me that it was an eternity, though strangely enough, I never uttered a cry, but willingly accepted the suffering. I was thinking that God was sending these sufferings to me, so that I might repent and give up visiting my master of penmanship. When my hands were terribly swollen and the skin lacerated all over, showing all sorts of colours, Reb Yosel laid down the rod and quietly observed:

"That will do! I do not think that you will knead wax any more."

But I continued to knead my wax.

3

I used to derive a considerable amount of joy from this occupation of wax-kneading; when I could shape it according to my wish, I felt that I was dominating something. It amused me to shape the head of a man which I turned into a cat or a mouse, and then again transformed into an eagle. And yet in the hands of others I was myself like wax. They could do what they liked with me, Reb Yosel, my master of penmanship, or my mother. As for Gittelé, she made me melt. They could shape me as if I had been a piece of wax, but it hurt. I recollect quite well that it *did* hurt. But why? Why did I worry so much about the soul? My comrades often made fun of me and gave me the nickname of "Soul-boy." And this nickname, stupid though it was, caused me a lot of suffering.

Sometimes, when I was deep in thought, considering how best I could escape from the hands of Satan; when I was examining my own soul, settling accounts with her, reading her a moral lesson, someone would suddenly give me a tap on the nose and call out, "Soul-boy!" At other times, trying to forget my suffering, I would try to plunge into deep study, and for a time succeeded in driving the thoughts of the master, of Gittelé and of the soul out of my mind. No sooner, however, has someone whispered into my ear, "Soul-boy," than I once more became aware of my suffering. During prayers I recited with fervour and devotion the words, "Heal us, O Lord," meaning not my body but my soul. "Lord of the Universe," I prayed, "heal my poor young soul!" But someone had only to point at me and say, "That is the soul-boy praying," and all my devotion was gone from me.

Thus I suffered constantly. Gittelé was generally considered to be a very intelligent girl; and her father used to refer to her as "my clever girl." The neighbours used to say that the girl was as wise as the day, and if only her piety had been as great as her intelligence, her mother would have rejoiced in Paradise. My own mother frequently praised her, and said that if she had only been able to prepare *kosher* meat according to the ritual prescriptions, she might have made a perfect daughter-in-law.

One day, coming for my lesson, I found my master out and Gittelé alone in the house. The thought suddenly occurred to me to question her about the soul. I was trembling all over, my heart was beating fast, and all my blood rushed up to my face. Lowering my eyes to the ground, I said :

" Gittelé, they all say that you are very wise and intelligent ; tell me, I beg you, what is the soul ? "

She smiled, and shrugging her shoulders replied, " I have not the least notion."

But suddenly she had grown very sad, and tears welled up in her eyes.

" I remember," she said, " that when my mother was still alive, my father used to call her ' his soul '—they loved each other so much."

I do not know how it happened, but suddenly seizing Gittelé's hands, I asked her : " Gittelé, would you like to be my soul ? "

In an almost inaudible whisper she replied, " Yes."

We were lucky in more than one way. First of all, it was lucky that both Gittelé and myself were orphans, and the only children of our respective parents. It was so much easier to obtain the consent of our parents for our marriage. It was also lucky that my master had saved up a few hundred roubles, as a dowry for his daughter, and my mother happened to need the money greatly for her shop. Then, again, it was lucky that I had gained the reputation of being a heretic, although, of course, I was innocent of the accusation. The rumour, however, had spread in the town, and no one was anxious to choose me as a prospective son-in-law. It was, above all, lucky that I had procured the services of a match-maker, Zippe the wadding-maker, to whom I had promised a lot of money. Being the most expert and clever marriage-broker in the town, this lady soon arranged everything satisfactorily. And yet my mother was always crying over me.

" Ah," she said, " if your father were to rise up and see

to whom you are affianced, he would return to his grave for very shame."

It was then that I saw what I must do. One night I began to cry in my sleep. When my mother hastened to wake me and anxiously inquired what was the matter, I told her that I had been in the next world, and seen my father. I said that he not only sent her greeting but had given me his blessing and consented to my marriage with Gittelé. Thus I had found a new soul.

III

THE MESSENGER

HE is walking along; the wind is lifting the skirts of his long garment and blowing back his white beard. From time to time he lifts his right hand and touches his left side, because he feels there something like a sudden shooting pain, although he does not care to admit it even to himself. In spite of the pain, he endeavours to persuade himself that he is only feeling his inner pocket.

"Provided only," he says, "I do not lose either the contract or the money!"

That is what he is pretending to be afraid of.

"And even if I do feel some sort of acute pain in my side, what of that? Of what importance is it? Thank God, I am still strong enough to go on such an errand. At my age, others would not have been able to walk even one *verst*, but I, praised be the Lord, I do not require the help of men. I am still capable of earning my own living. Heaven be praised, people are trusting me with considerable sums of money.

"Of course," he continues, "if I could call my own, such sums of money as people are entrusting me with, I should not go on errands at seventy years of age; but since such is not the will of the Most High, then it is well."

The snow begins to fall in thick flakes, and the old man wipes his face from time to time. "I have only another half a mile to walk. *Ouvah!* Call this an errand? I have already walked the greatest part of the way."

He turns round. Neither belfry nor church nor barracks are any longer to be seen. "Come on, Shmarya, get a move on." And Shmarya is moving along through the wet snow, his old feet are wading and sinking deeply into it. The wind, however, praised be the Lord, is not blowing too fiercely.

For this old man a fierce wind was evidently nothing less than a squall. Though, as a matter of fact, the wind was blowing quite fiercely and so mercilessly lashing his poor face that it was continually taking his breath away. The tears were flowing from his eyes, tears pricking like needles and making his eyes smart; but then he was always suffering from his eyes. An idea occurred to him. With the first money he was going to earn he would buy a pair of eyeglasses, those big, round glasses which completely cover and protect the eyes.

" If only God wills, then I shall soon be able to manage it. I should only have to get some commission every day, and go on long, very long, errands. Thank God, I am quite used to it; and thus I shall soon save the money for a pair of eyeglasses."

Of course, he would also require some sort of fur coat to enable him to breathe more easily. But he suddenly changes his mind. Has he not a warm overcoat? This coat is still quite excellent, if it would only not wear out and get torn. He smiles quite contentedly.

" This coat," he thinks, " has not been made out of that flimsy stuff, the mere cobweb they are selling nowadays. It is the strong serge of the good old days. Such a coat will outlive me, and last when I am no longer here. Then it has another advantage: it has no split at the back, whilst in front the skirts are covering each other to the extent of a good ell."

" It is true," he thinks, " that a little fur coat would be preferable, because it keeps one properly warm, very warm." Yes, but first he needed the eyeglasses. A fur coat is useful only in winter, whilst one always needs eyeglasses. When the wind is blowing strongly in summer, hurling all the dust into one's eyes, it is even worse than in winter.

So he makes up his mind to buy first the eyeglasses and then the little fur coat. May it please God that it should be he who would be sent to collect all the money for the wheat; then he could surely earn at least four gulden.

He continues to drag his legs; the wet snowflakes are lashing his face, the wind is blowing more fiercely and the shooting pain in his side is becoming more acute. Ah, if the wind would only turn, but no doubt it is better thus.

" On my return journey," he thinks, " I shall be rather tired, and then it will be an advantage to have the wind behind me. Oh, I shall walk much faster then!" So all has been arranged for the best, he thinks, and feels quite light-hearted.

He is compelled to stand still for a moment, so as to get his breath, and this rather worries him.

" What is the matter with me?" he is asking himself rather sadly, and a little frightened. " How many squalls and gales have I not faced in former days, when I was a Cantonist?"

And he remembers his years of military service, as a soldier under Tsar Nicholas I. Twenty-five years of service, all the time shouldering the gun; not counting the years when as a child he had served as a Cantonist. He had done some walking in his life, marching over mounts and dales, in snowstorms, in frost and gales. And what snowstorms! what gales! Trees were cracking and birds falling down stiff dead—whilst the Russian soldier had to march on, fresh and alert, singing a song while marching, a *Trepak* or a *Kamarinskaya*, beating the measure with his foot.

The thought that for twenty-five years he had been able to endure such service, such suffering, such snowstorms and gales, to undergo such torture, to suffer hunger, thirst and privations and yet come home in good health—the thought filled him with pride. Lifting up his head, he continued to march on, his heart swelling with renewed strength.

" Well, well," he thinks, " what is such a small frost to me ? It is as nothing to what I faced once in Russia."

He is marching on. The wind had somewhat abated, darkness was gradually spreading over the horizon, night was falling.

" Call this a day ? " he says ; " it is no worse than a little thaw."

He walks a little faster, afraid lest night surprise him. He was in the habit of studying the Holy Law on Saturdays at his little synagogue, and he knew that a traveller should leave with the sunrise and endeavour to reach his destination at sunset.

He is growing hungry, and when he is hungry—such is his custom—he becomes quite jolly. Appetite is such a good thing. The merchants who often send him on errands are always complaining of their lack of appetite, of not being hungry. Thank God, he is never suffering from lack of appetite—except, of course, when he is not quite well, as yesterday, for instance. He had been ill and the bread had tasted a little sour.

Nonsense ! sour, that brown bread of the barracks ? In former days, perhaps, yes, but not to-day. Nowadays the Russians, too, bake their bread in such a way as to put the Jewish bakers to shame. Besides, the bread he had bought was quite fresh ; it was a real pleasure to cut it. But he was not quite well yesterday, feeling a sort of cold shiver in his bones.

Thanks, however, to Him whose name he was not worthy to pronounce, such happenings were of rare occurrence with him. At the present moment he feels quite peckish ; but he has some bread and a piece of cheese in his pocket. The cheese had been given him by the wife of the merchant, may God grant her long life ! She is quite a charitable woman with a really Jewish heart, if only she did not swear and curse so much, he thought, she would be an excellent Jewess. He then remembers his dead wife.

She is quite like my Shprintse. Shprintse, too, had a good heart, but she was rather inclined to swear and to curse. Whenever I sent one of my children out into the world, she would weep and shed tears like a beaver; whilst when the children were at home she did nothing but hurl curses and maledictions at their heads. And when one of the children died! Oh, then for days she used to wriggle on the ground like a serpent, beating her head with her fists. One day she was even on the point of hurling a stone against heaven.

Ridiculous, he thinks; the Lord pays little heed to a silly woman. But then she would not allow the coffin to be carried out of the house. She boxed the ears of the women, and pulled the beards of the men of the Holy Confraternity. What strength there lay dormant in that Shprintse! To look at her you might have thought her a fly, and yet what strength, what strength there was in her!

May she forgive me; she was a kind woman at heart after all. She did not hate me either, although she never gave me a kind or tender word. She was always in the habit of shouting: "Divorce, divorce!" She would run away if I did not divorce her. But no fear! she never really wanted me to divorce her!

He remembers a certain incident and smiles.

It happened a very long time ago. Even in those days there existed the tax upon the consumption of spirits; and he was a nightwatchman then. His iron-shod stick in his hand, he used to walk about all night watching that no contraband alcohol was smuggled in.

He knew his job, for he had been at a good school; the Russians had been good masters. Once, at dawn in mid-winter, Hayim Jonah, the day-watcher, who is no longer of this world, came to relieve him. He, Shmarya, returned home, quite frozen and almost stiff, and joyously knocked at his door. From her bed his wife replied:

"Go to the devil! I was hoping to hear that something had already happened to you."

"Aha, she is still cross," thought Shmarya. To tell the truth, he could not recall to his mind what had really happened yesterday, but something must surely have occurred.

"Shut your mouth and open the door," he shouted.

"I will open your head!" was her curt reply.

"Let me get in!" he called once more.

"Go to the devil!" she replied.

He altered his mind, proceeded to the *Beth-ha-Midrash* and there went to sleep behind the stove. As ill-luck would have it, however, there was an escape of carbon fumes from the stove. He fell down from his bench unconscious and was carried home half-dead. And then it was really marvellous how that woman carried on. He had heard quite clearly how she was carrying on. They were telling her that it was nothing, merely the effect of carbon fumes, but she was not satisfied and clamoured for a doctor. She was going to faint, would throw herself into the river. And she was lamenting: "My own man! my husband! my treasure!"

He had then gathered up all his strength, made an effort, sat up and gently asked her: "Shprintse, would you like me to divorce you?"

"What the de—— Go to the——" she did not finish her sentence, however, but burst out into loud sobbing.

"Shmarya," she said, "what do you think? Will the Lord forgive me for my wickedness and my swearing?"

But directly he recovered she became the Shprintse of old. She had a tongue like an engine, was strong as iron and she could scratch like a cat. Poor, poor Shprintse! She has not even been allowed to witness the happiness of her children.

They must all be quite well off, wherever they are. They are all artisans, and a man who knows a craft never dies of hunger. They are all strong fellows, wherein they are taking after me. Yes, of course, they never send letters, but what of that? I can't blame them for it. They are too ignorant to be able to write themselves, and it is too much trouble to have recourse to others. And besides, what pleasure is there in reading a letter written by a stranger's hand? It tastes like mere ditch-

water. Then in the course of time, children, young
people, are apt to forget. Of course, they must be all
right, and have therefore nothing to write to me about.
But poor Shprintse, she is sleeping her last sleep. Poor,
poor Shprintse!

Soon after the abolition of the tax on consumption of
spirits, Shprintse was not the same woman. Before I
had grown accustomed to go on errands, to say " Your
Honour " in Polish, and not, as I had been accustomed,
to say in Russian, " Your Nobility," before the people
had deigned to entrust to me contracts and money, we
often used to lack bread.

As for myself, a man, an old Cantonist, well and good ;
I can do quite well without food for a day. But a delicate
woman grows faint immediately. She had no strength
even to curse, had lost all her insolence, and the whole
day long she did nothing but cry. Life became unbearable, I was thoroughly disgusted with it. She seemed to
be afraid of me. She did not eat, always fearing that
there would not be enough for me. When I saw that my
wife was afraid of me, I mustered up courage, and now
it was I who stormed and swore. " Have a blow out,
you wicked old woman," I shouted. Once I was carried
away by my fury so far as to want to beat her, but how
can you beat a woman who is weeping, who sits there
with arms folded, without moving ? I rushed up to her
with clenched fists, but she merely said : " You eat first
and I shall eat afterwards." What could I do ? I was
compelled to cut off a piece of bread, eat it, and leave
the rest for her.

Another time she even had recourse to a ruse to make
me leave the house. " I will eat," she said, " you can go.
Go out into the street, you might perhaps be able to earn
something." She made an effort to smile, even caressing
me several times. But when I came back I found the
bread intact.

" Why have you not eaten ? "

" I can't eat dry bread," she said, " I must have some
soup."

Shmarya lowered his head as if weighed down by a heavy burden, whilst those sad days were unfolding in his mind's eye.

And what a scene she made when I wanted to pawn my Sabbath garment, the one I am now wearing. Quickly she ran out and pawned her brass Sabbath candlesticks. Until the day of her death, she had to put her candles into candlesticks made out of potatoes on Friday nights.

Before she died, she confessed to me that she had really never wanted me to divorce her, and that it had all been the fault of her sharp tongue.

" My tongue ! my tongue ! " she cried. " God in heaven ! Forgive me the sins I have committed with my tongue." And she died in terror of being hung up by her tongue in the next world. " The Lord," she said, " will certainly never have pity upon me ; I have sinned too much. But when you join me in the next world— not soon, but after a hundred and twenty years, when you, too, come to the next world, don't forget to take me down from the gallows. You will tell the Celestial Tribunal that you have forgiven me."

Then she had lost the trend of her thoughts and begun to call for her children. It seemed to her that they were all there, surrounding her bed, talking to her ; and she asked them too to forgive her. What a silly woman ! Who would not have forgiven her ?

And how old was she, after all ? Fifty, perhaps. Poor woman, she died before her time. Of course, it is no wonder, since she was ruining her life with her own hands. Whenever something was taken out of the house to be pawned it was as if a piece of her own flesh had been cut off. Every day she was growing paler, more yellow, drying up, shrivelling up. She was saying that she felt as if the marrow in her bones was drying up. Oh, she had known that she was going to die. And how she had loved the house and our furniture ! Every time when a chair, a candlestick, or another object, was removed from the house, she would cover it with a flood of tears and bid it farewell as if it had been one of her children. She would seize the object, cover it with kisses, and exclaim in heartrending accents : " Ah, I will never see you again ; in the hour of my death you will not be here." How stupid ! A woman will always be a woman. She may be as brave as a Cossack at one moment, and the next a very small incident will be enough to upset her entirely, and make her act like a child. What does a man care whether he will see a piece of furniture at his death or not ?

" Fie," he interrupted himself. " Fie upon these vain thoughts, which are only muddling my brain and causing me to slacken my pace."

" Come now, my old soldier legs, get a move on," he commands them. He looks around and sees nothing but snow, whilst the grey sky above looks as if it had been patched with black rags. " Just like my undergarment," thinks he. " Lord of the Universe, are they refusing to sell even You things on credit in the little shop, so that You can't afford to give Your sky a decent garment ? ",

In the meantime it had started to freeze, and his beard and moustache were turning into icicles. He was, however, feeling warm all over ; his head was quite hot, and there were beads of perspiration on his forehead. Only his legs were icy cold and growing weaker every moment. He had now only a short distance to walk, but his need of rest was increasing. He felt ashamed of himself ; this would be the first time that such a thing had happened to him—to sit down whilst walking a distance of only two miles. He does not like to admit to himself that he is nearly eighty and it is high time he took a little rest. He must walk on ; he must. As long as a man is walking, his legs will carry him, but let him only yield to temptation and one never knows what might happen. " I will even catch cold if I sit down." He was trying to frighten himself, so as not to give in. Another short lap and he would be able to rest, yonder in the village which was not far away.

" Yes, I know what I will do," he thought. " When I reach the village, I will not go straight to the Squire, because one has often to wait an hour before one is admitted. I will first go to the Jewish Inn.

" It is lucky that I am not afraid of the dogs. Of course, towards evening, when they let loose Boury the big grey dog, who is a veritable wolf—it is rather dangerous. I have my supper in my pocket, bread and cheese, and Boury is rather fond of cheese ; but still it will be better to have a rest first. No, I will first go to the Jew, get warm, perform my ablutions, and have some food."

The very thought of soon having a meal made his mouth water, for he had not tasted anything since the morning. But that mattered little. Was he not used to being hungry ? As a matter of fact, he rather liked being hungry ; it was a sure sign that one was alive. But his legs—that was a different matter. He had only another two versts to walk ; he could already get a glimpse from afar of the big Manor. His legs, however, they did not see anything and were insisting on a little rest.

" Well, after all, what if I did rest a while, just a short moment. Well, well, my legs have obeyed me for such a long time, I could just give in to them for once." And Shmarya sits down upon a small heap of snow. It was then that he could hear how his heart was beating. It was like the blows of a hammer, causing him acute pain, and bringing out the perspiration upon his forehead.

He grows frightened. Was he going to be ill by any chance ? He had money in his pocket, money which did not belong to him. And if he were to faint on the road ? But he consoles himself. Praised be the Lord, no one is passing here. And even if someone did pass, he would surely not guess that such a ragged man had been entrusted with a considerable sum of money. Let us have a little rest, and then we will get a move on. But his lids are closing, as if they had been made of lead. No, no, he must not fall asleep, on account of the money he was carrying in his pocket. He commands himself to rise up : " Rise up, Shmarya ! "

He is still able to command ; but as for moving, that is

impossible. And yet it seems to him that he is walking, faster and faster. He can already see the whole village and distinguish all the peasants' huts. Here lives Antek, and there is the dwelling of Vassil. He knows them all, for he hires carts from them. The inn of the Jew is still farther away, but he liked it better than a peasant's hut, for in the inn one often found a *mezouman*. And it seems to him that he was getting nearer to the inn ; but, strange, the nearer he is the farther it is moving away ; but, no doubt, that was quite all right.

There must be a cheerful fire now in the chimney, for he could see the small window glowing red. Now stout Mirl is surely skimming a big pot of boiling potatoes. She always treats him to one, and it is quite a pleasure to eat a hot potato. He advances a little so as to be nearer —at least so he thinks ; although he is still seated upon the snow. It is not so cold ; and heavy, dense snow-flakes begin to fall. Gradually the snow covers him up entirely, and in his snow-garment he must no doubt feel quite warm, for it seems to him that he is already in the inn. Mirl is emptying the potatoes into a sieve, and one can hear the water running through the holes, *zyour, zyour* ; and from his serge gaberdine the water was running, too. Jonah, the innkeeper, is pacing up and down the room, as he always does after his evening prayers, because then he is hungry. He is continually repeating : " *Nu*, Mirl ! " But Mirl is in no hurry : slow but sure.

" Well, I never ! Have I by any chance fallen asleep, and is this only a dream ? " he exclaims, pleasantly startled. It seems to him that the door of the inn is being opened, and who is it that is coming in ? Fancy it, it is his eldest son, Honeh. He recognizes him quite well ! What is he doing here ? But Honeh does not recognize his father, and the old man pretends not to see him. What a joke ! He is telling Jonah that he is going to see his father, for he has not forgotten the old man. And that rogue of a Jonah does not tell him that his father is there, sitting on the bench. Mirl, she is too busy with her potatoes, and will not leave her work. A big white wooden spoon in her hand, she is crushing the potatoes; but she is smiling.

He will wait for his son to recognize him. In the meantime he will enjoy looking at his son. Honeh must be rich, very rich. His clothes are so clean, and not a tear on them. And look at his watch-chain! It is surely gold, oh, surely not imitation. He is turning his head towards the big stove, and bursts out into loud laughter. What a joke! Here are Jekel, Berl, and Zacharya, all the three hiding behind the stove. Ah, the brigands, the bandits! Ha, ha, ha! he laughs. But what a pity that Shprintse is not here, a great pity. If she could only share this joy! In the meantime, Honeh is ordering two roast geese!

"Honeh, Honeh!" he cries, "don't you recognize me? It is I, your father." And it seems to him that he and Honeh are embracing each other. "You see, Honeh, it is a pity your mother is not here. If she could only see you? And you, Jekel, Berl, Zacharya, come out of your hiding-place! I recognized you at once. Come out! I knew you were coming. See, I have brought you a bit of cheese, real goat-cheese. Come along, my children, look at this soldier's bread. You like it, don't you? It is a great pity indeed that your mother is no longer here, to witness our meeting."

And it seems to him that his four sons are surrounding him, hugging and kissing him.

"Gently, gently, my dear children, gently; don't squeeze me so hard. You see, I am not so young any more. I am nearly eighty. Gently, you are stifling me; gently, my little ones. My bones are old, and then, you see, I am carrying money on me; yes, a lot of money that has been entrusted to me. That's enough, my little ones, enough."

It was enough indeed! They found him stiff, frozen to death, his hand upon the inner pocket of his coat.

IV

MARRIED

(Told by a Woman)

———

I remember the time when I was still playing hopscotch in the courtyard and making bread from clay. I remember my little brother with his emaciated wax-like figure, who had been ailing ever since he had been born; he was ill for seven years and then died. In summer I used to place him in the sun so that he could watch me playing with the other children. In winter he never left his cradle, and I used to sing him songs and tell him stories. My other brothers were at school.

My mother was always very busy. She had a number of different occupations—perhaps ten—that poor mother of mine. She was a street-hawker; a pastry cook; an assistant cook on special occasions such as banquets, weddings, and circumcisions; a servant at the ritual baths; an official weeper at funerals; a reader of prayers for the women in Synagogue; and last, but not least, she also did the marketing for several households. My father was a clerk in Mr. Terkelbaum's employ, superintending the timber-cutting in the forest. He was earning three roubles a week. Those were the fat years in our house, for both father and mother were earning. Both the boys' teacher and the landlord were paid almost regularly, and there was always bread in the house. Sometimes mother made us delicious buckwheat soup, and that, of course, was a great treat. But such occasions were rather rare. Most of the time she used to come home late, tired and worn out, and very often shed bitter tears. She complained that many of the ladies for whom she did the marketing refused to pay their debts. They would, for instance, ask her to buy such a thing for them in the market, but instead of paying her at once would postpone payment for the next day or the day after. In the meantime mother had bought other things for the lady of the house, and when it came to settling accounts the lady no longer remembered whether she had paid for the quarter of a pound of fresh butter, or the eggs she had the other day. The matter was put aside for the moment.

" I will ask my husband," the lady would say, " for he was present when you delivered the goods ; he has such a splendid memory."

The next day it appeared that the husband had come home rather late from the *Bethhamidrash*, and Madam had forgotten to ask him.

The day after, Madam says quite gleefully that she had asked her husband about the matter, but that he had scolded her for bothering him. Did they imagine that he had nothing else to think of than these paltry women's accounts ? However, Madam promised that she would try to remember herself whether she had paid or not. A few days later, she actually began to remember that she had indeed paid my poor mother for the butter. A little later she was quite sure of it. And when my mother ventured once more to claim for the butter, she was treated as an insolent hussy and accused of trying to extort money under false pretences. In the end Madam would warn mother that if she said another word she would never be allowed to step over the threshold of the house and would lose their custom. Mother, too, came from a respectable family, and had it not been for the Squire who had taken away her dowry, she herself would have been a lady. Mother therefore did not easily submit to such treatment. More than once she came home, her eyes swollen from weeping, and threw herself down upon her bed sobbing aloud. And so she would remain for a long time, shedding bitter tears. Then she would get up and cook some supper for us. Sometimes she vented her wrath on us. I say *us*, but I really mean myself. She never said a word to my little brother Berl, and very rarely did she scold my other brothers ; for the poor boys frequently came home from school with swollen eyes, their cheeks black and blue, belaboured by the cruel hands of the master. It was I, therefore, who was the scapegoat. I often had my hair pulled or received some other gratuitous attention.

" Could you not have lit a fire and put the pot to boil ? " she cried.

And yet, when I actually did it, then it was even worse.

" Look at that housewife. She has suddenly taken it into her head to make a fire. Of course she can afford to waste wood. Do you imagine I get wood for nothing that you use it so lavishly ? What does she care whether I am drudging ? All she can do is to waste my substance."

Sometimes it was father's turn to be scolded—in his absence, of course. Sitting down upon her bed, her face turned to the window, she would sigh :

" Much does he care about us. He is living there in the forest like a lord, inhaling the fresh air, the whole day lazily stretched out in the grass, gorging himself with fresh milk, and perhaps even cream, for all I know. And we here have empty and tortured bowels."

But in spite of all this, those were good days. We did not suffer the pangs of hunger, and after a week of work and petty miseries came a joyous, or at least a restful, Sabbath. Father often used to come home, and then mother was flitting about the house busily engaged, a happy smile discreetly playing round her lips. Often towards sunset, before the candles had been lit, mother would kiss me upon the head. I knew, however, what these kisses meant, because when it happened that father had not come home for the Sabbath, then I was a witch. When I was being washed and combed in honour of the Sabbath, mother would tear out handfuls of my hair with her comb, and treat me from time to time to a box on the ears, to a blow or a cuff. I did not cry, for my childish heart felt that mother was not angry with me ; but was revolting against her sad and miserable fate.

Afterwards when the cutting of timber in the forest had been completed, and father came home for good, we began to suffer hunger. That is to say, only father and mother and myself were lacking bread ; the other children did not feel the want so much. The sick little brother did not require much. He sometimes drank a little gruel, when he got it ; and then he lay in his cradle staring at the ceiling. The other children *nebbich*, were going to school, and when they came home one had to give them some hot food, whilst I alone often went to bed hungry.

With tears in their eyes my parents often used to remember the good old times ; but I, on the contrary, felt much happier in our present state. Since we had begun to lack bread, my mother had grown much fonder of me, did not tear my hair when combing me, never treated me to a cuff or a box on the ears. During meals my father used to pat me on the head, caress me and thus divert my attention so that I should not think that I was being overlooked. I was rather proud of being allowed to fast and starve together with my parents. I felt that I was now a grown-up maid. It was about that time that my sick little brother died.

It happened in this way. One morning mother woke up and called out to father :

" You know, Berl must be much better ; he has slept all the night without even once waking up."

Being a rather light sleeper, I heard what my mother was saying, and joyfully jumping up from my improvised bed, I hastened to my little brother, whom I loved dearly. I expected to see a smile upon his little parchment face— a smile which very rarely illumined it—but, alas, I found a dead body !

The week of mourning followed. Then my father fell ill, and the barber-surgeon became a frequent visitor in our house. As long as we could afford to pay him in cash he came himself. But afterwards, when the bedding, the chandelier, and father's books, which mother would not touch for a long time, had all been sold to pay for medicine, then the barber-surgeon began to send his assistant.

Mother intensely disliked the boy. He had a curly moustache, was dressed like a Gentile, and often used Polish words in his conversation. As for myself, I was afraid of him, although to this day I do not know why. But whenever I knew that he was coming to our house, I rushed out and waited until he had left.

Once one of our neighbours, also a poor man, had fallen ill, and as he, too, had evidently already sold out all his furniture, the boy came to see him. He (even to-day, I do not know his name) went from our house to the neighbour, and crossing the yard saw me seated upon a log. I had lowered my eyes, but feeling that he was coming near to me, I grew stiff and cold all over, and my heart began to beat furiously. He approached me, took me by the chin and raising up my head, said in plain Yiddish :

" Such a beautiful girl as you are should not go about with hair so dishevelled, nor should she blush and be so bashful at the approach of a young man."

As soon as he had left me I hurried into the house. I felt that all my blood was rushing into my face and I hid in the darkest corner behind the stove, pretending to count the dirty linen. This happened on a Wednesday, and on Friday I reminded my mother for the first time to wash my hair as it was rather entangled.

" Woe is unto me ! " cried my mother. " I have not combed her hair for three weeks." But suddenly she grew angry. " Witch," she shouted, " such a big, grown-up maid cannot comb her own hair ! Other girls in your place would have washed the other children, too."

" Sarah, dear," begged my father, " please do not shout " ; but my mother's anger was increasing.

" Witch," she shouted, " you hear ; go at once and wash your hair ; you hear, this very instant ! "

I was afraid to approach the stove where the hot water stood, as I should have to pass mother, who would certainly have treated me to a blow, but, as usual, it was father who saved me.

" Sarah, dear," he groaned again, " please do not shout, I have such a headache."

This was sufficient ; mother's anger disappeared completely, and I was free to go near the kettle of boiling water. I was washing my hair clumsily, and I saw mother approaching father and pointing to me she whispered, although I heard every word :

" She is growing up as fast as she can, and is as beautiful as beautiful can be. Lord of the Universe," she sighed, " what is to become of her ? "

A deeper sigh was father's only reply.

Several times the barber-surgeon had asserted that father was not ill at all, that it was only worry that had caused his liver to swell ; and being swollen, the liver was pressing against his heart ; that was all. All that he needed was to drink milk and avoid worry.

" Go out into the street," he said, " talk to people, and find some occupation."

My father, however, replied that his legs refused to carry him. I learned the reason a little later. One summer day, at dawn, I overheard a conversation between my parents.

" Thus you have caught your illness in the forest ? " asked mother.

" Of course," replied father. " They were felling the trees in twenty places at once. The forest, you see, belongs to the Squire, but the peasants have certain rights. Any dead branches, trees, or wood that is thrown down by wind and thunder, belong to them. So when one is felling the trees, the peasants naturally stand to lose by it, as they are then compelled to buy timber, both for building and heating. They were preparing to take out an injunction ; to bring the commissary and stop the

felling of the trees.   But their decision had been delayed.
As soon as Reb Zanvill saw them scratching their heads
—a sure sign of meditating deeply—he gave instructions
to engage an extra forty workmen and proceed with the
felling as quickly as possible.   It was a veritable hell, and
they were working in twenty places at once.   I had to be
everywhere ;   and you can easily imagine that my feet
grew swollen, compelled as I was to run backwards and
forwards."

" And I," sighed mother, " I was so sinful and wicked
as to imagine that you had absolutely nothing to do there."

" Yes, of course," smiled father rather sadly ; " from
grey dawn to late night I was on my feet."

" And all that work for three roubles a week," said
mother indignantly.

" He promised to give me a rise, but in the meantime,
as you will remember, a load of timber was wrecked, and
he said that he had lost every penny."

" And you believe him ? "

" It is possible—— "

" Yes," continued mother in an angry voice, " he is
always doing bad business and losing, and yet he is
growing richer every day."

" When God wills it—— "

There was silence for a while.

" Do you know what he is doing now ? " asked father,
who had not left the house for nearly a year.

" What he is doing ? " answered mother.   " What do
you expect him to do ?   He is dealing in hemp and eggs
and has a wine shop."

" And she, how is she ? "

" She ? she is *nebbich* ill."

" A pity, she is such a good soul."

" A gem, the only madam who never swindles me to
the amount of one penny ; she would even pay me very
promptly, but unfortunately she has little influence over
him."

" I think she is his third wife ? "

" Of course," said mother.

"You see, Sarah dear, here you have a wealthy Jew, and yet he has no chance as far as wives are concerned. Everybody has his share of troubles."

"And she is so young," added mother, "she cannot be more than five and twenty."

"There you are; and he is sixty at least, and still as strong as iron."

"I should think so; he cracks nuts with his teeth."

"And uses no eyeglasses."

"And how he walks; the floor shakes under him."

"Whilst I," added father, "am lying ill in bed."

The last words cut me to the quick.

"God will help," said mother by way of consolation.

"But the girl," continued father, groaning and sighing; "the girl," casting a look in the direction of my improvised couch, "she is growing up fast. Have you noticed her chest?"

"For sure," said mother.

"And as beautiful as the sun."

Another silence followed.

"Do you know Sarah, dear," father began again, "we are not doing our duty by her?"

"How's that?"

"How old were you when you married?"

"Younger than she is now."

"Nu?"

"Nu, what?"

At that moment someone knocked twice against our window shutters. Mother immediately jumped out of bed, tore off the cord with which the shutters had been fastened, and opening the window asked what the matter was.

"Rivka, Zanvil's wife is dead," someone replied.

Mother hastily retreated from the window.

"Blessed be the Just and Equitable Judge," father recited the traditional formula at the news of a demise.

"Blessed be the Just and Equitable Judge," mother repeated after him, "and, fancy, we had just been talking about her."

It was a strangely restless time for me in those days. I do not know myself what was the matter with me. I passed sleepless nights, my temples were hammering, and my heart within me was weeping. I felt as if afraid of something or yearning for something unknown. Again at other times I felt a pleasant warmth in my heart, and I was tempted to hug and kiss everybody. But whom? My brothers would not let me touch them, and even the five-year-old Jochanan kicked and cried that he did not care to fool about with a girl. Mother, of whom I was afraid, was always in a bad temper and worried—whilst father was daily growing weaker. In a short time his hair had become as grey as a pigeon, his face shrivelled up like parchment, and his eyes were looking out so help-lessly, with such a dumb supplication, that whenever I caught sight of him I had to rush out of the house, sobbing aloud.

It was at such moments that I recalled little Berl to my mind. I could have unburdened my heart to him; I could have told him everything; I could have kissed and hugged him. But, alas, he was lying under the cold earth, and I burst into tears.

Sometimes, as I looked out of the window, I fancied the moon was gliding and gliding—nearer and nearer to the white wall opposite our window, but she could never glide over the hedge. Then I was filled with great sym-pathy for the moon, and I began to weep.

Sometimes, again, I used to walk about tired out, list-less, pale-faced and heavy-eyed. There was a noise in my ears, my head was heavy, and I thought that life was very sad. At such moments I again remembered little Berl and envied his lot. He, I thought, is lying there in sweet repose. Very frequently I dreamed that I was dead and lying in my grave, or that I was soaring about in heaven in a nightgown, with my hair loose, and that I was looking down upon the earth.

It was at that time that I had lost all the comrades and playmates with whom I had played at hopscotch. I was not anxious to find new playmates. One of them was already walking out on Saturdays, arrayed in a silken skirt and wearing a golden saltire and watch ; being engaged and soon about to be married. Others were marriageable girls, and the marriage-brokers were besieging their houses. Their respective mothers were combing, washing and dressing them up ; whilst I was still running about barefooted and clad in rags and tattered garments. The marriageable girls avoided me, and I, in my turn, was ashamed to seek out companions among girls much younger than myself.

Hopscotch, too, no longer appealed to me or interested me. During the day I never showed my face in the street, and mother gave up sending me out on errands. She even refused to send me when I asked her. But towards evening I used to go for a walk behind our house, near the barns, and even went so far as the river, where, during the summer, I remained till late at night.

At first I noticed that mother was following me, although she never came quite near. She would stand at the gate, watch me from a distance, and then go in, but I heard her sighs. Gradually she ceased to follow or watch me. I would remain thus for hours, listening to the murmur of the rushing river, to the noise made by frogs jumping from the grass into the water, or following with my eyes a swift cloud in the sky. Sometimes I would fall asleep with open eyes.

Once the sound of a sad song coming from a distance reached my ears. The voice was young and fresh, and a sudden sadness seized me. It was a Jewish song.

" That is the barber-surgeon's boy singing," I thought. " Anyone else would have sung a hymn instead of a worldly song. I had better go into the house, and neither listen to such songs nor meet the boy." And yet I did not rise from my seat. As if in a trance I remained chained to my seat, tired out, although my heart was strangely agitated.

Nearer and nearer came the song ; coming from the other side of the river and crossing the bridge. I heard footsteps on the sand, and once more I tried to rise and

run away, but my feet refused to obey me and I remained
At last he stood before me.

"Is it you, Leah?"

I did not reply. The noise in my ears became louder,
my temples were hammering more violently, and it seemed
to me that I had never heard such a sweet voice. Not at
all offended by my silence, he sat down by my side on the
log, looking straight into my face. I did not see his gaze,
because I dared not raise my eyes, but I felt how it was
scorching my face.

"You are a beautiful maid, Leah, but a pity . . ."

I burst out into loud sobbing and ran away.

On the two following evenings I did not leave the
house, but on the fourth day, it was a Friday, I was so
lonely and my heart was so heavy, that I felt compelled to
go out for a walk. It seemed to me that I should choke in
the house; it was so stifling. He must have been waiting
for me in the shadow in some obscure corner, for I had
scarcely sat down when he stood before me.

"Don't run away from me, Leah," he begged in such
a soft and tender voice. "Don't be afraid, I will do you
no harm."

His tone reassured me.

He now began to sing slowly and softly a very sad
melody, and once more tears welled up in my eyes. I
could not keep back my tears, and I began to sob softly.

"Why are you crying, Leah?" he asked, seizing my
hand.

"Your song is so sad," I said, withdrawing my hand.

"I am an orphan, lonely and miserable . . ."

Someone was approaching, and we hastily separated
and ran away.

He taught me his song, and I used to hum it in my bed.
I went to sleep with it, and in the morning I awoke with
it. Frequently, however, my heart smote me and I
regretted having made the acquaintance of the boy who
dressed like a Gentile and shaved his beard. If he had
only behaved like the old barber-surgeon, if he had only
been a pious Jew. . . . I knew that if my father became

aware of my acquaintance with the boy, he would die of a broken heart; whilst mother would be capable of committing suicide. The secret was weighing heavily upon my heart.

Whenever I approached father's bed, bringing him something; or when mother came in and I remembered my sin; I began to tremble violently and my face seemed to become drained of the last drop of blood. And yet every day I promised the boy that I would meet him on the morrow. There was no reason why I should run away from him. He no longer attempted to seize my hand, he no longer told me that I was a beautiful maid, but he simply talked to me and taught me songs . . . once he gave me a piece of St. John's bread.

"Take it, Leah," he said.

I refused.

"Why not," he asked sadly, "why do you refuse to take this from me?"

Taken unawares, I let the answer escape my lips: "I would have preferred a piece of bread," I said.

I do not know how often this meeting and singing had occurred, but I remember that one evening he seemed very sad. I saw it at once, and asked him what was the matter.

"I must leave here," he said.

"Leave here? Where are you going?" I asked.

"I must go before the military examining board."

Seizing him by the hand, I anxiously inquired:

"You are going to be taken as a soldier?"

"No," he replied, squeezing my hand, "no, there is no fear of that, I am not strong enough; my heart seems to be rather weak. I shall no doubt be discharged, but I must nevertheless go before the board."

"You will come back?"

"Of course."

We were silent for a while.

"It will only be for a few weeks," he said.

I was silent, whilst he was looking at me with eyes full of supplication.

" You will miss me ? "

" Yes," I whispered in so low a voice as to be inaudible even to myself.

" Let us say good-bye," he said. My hand was still lying in his.

" I wish you a pleasant journey," I said in a trembling voice. Bending over to me, he kissed me on the lips and then disappeared.

For a long time I remained like one intoxicated.

" Leah," I suddenly heard mother's voice calling me. It was her voice of olden times ; the soft, sweet voice with which she used to call me sometimes when father was still well.

" Leah, darling ! "

I had not been called with such endearing terms for a long time. Once more a tremor passed over me ; my lips still burning from the kiss, I hastened back into the house. I hardly recognized our living room. There were two unfamiliar chandeliers upon the table with lighted candles ; there were also brandy and cakes. Father was seated in an easy chair propped up with pillows, and a happy smile seemed to be emanating from every wrinkle in his dear old face. There were more chairs round the table, also unfamiliar to me, and there were strangers present. Mother took me into her arms and began to hug and kiss me.

" *Masoltov*," she cried, " *Masoltov*, my daughter, my pet, *Masoltov*, Leah darling."

I did not understand what it all meant, but a wild fear of something unknown seized me, and my heart began to beat furiously. When mother let me go, father called me to him. Being too weak to stand, I knelt down in front of him, placing my head in his lap. Patting me upon the head and caressing my hair, he said :

" My child, you will no more suffer the pangs of hunger, nor will you know want ; you will no more walk about in rags, naked and barefoot, for you will be a rich woman now ; you will pay the schooling for your little brothers and they will not be sent away from school. You will also help us, and I shall get quite well again."

"And do you know, my child, who is your fiancé?" asked mother, full of joy. "It is none other than Reb Zanvil himself. Reb Zanvil has sent a marriage-broker."

I do not know what really happened, but when I regained consciousness towards noon on the following day, I was lying on my couch.

"Praised be the Lord," exclaimed mother.

"Praised be His blessed name," said father.

And once more I was being hugged, embraced, and covered with kisses. I was offered jam, and asked whether I would like a drink of water mixed with preserve, or perhaps a sip of wine. I shut my eyes and stifled my sobs.

"That is all right," mother said joyfully, "that is quite all right; let her have a good cry, the poor child. It is all our own fault. It was wrong of us to spring such good news upon her so suddenly and unexpectedly. It was enough to stun her; a vein might have burst—heaven forbid—but now, praise be unto the Lord, all is well. Cry your fill, my child; may your tears wash away all your past sufferings, and may a new life begin for you, a new life——"

Two angels are supposed to accompany every man, a good angel and a bad angel. I was sure that the good angel was commanding me to forget the barber-surgeon's boy, to eat Reb Zanvil's jam and his sweets, to drink his wine and his water mixed with preserve, and to dress at his expense. But the bad angel was whispering into my ear, bidding me tell my parents once for all that I refused to accept my fiancé.

I did not yet know Reb Zanvil. I might have seen him once, but I had either soon forgotten him or did not know him. But I hated him. The following night I dreamed that I was standing under the nuptial canopy. Reb Zanvil was the bridegroom, and I was being led round him seven times. My feet refused to obey me, and I was being carried by the bridesmaids, and was led home. Mother came to meet me, dancing in front of me with a

Koiletsh in her hand. Then there came the golden soup.[1]
I was afraid to raise my eyes, feeling sure that I should
behold a blind man, with a long, terribly long, nose, and
a cold sweat broke out all over me. Suddenly someone
was whispering into my ear : " You are a beautiful maid,
Leah darling." It was not at all the voice of an old man,
it was the voice of *the other* ; I opened my eyes and beheld
the face of *the other* !

" Sh," he whispered into my ear, " keep it secret ;
don't tell anybody. Under some pretext, I have lured
Reb Zanvil into the depth of the forest. There I put him
into a sack ; tied it with a cord and, attaching a stone to
it, threw him into the river (I remember that mother had
once told me a similar story) ; and now I have taken his
place."

I woke up all in a tremble. Through a chink in the
shutters I could just see the rays of the moon illuminating
the room. I first perceived the chandelier hanging down
from a beam on the ceiling, then I saw my parents in their
beds, and the bedding that had come back. Father
was smiling happily in his sleep, whilst mother was
breathing peacefully. And then the good angel said
unto me :

" If you are good and obedient, your father will soon
get well, and your mother will not have to work so hard
in her old age. Your little brothers will go to school
and become learned men—Rabbis, scholars, great Jews—
for you will defray the expenses of their studies."

"But it is Reb Zanvil who will kiss you," said the bad
angel. " He will touch you with his moist lips and
moustache. He will press you with his bony hands. He
will also torture you, as he has tortured his other wives,
and will send you to an early grave. And then *he* will
come back and will be very grieved. He will no more
teach you songs, nor will you sit by his side in the evening,
for you will be sitting with Reb Zanvil."

" No ! " I cried, " may the heavens fall, but I will tear
up the marriage contract ! "

For the rest of the night I knew no sleep.

It was mother who awoke first in the morning. I wanted to speak to her, but I was so used to turn to father when in trouble. Father is waking up.

"Do you know, Sarah dear," were his first words; "do you know, I feel much better? You will see, I will go out for a walk to-day."

"Praised be His blessed name; it is all thanks to our dear daughter, it is due to her merits, this noble and pious child."

"And the barber-surgeon was quite right, the milk I am drinking is doing me a lot of good."

My parents were silent, and once more the good angel was saying to me:

"If you are good and obedient, your father will get quite well again; but if one sinful word escapes your lips, then your father will die."

"I say, Sarah dear, I think you had better give up doing the marketing for people."

"Are you serious? What do you mean?"

"What I am saying. This very day I will see Reb Zanvil; he will either take me into his business, or lend me a few roubles, and we will open a small shop that we can both look after. Then I will try and begin to deal in wheat."

"May the Lord fulfil your wishes."

"Of course He will. Listen, dear, when you are going to buy material for the child's wedding dresses, you had better also buy some for yourself—for two dresses at least. Why not? Has he not told us to buy all that we require at his expense? You do not intend, I expect, to go to Synagogue in your old dress, when the fiancé will be called up to the Law?"[1]

"Come now! Don't talk so foolishly," said mother. "It is much more important to buy some clothes for the children. Ruben is going barefooted; last week a piece of wood pierced his foot and he is still limping. Winter, too, is approaching, and the children will require some warm underwear and some winter garments."

"Then buy some, by all means."

"You hear," said the good angel, "you need only utter one sinful word, and your mother will have to do without a new dress, and you know quite well that her old dress is falling to pieces. During the winter your little brothers will have to run barefoot over the frozen snow in the severest frosts; in summer splinters will enter their poor little feet."

"To tell you the truth," continued mother, "I feel that we shall have to talk quite plainly to him. We shall have to tell him, as the saying goes: 'Rachel, your youngest daughter';[1] for, after all, he is not exactly a model of generosity. We shall have to make sure how much he will settle on her, because there are plenty of heirs who will come to claim his inheritance. If he refuses to make a settlement, then let him at least make a solemn promise sanctioned by an anathema; because, after all, how long can you expect such a man to live? another year, or two, at the utmost——"

"Wealthy and opulent people live long," sighed father.

"Long! You forget that he is nearly seventy, and I have noticed sometimes that he has the look of a dead man behind his ears."

"If you keep silent," whispered the bad angel, "you will go under the canopy with a lifeless man; you will live with a dead body, you will lie by the side of a corpse."

Mother sighed, whilst father said:

"Everything is in the hand of God."

Another sigh from mother.

"Well, what can we do?" said father. "Could we have acted otherwise? Had I been well and earning my living, were it only a dry crust of bread——" His voice failed him, and I thought that his heart was weeping within him.

"If she had at least been younger, I would have tried my utmost—I know not what—but I might have bought a ticket in the lottery."

And I kept silence.

My septuagenarian bridegroom gave for money for my trousseau, advanced my father a few hundred *gulden*, and

4

settled on me 500 *gulden*. People said that I was making an excellent match. I got new friends and companions. The girl with the silken dress and gold watch and chain came to visit me three times a day ; she was extremely happy that I had caught her up and that we were going to be married in the same month. I had other comrades too, but she had grown quite fond of me, and we became quite inseparable.

" Who are the other girls ? " she used to say. " Only horrid kids ; it will take a long time before *they* get married."

Rivka, the girl with the silken dress and gold watch and chain, was going to be married to someone from another town, but the couple would board and lodge in her father's house for another two or three years.

" All this time," she said, " we shall remain stanch friends, dropping in frequently for a cup of chicoree, or on Saturday afternoons for a plate of chicken soup. And when I am delivered," she continued, her face beaming, " you will come and nurse me."

I was silent.

" Nonsense," said Rivka. " Why are you so sad ? It may happen also to people of seventy. Go on, you silly," she consoled me, " if God wills it, then even a broomstick can shoot. And if not, well, how long do you think it can last ? People do not live for ever. May I have such a good year ; what a fine, young, nice little widow you will make, to smack the lips and lick the fingers."

Rivka did not wish Reb Zanvil any ill.

" Of course," she added, " he *is* a beast, for he tortured his last wife. But then again she had always been ailing, whilst you are healthy and well. He will treat *you* well; you will see how well he will treat *you*."

He came back.

My father got much better, but he took it into his head to have cupping, otherwise he was still afraid to go out into the street. He said that having remained in bed for a long time it seemed to him as if his blood had all accumulated in one place, and that cupping would do him a lot of good. He was also suffering from backache, and for this cupping was the best remedy.

A great fear seized me, for cupping was usually the business of the assistant.

"Will you go and call the barber-surgeon?" said father.

"What are you talking of?" said mother;   " ; girl who is on the eve of her marriage to go out on errands?"

She went herself for the barber-surgeon.

"Why did you grow so pale?" asked father, somewhat frightened.

"It is nothing, father."

"I have already noticed it for some days," father went on.

"It is only your imagination, father."

"Mother, too, is telling me——"

"What?"

"To-day," continued father, anxious to tell me something pleasant, "the dressmaker will come to try on your new dresses."

I remained silent.

"You don't seem to rejoice at the news?"

"Why not?"

"You don't even seem anxious to know what dresses you will get."

"Yes, of course, I know; have I not been measured for them?"

Mother had in the meantime returned, together with the barber-surgeon. I felt relieved, and yet my heart within me was weeping. You will perhaps never see him again, I thought.

"What a world we are living in!" said the barber-surgeon, who had arrived quite out of breath and groaning. "What a world we are living in! Here is Reb Zanvil marrying a young maiden, whilst Leiserl, the son of the president of the community, is becoming an anchorite and is running away from his wife."

"Leiserl!" exclaimed my mother, greatly astonished.

" As I am telling you. Here am I, a man of sixty, running about from morn till evening, whilst my assistant —a young man—is lying ill in bed."

Once more I began to tremble all over.

" Serves you right," said mother, " for keeping in your employ such a heathen."

" A heathen ? " said the barber-surgeon. " What do you mean by a heathen ? "

" What is the good of all this talk ? " my father interrupted him rather impatiently. " You had better proceed with your work."

By nature my father was rather kind-hearted, and it always seemed to me that he could not harm a fly on the wall, and yet his words were rather humiliating to the barber-surgeon. When he was lying ill in bed he was very pleased when someone came in for a chat ; but with the barber-surgeon he could never talk without interrupting him. He would always interrupt him and tell him to go on with his work. This time, however, I felt it more keenly ; and my heart ached within me. I imagined how he would have treated the *other* and humiliated *him* —who was now lying ill in bed. What ailed him ? . . . He had told me once that he was suffering from a weak heart. What a weak heart really meant I did not know, but I fancied that it must be some disease, which sometimes compelled people to be laid up. And yet I felt that I myself was somehow responsible for his present illness.

During the night I cried in my sleep. Mother woke up and sat down on my bed.

" Hush, my child," she said, " let us not wake father," and we conversed in whispers.

I noticed that my mother was greatly agitated. She was scrutinizing me with her eyes, as if trying to find out my secret ; but I had made up my mind not to tell her anything, certainly not whilst father was asleep.

" Why did you cry, my child ? " she asked.

" I don't know, mother."

" Are you well ? "

" Yes, mother dear, although my head does sometimes ache."

She was leaning over me on the bed, and, nestling close to her, I put my head upon her chest.

" Mother," I asked, " why does your heart beat so fast ? "

" Because I am afraid, my darling."

" Are you also afraid of the night ? "

" By night and by day, I am always afraid."

" Afraid of what ? "

" I am afraid for you—— "

" For me ? "

My mother did not answer, but I felt that one of her hot tears had fallen upon my face.

" You are crying, mother ? "

The tears began to fall faster. I made up my mind not to tell her anything. Suddenly my mother asked me :

" Has Rivka told you anything ? "

" What about, mother ? "

" About your fiancé."

" How should she know my fiancé ? "

" If she had known him she would not have talked ; but as there are rumours in the town . . . you know, of course, envy, and when a wealthy old man is marrying a young maiden, then people will talk. They have not been telling you that his last wife died because he had been tormenting her ? "

With an air of indifference, I said that I had indeed heard something about it, but did not remember who told me.

" It must have been Rivka. May her mouth be shut for ever ! " replied my mother in an angry tone.

" But why did she die so suddenly ? " I asked.

" Why ? because she was suffering from heart disease."

" And people die when they are suffering from heart disease ? "

" Of course they do."

Something seemed to have snapped in my brain.

I had become a dear child, and was being praised all

over the town.   My parents could not understand it, and the dressmaker least of all.   I took no interest in my dresses.   It was my mother who chose the material and decided upon the cut and fashion.   I left it entirely to her to do as she liked.   Rivka was furious and came to scold me.

"Whoever heard of such a thing?" the girl cried. "How can you leave everything to your mother, a woman of the old world?   I tell you that you will not be able to show yourself anywhere on Saturdays, neither in the Synagogue, nor in the streets.   You are simply killing yourself," she concluded.

It occurred to me that I had already been killed long ago, and I calmly awaited the *Sabbath Nahmu* when my fiancé was to be invited for breakfast.   Then there would come the Sabbath on which the fiancé and my father would be called up to the reading of the Law, and then the wedding.

Father was really feeling much better.   He was now going out more frequently, and began to take an interest in the grain market.   But he considered it would be premature to ask my fiancé for a loan.   On *Sabbath Nahmu* he would invite him for the third Sabbath meal,[1] and then after the meal he would let drop a few words on the subject.

As we were already well off, my parents decided to pay the barber-surgeon his fees.   He was, of course, giving us credit now.   He never sent his assistant to us, but came himself, yet my parents felt that it was time to pay him.   I do not know how much they sent him, but it was Avrehmel, one of my brothers, who, on his way to school, was to take the few *gulden* to the barber-surgeon.   A little later the assistant suddenly came to our house.

"Well?" asked father.   "What is the matter, not enough?"

"No, Reb Jehouda, I have only come to say good-bye."

"Say good-bye to *me*?" father asked, greatly astonished.

When he came in I had almost fallen on to the nearest chair; but at these words I suddenly jumped up again. A thought had flashed across my brain that it was my duty to protect him, and not allow anybody to humiliate him. My fear, however, proved groundless.

" I used to be a frequent visitor in this house," he said in his gentle, sad voice, which was like balm poured upon my heart. " I used to be a frequent visitor here, and now I am leaving this town for ever, so I thought——"

" *Nu*, *Nu*, well, that is right," said my father more calmly. " Sit down, young man; it is quite thoughtful on your part to remember a customer, that's right."

" Darling," he added, turning to me, " we ought to give him something."

He grew pale, his lips were trembling, and his eyes were flashing; but the next minute his face changed again, assuming its former melancholy expression.

" No, Reb Jahouda," he said, " I don't want anything, thank you; good-bye."

He did not extend his hand and scarcely gave me a look. There was reproach in his eyes, and it seemed to me that he was accusing me of something, that he would never forgive me. For what? I did not exactly know myself. And once more I had fainted.

" It is the third time," I heard mother saying to father.

" That does not matter, it is a frequent occurrence nowadays; but should Reb Zanvil—heaven forbid—hear of it, he would be quite capable of breaking off the match. He has had enough of it with his other wife— the invalid."

But I did not become an invalid. Only once more did I faint, and that was at the Golden broth, when for the first time I had a good look at Reb Zanvil. That was all.

Even yesterday, when the barber-surgeon who comes to visit my Reb Zanvil every month to trim his nails which are growing into his flesh—even when he asked me whether I remembered his old assistant, I did not faint. And even when he told me that the boy had died

in hospital at Warsaw, I did not faint. Almost unconsciously I shed a tear. It was the barber-surgeon who
rather liked that tear, and called my attention to it.

" You are very kind-hearted," he said ; and it was only
then that I felt the tear upon my cheek.

That is all.

I am quite well, and I have been living with Reb Zanvil
for the last five years.

How ? This I will tell you on some other occasion.

V

THE REPUDIATED DAUGHTER

DURING the whole month of May wind and rain had worked havoc on the earth. It seemed as if summer would never make its appearance, that the rain and frost would continue for ever. On the eve of the feast of Pentecost, however, the sun suddenly unveiled its brilliant countenance.

"The *Torah* is light," said our father, full of joyous pride; and he straightway began to look for the book containing the special prayers for this solemn anniversary.

"The sun is shining in honour of the holy festival," exclaimed my mother, and immediately turned her attention to the making of cakes. "I will bake for you a *Halah* made with yolks of eggs," she informed us.

Soon the smell of fresh dough, of saffron, of cinnamon and clove, of sour and sweetened cheese, mixed with the vapours of melted butter, filled the room.

My younger sister, Hannah, took no part in these festive preparations. Seated at the open window, she was bending over a novel. She was not reading, however, but in a state of restlessness was looking out into the street. Several times my mother had invited her to come and lend a hand, but Hannah vouchsafed no reply. A mocking smile flitted across her pale countenance. She opened her lips as if to make some reply, but soon again turned her attention to her book.

" Lazy one," murmured my mother, " always busy with her silly books ; the preparations for the festival are no concern of hers."

Father, who never meddled in household matters, had now found the prayer book and dusted it. Before proceeding to the bath he decided to lie down for a while, so that he could sit up all night. Mother now ceased to grumble and scold my sister, for fear of waking father.

Softly she called me, and giving me a few coins, sent me out to buy some green plants and coloured paper, destined for the symbolical decoration of our windows. Heaven is my witness that I was loath to leave the house at that moment. There was a bowl full of cream and another containing sugared cheese, and there were also paper-bags full of dry raisins. But to go out alone into the street, marketing and buying things and paying for them, was a great temptation, and I hastened to run out.

Then we had a sad Pentecost. My sister Hannah had left us. Father and I were at the Synagogue, whilst mother, before lighting the candles to welcome the incoming sacred festival, lay down for a moment. It was then that they signalled to Hannah ; mother in her sleep had distinctly heard a loud whistle—and my sister had gone over to them—to our enemies. . . . And it was the eve of the Pentecost, the holy day on which we had once received the Holy Law on Mount Sinai, that she had chosen as the moment of her desertion.

Everything passes, happiness and misfortune, the good and the bad. We advance in life, drawing nearer to the place where everything is forgotten, or remembered anew. All that we have undergone remains behind us like stones on the road, like tombstones under which lie buried our dear friends and our enemies. But I could never forget my sister Hannah.

The life into which she had so recklessly plunged, soon threw her out. The happiness she had once pictured unto herself was soon destroyed and crushed, and for the flowers of her dream, there remained only the pricking of thorns.

But she could not return to us any more. The Law now forbad, and there were also two tombstones, the tombs of my father and my mother. Where is she now?

At every Pentecost, at sunset, she appears to me. I behold her standing in the street, near our window, as if afraid, or as if unable any more to enter a Jewish house. Her eyes wide open, she is casting a glance into our house, but she sees only me. There are supplication, fright, and anger in her look; and I, I understand her so well.

" Where are they ? " she asks me in a trembling voice.

" Forgive me," she begs. Then again anger seizes her and she vehemently accuses us of her misfortune.

" What did I know," she cries, " of your terrible quarrel with the others ? You, you knew of it, for you went to school. My books, the books I used to read, never told me anything. I have lived the life of a stranger in your house, a beautiful outside life which appeared to me even more beautiful through my books. Am I guilty of treason ? have I perjured myself ? I have only exchanged the *Halah* made with yolks of eggs for another sort of pastry. I have exchanged the legends of mother's *Tseno-Urenoh*[4] for other legends—perhaps more beautiful and more vivid. I have left the few sprays of green scattered over our house for the free and perfumed green of pastures and woods. I gave up the stale prayers for the sake of Romance. I abandoned the narrow, suffocating, shut-in life for the sake of sunshine and flowers, of joy and love.

" I have never been false to you, for I hardly knew you. I knew nothing of your sufferings, for you never told me of your life. Why did you not tell me anything of your love, that love that is nurtured with your life blood ? Why did you not speak to me of your beauty, of your eternal blood-stained beauty ? The beautiful, the sublime, the elevated, all that you have jealously guarded as a secret, keeping it for your men alone. What did you ask and expect of me, of all your women who are sadly yearning for life with all our youthful strength? Tarts and a *Halah* made with yolks of eggs.

"You had shut me out of your real life," she angrily exclaims.

May He who is above all nations; who is above their complicated quarrels and their bloody fights; may He alone judge her.

VI

DOMESTIC PEACE

———

HAYIM is a carrier. When he passes in the street, bent
under his heavy burden, you can hardly see him ; one
might think that it was a box walking upon two human
legs. And yet, one can hear from far the rhythm of his
heavy breathing.

But here he is unloading his burden, is receiving a few
groschen for his job. He straightens himself, draws a
deep breath and letting down the corners of his gaberdine
which he had pulled up so as to walk more easily, wipes
his perspiring brow. He wends his way to the fountain,
refreshes himself with a sip of clear water, and then hurries
away swiftly and enters the courtyard of his house.
Leaning against the wall he lifts up his giant head so that
his pointed beard, his nose, and the vizor of his cap, are
all in one line. He calls aloud :

" Hannah ! "

A narrow window is opened just underneath the roof,
and the small head of a woman in a white bonnet appears.

" Hayim ! "

They look at each other with a smile of content. The
neighbours, when talking about the couple, say they are
still courting. Hayim throws up to the window his
meagre gain, a few coins wrapped up in a piece of paper.
Hannah catches the money, being used to this game, as
it is not the first time.

" Wonderfully clever of you," says Hayim, who does
not seem to be in a hurry to go away.

" Go, go, Hayim," she says smiling ; " I cannot leave
the sick child. I have moved the cradle near the cooking
stove, and whilst I am skimming the pot with my hand,
I am rocking the child's cradle with my foot."

" How is the poor mite ? "

" Better."

" Thank God ! And Hena ? "

" She is working at the dressmaker's."

" And Yossel ? "

" At school."

Hayim lowers his beard and walks off, whilst Hannah
accompanies him with her eyes until he disappears from
her view. On Thursdays and Fridays their interview lasts
a little longer.

" How much have you got in that paper ? " asks
Hannah.

" Twenty-two *groschen*."

" I am afraid that it is not enough."

" What is it that you still require, Hannah ? "

" I want six *groschen's* worth of ointment for the child,
a few *groschen* for candles. I have already the Sabbath
loaves and the meat—a pound and a half—I have no wine
yet for the *Kiddush*, then I also require a few logs—— "

" Logs I will try and find, there ought to be some in
the market-place—

" Then I also require—— "

And Hannah enumerates all the things that she still
requires for the Sabbath. They at last decide to do
without a good many things, and to recite the benediction
of *Kiddush* over bread instead of over a cup of wine.
They could do without a good many things. What they
would have to get first of all are the Sabbath candles and
the ointment for the child.

And yet, if such is the will of God, when the children
are all in good health, when the copper candlesticks are
not pawned, and especially when there is a *Kuggel* for the
Sabbath meal, then the household passes an enjoyable

Sabbath. For Hannah is quite an expert in the art of preparing a *Kuggel*. Of course, it frequently happens that she has not all the ingredients required for the *Kuggel*; one Friday it is flour, another, eggs, and a third, fat; but always the *Kuggel* proves a great success, succulent and delicious.

"It is an angel who has cooked the *Kuggel*," says Hannah, her face shining with happiness.

"Yes, it is surely an angel," replies Hayim, "and you yourself, are you not an angel, bearing so patiently with me and the children? They are often unkind, and I myself am sometimes short-tempered. Well, have I ever heard an unkind word, much less an oath, from you, as so many husbands hear from their wives? Well, have you so much happiness with me? You yourself and the children are walking naked and barefooted. And what good am I? I am not much good either at orisons or prayers, at *Kiddush* or *Habdalah*. I cannot even properly sing the Sabbath hymns."

"Never mind," Hannah persists, "you are still a good father and a good husband, and I pray to the Lord of the Universe that he may let us grow old together."

And the couple look into one another's eyes with so much tenderness, with so much warmth and cordiality, that you might think they had just left the nuptial canopy. And the happiness and joy reigning at the table become even greater.

On Sabbath afternoon, after a short nap, Hayim goes to the small Synagogue to hear the Divine Word. A school-teacher is explaining to the people a passage from the *Alshech*. It is rather hot in the Synagogue, and the faces of the worshippers are still sleepy; some of them are dozing, whilst others are yawning loudly. But when the teacher reaches the right passage, the interesting subject of heaven and hell, where the author is describing the next world, how the wicked are being flogged with iron rods in hell; when he is giving a word picture of the glories of Paradise, where the just are sitting, golden crowns upon their heads, and studying the holy *Torah*,

then the general attention is riveted at once. The
worshippers, mouths agape and faces flushed, hardly
daring to breathe aloud, are listening to what will happen
in the next world.

Hayim as a rule takes up a seat neat the stove. His eyes
are tear-filled, and his limbs are trembling ; he is entirely
in the next world. He is suffering together with the
wicked ; together with them he is being immersed in
boiling pitch, is thrown into the abyss, or is collecting
prickles in dark forests. All these torments he is under-
going himself, is imagining so vividly that a cold sweat
covers his whole body. But, in return, he soon partici-
pates in the reward meted out to the just and pious. He
sees so clearly the glorious dazzling Paradise, the angels,
the *Leviathan*, the *Shor-habor*, and the many other good
things dished-up for the pious, sees them so vividly and
so clearly that when the preacher at last closes his book,
kissing it devoutly, Hayim wakes up as if from a dream,
as if he had really just returned from the next world.

" Great and Mighty Lord of the Universe," sighs
Hayim, drawing again a deep breath, " only one tiny bit,
one crumb of Paradise for me, my wife and all n'
children."

Then Hayim grows sad. " Unhappy man that I am,"
he sighs, " what claim have I to Paradise ? What right
to enter it ? "

Once he mustered courage enough to approach the
preacher after the conclusion of his lecture.

" Rabbi," says Hayim in a trembling voice, " give me
advice. What can I do to deserve Paradise ? "

" Study the *Torah*, my child," is the reply.

" I am too ignorant."

" Study the *Mishnah*, or the *Ayn Yaakov*, or at least
the *Maxims of the Ancients*."

" I am too ignorant," again replies Hayim.

" Recite the Psalms of David."

" I have no time."

" Pray devoutly."

" I do not understand the meanings of the words."

The teacher gazed at him with a look of pity.

" What is your occupation ? "

" I am a carrier."

" Then try and make yourself useful to the pious students of the Law."

" How could I do it ? "

" Bring, for instance, every evening to the *Beth-Hamidrash* a couple of cans of water so that the learned may have something to drink."

Hayim is quite happy.

" Rabbi," he queries again, " and what about my wife ? "

" When the husband occupies a chair in Paradise," replied the Rabbi, " his wife is his footstool."

When Hayim returned home to recite the *Habdalah*, Hannah was just singing the prayer beginning with the words, " God of Abraham." When Hayim perceived his wife, a deep emotion swept over his frame.

" No, Hannah," he cried, taking his wife into his arms, " no, I don't want you to be my footstool in Paradise. I will stoop down to you, lift you up, and place you by my side. Together, we shall be seated in the same easy chair just as here below. It is so nice to be together. You hear, Hannah ? You shall sit with me in the same easy chair. The Almighty will *have* to grant our request."

VII

IN THE BASEMENT

A VAST basement full of beds.

In her corner between the stove and the wall Frida is already asleep on her box. She had gone to bed early to-night because she would have to rise up with dawn to-morrow morning and start with her barrel of tar for the fair. Her sleep, however, is rather restless and she is tossing about on her improvised couch. She knows that she will have trouble with the driver of the coach. She had arranged with him to take herself and her *small* barrel, but before falling asleep it had occurred to her that it would be best after all to take the large barrel. She was very angry with herself for her thoughtlessness. How stupid women are, she grumbled, why ever did I tell him that it would be the small barrel? What business is it of his? What? He would have to treat his horses to another mouthful of oats. And thus grumbling and abusing herself for her "wicked tongue" she had fallen asleep. From beneath her blankets a red shawl emerges falling over her face, framing her long pointed blue nose. She is breathing heavily, probably because her bony hand is lying upon her old chest. God alone knows what she is dreaming about. In her sleep she is perhaps having a quarrel with the driver, who is chucking her and her barrel out of the cart, and she will thus be unable to earn her living for six months.

The opposite corner is inhabited by Yosel, the water-carrier. His wife and two children are sleeping in one bed, whilst he himself and his eldest *Cheder*-boy occupy the second bed. In this corner, too, groans are frequently heard coming from the beds. The schoolboy had come home in tears because the master demanded his money, whilst the eldest daughter had lost her situation. She had an excellent place with a childless couple ; but unfortunately the mistress had suddenly taken it into her head to die, and the girl was compelled to leave the house, as she could not very well stay on alone with a widower. They still owed her part of her wages, which would have come in handy and enabled the parents to pay for the boy's schooling, but the widower had refused to pay. " I know nothing about the debt," he said, " my wife has not told me about it, and I never bothered about the household management, which is woman's domain."

Before going to sleep there had even been a little quarrel in Yosel the water-carrier's household. The mother was of opinion that the widower should be summoned before the Rabbi, whilst the daughter preferred to address a petition to the local Justice of Peace. Yosel, however, would hear neither of the Rabbi, nor of the Justice of Peace.

" The widower," he said, " will take his revenge and do me a great deal of harm in my business. He wields a good deal of influence in the town and has only to say a word, to whistle, and it will be all over with me. You have no idea how many water-carriers there are going about idle."

A little higher up, Berl, the carrier, is snoring alone like a prince in his bed, whilst his two children are sleeping in the next bed. Berl's wife is a cook in a big house, and there is a wedding banquet to-night. In this corner, too, the sleep of the occupants is restless. For some time already Berl has been feeling an acute pain in his bones. The eldest boy is groaning in his sleep because he is working in a chalk-kiln and had burned his foot.

A little farther down there sleeps like a perfect lady,

alone in her bed, Zirl, the watcher of the dead; whilst
her three children repose in the second bed. Zirl's
husband, the night watcher, will only return with the
break of dawn, and then she herself will go out on her
daily round, selling bread and fresh rolls.

We have now reached the third corner, where stands
an iron bedstead. An unhealthy-looking woman's head
emerges from a heap of rags, serving the sleeper as a
pillow. The young dry lips frequently part, and a deep
sigh escapes them. Her husband's is a difficult profession;
and, besides, fortune never seems to favour him. With
great risk to limb and life, he had managed last week to
carry off a copper basin, which he had hidden in the
ground on the outskirts of the town. As ill-luck would
have it, he was found out, and heaven only knew what
result awaited his efforts to-night; maybe he has been
arrested. For three weeks already, the woman is thinking,
we have not put the pot upon the fire to boil, and the
landlord is threatening to throw us out from our corner.

"It is a hard profession indeed, and no luck," sigh
the fever-parched lips. "Besides, I have to keep it secret
from the neighbours, who are constantly worrying me
with their questions: 'What is your husband doing?
Why is he coming home so late?'"

Above all these beds a dim light is trembling, coming
from the middle of the room. The light issues from
behind the Spanish partition that marks the boundaries
of a domain belonging to a newly-married couple, known
among the inmates as *Trinah's four-yard kingdom*. Trinah,
who has been married only for two months, is not asleep
yet, but is expecting her husband back from the *Beth-
Hamidrash*. It is in Trinah's domain that the night-light
is burning, casting its reflection upon the black ceiling,
and sending out through the slits in the Spanish partition
the few poor rays of light which are dancing over the
miserable beds and the bored, extenuated faces of the
occupants.

In Trinah's kingdom there is a little more light and
greater cleanliness. Between the small beds stands a

white little table and upon it lies a woman's prayer book (*Korban Minha*) between two small copper candlesticks, Trinah's wedding present. On the wall are hung up the couple's new garments, a *Talith* satchel with a tower of David embroidered upon it. There are no chairs, however, within the precincts of this domain. Trinah herself is seated upon one bed, mending a net, to carry the onions which are spread out all over the sheet. She has heaped up all the pillows on the other bed to keep warm the pot containing the supper.

The door is very quietly opened and a faint flush suffuses Trinah's countenance. Throwing down her net, she rises as if about to rush out and meet her husband, but she soon checks her impulse. No, she thinks, it is not decent on account of the neighbours. If any one of them were to wake up and see her going to meet her husband, she would, on the following morning, become the laughing-stock of all the inmates. Trinah has to suffer a great deal from her neighbours, and, above all, from that abominable Freidel. The old hag could not understand how a woman was able to refrain from cursing her husband, even on the morrow after their marriage.

" You wait a bit, my beauty," Freidel was wont to repeat, " you wait and see what life he will soon lead you. You have only to show him one finger, and—— "

Freidel never gave Trinah any respite. " If you do not lead your husband by the nose," she was constantly repeating, " he will turn out to be worse than a wolf ; he will suck the very marrow from your bones and the blood from your veins. Look at me," the old hag argued, " here have I been husbandless for ten years, and I have not yet managed to regain the strength I lost in the course of my married life."

She was a clever woman, that Freidel, a learned woman, nd she used to say :

" Whatever is due to him according to the Jewish Law, give it to him by all means ; but give it to him as if you were throwing a bone to a dog. As for the rest, keep off the grass ! And never forget to hurl curses at his head."

Trinah has plenty of time to recall to her mind Freidel's advice and teaching, for it takes *Yosele*, her husband, a little while to wend his way on tiptoe between the numerous beds of the neighbours. At every step Trinah's heart beats faster, but as for going out to meet him, she would not do it for anything in the world. Ah, he has nearly stumbled in the dark and fallen ; thank God, he has reached the partition, and Trinah is breathing more freely.

" Good evening," he says in a low voice, his eyes downcast.

" Good year," replies Trinah, even more softly.

" Are you hungry ? " she asks.

" And you ? "

" Hm."

He goes behind the partition to perform the ritual ablution of his hands, and soon returns. She hands him a towel. The bread and salt and the hot supper are on the table already, waiting for him to say the blessing.

They sit down, he on the bed covered with the cushions and pillows, she on the other with the onions. They eat very slowly, talking to each other with their eyes, after the manner of a newly-married couple, whilst with their lips they converse in a low voice about business and earning a living.

" Well," asks Trinah, " how far have you succeeded ? "

" I have already three pupils," he replies.

" That means that it will be teaching after all ? " she asks rather sadly.

" Well," says he, " what can I do ? "

" Thank God even for this," she says, trying to console both him and herself.

" Yes ; thank God for this," he repeats after her, " but this only means a hundred and twenty roubles."

" Well, why are you sighing ? "

" Well, count for yourself," he replies. " We require one rouble a week for rent, that makes twenty-six roubles for six months. Then I still owe for the wedding expenses—— "

" What do you mean by owing ? " she asks in astonishment.

He smiles.

" Little silly, did you really imagine that father could do more than promise ? "

" Well," she interrupts him, " that makes how much ? "

" It makes," he continues, " twelve roubles—that is thirty-eight roubles in all. Well, how much will there remain for food ? "

She is calculating.

" I think eighty-two roubles."

" For twenty-six weeks."

" Well," she says, " that makes a little over three roubles per week."

" And what about heating, lighting, and extra expenses for the Sabbaths and festivals ? " he asks sadly.

" *Atj*," she replies by way of consolation, " God will not forsake us. I can also earn something. Look, I have bought onions, and eggs being cheap now I will buy some. In a couple of weeks, when prices go up, I shall have earned something. And now," she continues, " let us reckon out how much we require for heating and lighting. I do not think that it will cost us much—at the utmost one rouble a week, so that there still remains—— "

" But you are forgetting the extra expenses for Sabbaths and festivals. What are you talking about, my child ? "

The word *child* he had pronounced so softly, so tenderly, that a happy smile spread over her face.

" Never mind," she replies, " say your grace after meals and leave the calculations for to-morrow. It is time to go to bed."

She suddenly blushes, droops her eyes, and as if to excuse herself, adds :

" You come home so late," she said, making a pretence to suppress a yawn.

He bends over to her across the table.

" You silly child," he says in a whisper, " I am purposely coming home so late, that we might eat together. Otherwise the neighbours would talk, as it is not supposed to be decent among us for a school-teacher to be so intimate with his wife, you understand ? "

" Well, hurry up and say your grace," she repeats, her eyes shut.

He, too, shuts his eyes, that he may recite his grace with devotion ; but, against his will, his eyes open every moment. He is shutting his eyes more firmly still, but there seems to be a slit through which he can see his wife wonderfully illuminated, so that he is unable to take his gaze from her. She is tired, he thinks, and he feels pity for her. He sees how she is pushing up a little higher upon her bed and leaning her head against the wall. She is going to fall asleep like that, he thinks. But why does she not take a pillow for her head ?

He feels annoyed, but he must not interrupt his prayers, and only tries to call her attention by uttering a loud " *Hm, hm.*" She does not seem to hear him, and he hurries on with his prayers, finishes them, and rises from his bed. But he suddenly stands still, not knowing what to do.

He calls out " Trinah ! " but in such a low voice that it cannot wake her. He approaches her bed, bends over her. What a sweet smile is hovering round her lips ! She must be dreaming of something very pleasant. Oh, how beautiful her smile is ! It is a pity to wake her. But she will have a headache, sleeping without a pillow, her head leaning against the wall. What beautiful hair she once had ! He had seen it on the night of their engagement, dark long tresses, but now they have been shaved off,[1] although her hair is very becoming, it seems to be smiling too.

But he must wake her up after all. He bends lower still and fells her breath, which he eagerly inhales. She is drawing him like a magnet, and almost against his will, his lips touch hers——

" But I am not at all asleep," she cries, opening her

mischievous, laughing eyes. Throwing her arms round his neck, she draws him to her.

"Never mind," she whispers into his ear, "it is so sweet, so lovely; never mind. God, the Merciful One will help us. Did He not bring us together? He will not forsake us, but send us heating and lighting and maintenance. All will be well. Is it not so, my Yosele?"

He is silent, trembling all over.

She pushes him back a little.

"Look at me, Yosele," she suddenly begs him.

He would like to obey her, but cannot.

"You *batlen*," she says in a very soft voice. "Have you not yet grown accustomed to me?"

He tries to hide his face on her bosom, but she will not let him.

"Why are you ashamed, you silly? If you can kiss me, why not look at me?"

He prefers to kiss her, but again she holds him back.

"Look at me, I beg you."

Yosele opens his eyes, but almost against his will they close again.

"I beg you," she says again, in an even softer, more gentle and tender voice.

Yosele is looking, and now it is Trinah's turn to lower her gaze.

"Tell me," she asks him; "tell me the truth, Yosele, am I a beautiful woman?"

"Yes," he whispers, and she can feel his hot breath pressing upon her.

"Who told you that?".

"I see it myself; you are a queen, a veritable queen."

"And tell me, Yosele, will you always be like that?"

"What do you mean, Trinah?"

"I mean," she replies in a trembling voice, "I mean will you always be so good to me?"

"Of course."

"Always so tender?"

"Of course."

"Always?"

" Always," he assures her.

" You will always eat together with me ? "

" Always," he replies.

" You will never grow angry with me or scold me ? "

" Never, please God."

" You will never make me suffer ? "

" Make you suffer ? I ? You ? Why should I ? "

" I don't know, but Friedel says—— "

" Oh, that hag—— "

He moves closer to her, but she still holds him back.

" Yosele ? "

" Yes ? "

" Tell me, what is my name ? "

" Trinah ! "

" Fie ! " she makes a grimace.

" *Trineshou*," he corrects himself.

She is not satisfied.

" *Trinenyou*."

" No," she says.

" Then, Trinah darling, my life, my crown, my heart Is that better ? "

" Yes," she answers happily, " but—— "

" But what, my life, my joy ? "

" But listen, Yosele, and—— " she begins, but suddenly hesitates.

" And what ? "

" And if we should be in want, heaven forbid, if I should not earn anything myself, will you not scold me ? " Tears well up in her eyes.

" Heaven forbid, heaven forbid ! " he assures her.

Freeing his head from her hands that were holding it fast, he covers her still parted lips with hot kisses.

*   *   *   *   *

" A plague upon them ; a disease into their hands and feet ! " A voice is suddenly heard from behind the partition. " Disgraceful ; only kissing and smacking ; can't they let decent people have any rest ? "

It was Freidel's hoarse, harsh voice.

VIII

THE POOR BOY

(A Story Told by a Committee Man)

———

" Give me eight *groschen* for a night's shelter."

" No," I answer harshly and go my way.

He is running after me, begging like a dog with his sparkling eyes, kissing my sleeve; but it is of no avail. My income does not allow me to indulge in such charities every day. You soon have enough of these poor people, these beggars, think I, leaving the soup-kitchen where I had just treated the begging boy so harshly.

The first time when I beheld the dirty emaciated young face with its sunken but darkly glittering, melancholy, small eyes, I was moved to the quick. Even before I heard his request, my heart was moved and a coin quickly came out of my pocket, disappearing in his palm. I remember perfectly well that it was my hand alone that did it. The hand never inquired either of my heart whether it registered pity or of the brain—the accountant —whether one could afford to give away five copecks n charity out of a pension of forty-one roubles and sixty-six copecks a month.

The boy's request had simply been an electric spark, setting into motion every limb in my body, every cell in each limb, and it was only later on that the brain—the accountant—had been informed of the new expense. It was much later when the boy, skipping for joy, had already left the soup-kitchen.

Busy with my own and other people's affairs, I soon forgot the boy, but, as it proved, not entirely. Without my knowing it a meeting of *practical* thoughts must have taken place in some corner of my brain, because as soon as the same boy accosted me on the second evening, begging for the price of a night's lodging, ready thoughts at once emerged in my mind. These thoughts were as follows : A boy of seven or eight should not beg ; nor should he hang about in the soup-kitchen getting his food there, because this habit would make an idler of him, a beggar, and he would never get on in the world. My hand was unconsciously creeping towards my pocket, but I caught it in time and stopped it. Had I been a religious man I might have thought : Is this action worth eight *groschen* ? Could I not perhaps recite the afternoon prayers instead, or show more devotion, groan more deeply, whilst praying ? Not being a very pious man, I only had the boy's welfare in my mind. With these eight *groschen*, I thought, I should only do him harm, make a beggar of him.

And yet I gave him again what he asked me for. My hand was making an effort to get out of my pocket, and I no longer kept it back ; my heart was aching and my eyes were moist. Once more he left the kitchen in great glee. I felt as if a load had been lifted from my chest, my heart was lighter. I felt a smile flitting across my face.

The third time it took me longer, much longer, to make up my mind. I had already decided that my pension would not allow me to give away eight *groschen* every day. True, it was quite a pleasure to see the tear-stained lad dance and skip for joy, to watch the light flash up in his eyes, to know that with these eight *groschen* he would be able to pass the night not in the street, but in a lodging house, where he would be warm, that he would also receive a cup of tea and a roll in the morning. All that

was a pleasure, but with my income I could not afford
such pleasures.

Of course, I did not tell the boy all this. I preferred to
preach morals to him. I preferred to give him a moral
lesson, how else ? I gave him to understand that he was
ruining himself with this begging ; it was the duty of
every man to work ; that he, too, must grow up to be
a man. Work is a sacred thing and when one looked
for it one found it. I gave him much good advice, which
I had gleaned from books ; I gave it to the boy freely,
although it served him but little, either as a substitute for
a night's lodging or as a borrowed umbrella to protect
him during the night against rain or snow.

He stood there, continuing to kiss my sleeve, raising
his eyes to see whether he could surprise a spark of pity
in my face and whether his words were producing any
effect upon me. I began to feel that his hopes were after
all not in vain, that my emotion was getting the better of
my reason and discretion, that his dog-like pleading eyes
were after all subduing me, that, in spite of my batteries of
accounts and moral lessons, I should soon be compelled
to surrender. I decided to give him the coin this time,
but to tell him in a sharp tone that he must give up begging.
I had no small change, so I changed a coin and handed
him the eight *groschen*.

" Now," I said, " no more begging, you hear ? Never
beg again from me ! "

" From me ! " Where on earth had these two
additional words come from ? Anyhow, I had never
intended to utter them, and I would willingly have taken
them back. It seemed to me that a cold breeze had
suddenly passed over me, that somewhere I had torn off
the covering and my soul lay bare. The thought, however,
passed like a flash of lightning through my brain, whilst
my severe mien, my metallic hard voice, my extended
right hand, and my advanced left foot, continued to do
their work. They produced the desired effect upon the
boy. Standing as if on hot coals, anxious to run away
and reach the lodging-house as early as possible, he had

grown pale on hearing my words, and a tear trembled on his eyelash.

" Don't beg again," I concluded my exhortation ; " you hear ! This shall be the last time."

He drew a deep breath and ran away.

To-day I had refused to give him the coin he was begging for. I must keep my word. A word is precious, and a man must keep his word, otherwise there would be no order in the world. I once more make a mental examination of my action, and I feel satisfied with myself.

I cannot afford to give away eight *groschen* in charity every day, but that was not the real reason of my refusal. The real reason was my anxiety for the boy's welfare. I had had in mind his own good and also the good of the community at large ; because charity distributed without any system is worthless, and how could there be any system if we are not firm ?

I had spoken plainly, in ordinary Yiddish, to the boy, but to myself I used more learned language, employing scientific expressions. " Begging," I said to myself, " is the most pernicious microbe in the social body. He who refuses to work has no right to life," etc., etc.

Hastily I closed the door of the soup-kitchen behind me and was soon swallowed up by the dark night, my retreating feet sinking in the mud. The wind was fierce, the flames of the street-lamps were trembling as if they felt the cold, and their lights were reflected in puddles of mud that made me almost giddy. The wind was whistling in a plaintive tune, as if a thousand souls were pleading for salvation, or a thousand boys begging for eight *groschen* for a night's lodging.

Dash it ; again the boy !

One would not drive a dog into the street on such a night ; and yet, the boy will have to pass the night in the streets ! Well, what can I do ? It was quite sufficient for me to have given him the eight *groschen* three times ; let others give him something now. I have done enough. I have a weak throat and am coughing, and yet I visited the soup-kitchen. True, I am a member of the Committee, but no one had compelled me to come out and pay a visit of inspection, especially on such a night; and I had no fur coat! Had I been a pious man, a believer, I might have attributed my visit to the kitchen on such a night to selfishness, having in mind my own profit. I could have returned home and quickly gone to bed, to give my soul a chance to soar up to heaven during my sleep, and credit it with a good action in the account book, the reward for which would be a piece of *Leviathan*. Was I, however, thinking of reward and *Leviathan* when I went out to visit the soup-kitchen? No, it was only my kind heart that had made me venture out on such a night.

Thus praising myself, I felt a little warmer, and my gnawing heart grew calmer. Had others praised me, I should have felt ashamed and waved them off, but I can praise myself without feeling ashamed. I should have continued to sing my own praises, to discover new virtues in myself, but unfortunately, I got deep into the mud, with my thin shoes. Heaven alone knows that I had worn out the soles of my shoes in my too frequent visits to the soup-kitchen.

The *Talmud* says that the messengers engaged on a pious errand never come to any grief. I suppose that this must apply only to the messengers who are still on their outward journey, who are still hastening to perform the good deed. On their return journey, when the angel they have called into being through their good action is already soaring up to heaven, then they often run the risk of breaking their necks!

My feet are wet and I am cold all over. I feel sure that I am going to catch a cold. No, I am quite convinced that I have already caught it. In another moment I shall have a fit of coughing, and feel an acute pain in my side. Terror seizes me ; only recently I was laid up for four weeks.

" You really must not do it," something in me is whispering, revolting against my own conduct. " Of course, you can sacrifice yourself, if it so pleases you,

5

but what about your wife and children? Have you a right to deprive *them* of their support and protection?"

Had these words been uttered by another, not by myself, had I read such a sentence in print, I should have known how to deal with it, how to criticize it. But the words were uttered by myself.

I am quite sure that I have caught a cold. I am still a long way from home, and my boots are full of water. I suddenly perceive the lighted windows of a café, the worst in Warsaw—abominable tea; but I have no choice. Hastily I cross the street and enter a warm, lighted room.

I order a cup of tea and take up an illustrated paper. The first illustration that catches my eye seems to have some reference to the weather. It represents the following incident: The weather is bad (like that from which I have just escaped); two persons are meeting on the pavement. From one side comes a stout middle-aged lady, well fed, wearing a silk dress, a velvet coat, and a hat with a white feather upon her head. She had evidently left her home when the weather was fine, going out to pay some visits, and now on her way home she has been surprised by the rain. She looks somewhat frightened, afraid of the rain on her own account and perhaps even more for her velvet coat. She is hurrying, and beads of perspiration appear upon her white brow. She is hurrying, but her footsteps do not seem to be quite firm, on account of the wind which is blowing so fiercely. She has both her hands full. With her right she is holding up the train of her mud-stained and bedraggled silk dress, whilst in her left hand she carries a silken sunshade, hardly large enough to cover the white feather on her hat. The lady is only lacking one thing, and that is an umbrella, whilst she seems to possess everything else in abundance and to be leading a life without care and worry.

From the opposite side comes a young girl, all skin and bones. She has, perhaps, a wealth of beautiful hair, but, no doubt, she has only little time to bestow upon her hair. She is, of course, hatless, and it is being blown by the wind.   Her skirt is torn, tattered and patched up, and the wind is mercilessly blowing into her face, enveloping her frail body, penetrating through her scanty clothing to her very bones.   Her bare feet are mud-bedraggled.   She, too, is fighting against the wind and has both her hands full.   In her left she is carrying a pair of man's boots which she is evidently taking to the cobbler to be mended ;   the broken soles make this clear.   Her father must have come home from work tired out, and the mother is cooking supper.   She, the eldest child, has been sent out to the cobbler with the boots, for they must be mended at once and ready by the next morning for her father to go to work.   She, too, is in a hurry, for should the cobbler not be able to mend the boots at once, there would be no fire and no food in the house to-morrow.   The boots she is carrying in her left hand seem to be too heavy for her, but still heavier is the object that she is proudly holding in her right hand—a big, though old, umbrella ;   her father's umbrella.

The scantily clad child must be lacking a good many things in life—warmth in winter, clothes both in winter and summer, food all the year round—but she has something at the present moment and plenty of it, and that is an umbrella.   I am quite convinced that at the moment when the two met, the wealthy stout lady must have envied the poorly clad child her big umbrella.

With mischievously laughing eyes, the little girl, though tossed about by the wind, is looking up at me from the page of the illustrated paper.   Her eyes seem to be saying : " You see, we, too, have sometimes our pleasures in life ! Just now, I am better off than the stout lady."

Paying for the cup of tea which I had scarcely tasted, I once more remember the beggar boy.   He has no umbrella, I think, and no home to go to ;   no home whatever, where he might at least expect to find some hot potatoes, even without butter.   No bed, no parents are waiting for him anywhere.   He has nothing which the wealthy lady could have envied even for one brief instant. But how did I come to think again of the boy ?   Oh, yes,

I remember. When I was paying my bill for the tea which I had scarcely tasted, it flashed across my brain that with the money for the tea I had just ordered, the boy might have been able to get a piece of bread or half a portion of soup, in addition to a night's lodging.

And why had I ordered a pot of tea ? Tea and supper would be ready for me when I came home, and someone with a pleasant smile would be sitting up for me. Why had I ordered a pot of tea ? Well, I answer my own question : I had to order something when I entered the café.

The storm in the streets had not abated, but, on the contrary, had grown fiercer. The wind is fiercely pulling and tearing at the roofs, as if they had been Jews and he an anti-Semite, but the roofs are of iron and in their own homes. With tremendous fury down goes the storm to the street-lamps, but the street-lamps remain erect, continuing to shed their light, somewhat like the martyr-scholars in the days of the Inquisition. Deeper still goes the storm, attacking the very pavement, but the paving stones are deeply embedded in the ground, and the earth does not so easily give up her tenants. With increased fury the storm rises up again, raging fiercer and fiercer, rising heavenwards, but the heavens are far away, and the skies are looking down either indifferently or with a mocking smile. The people in the streets are bending their backs, lowering their heads, almost shrinking into themselves, shrivelling up so as to occupy as little space as possible, but they continue their way.

" How will the poor boy fare ? " I ask myself in a fright. Gone was all my philosophy ; pity had taken its place. Suppose it had been my own child ? Suppose I had now been thinking about my own flesh and blood tossed about by the storm ? Suppose it had been one of my own children who was compelled to pass such a stormy night in the streets, or having obtained eight *groschen* by begging, had to cross the bridge over the Vistula, and walk for miles in search of a lodging-house ? Is he less deserving because he is not my own child ? Is he worse because those to whom he belonged are lying somewhere in a grave under a tombstone ? Does he feel the storm less, or is he trembling less for cold ?

I lose my inclination to go home. Methinks I have no right either to the cosy room, the hot tea, the warm bed, or to the pleasant smile of those who are sitting up for me. Methinks that upon my brow there are engraven the words, " Assassin, Cain." Methinks that I dare not face my fellow-creatures. And once more I begin to think about piety and religion.

" Devil take it all," I scold myself, " if I had only been a believer, a religious man, I would have been all right then ! I would have felt sure that He who is dwelling above the stars yonder up in the highest heaven does not take off his eyes from the world, not even for one instant. I could have consoled myself with the thought that *He* would not abandon the poor boy ! "

Why should the boy weigh so heavily upon my heart ? I would sooner throw him upon the heart of the universe. I would not think for a moment of the boy, were I sure that he is safe under the eye of the cosmos. Were this universal eye to close for one moment, the universe would go to the devil, but as long as this eye is watching, the smallest worm will not perish unaccounted for, without justice or equity.

And now, not being a believer, I am compelled to trudge the streets with wet feet, suffering from my throat, in search of the strange orphan. It is a shame and a disgrace. Wherein my shame and disgrace lay, what I was ashamed of, I know not even to this day ; and yet, on account of this shame and disgrace, I trudged back to the soup-kitchen. I did not walk straight there, but I reached the place at last, after wandering about through several streets. The first room, the dining-room, is empty. The turmoil and hubbub of the day is beginning to cease, and the vapours are rising up higher and higher from the wet floor, forming a new sky, a new *Rakia*, separating the lower waters, running from the boots of the poor, from the upper waters, the drops dripping down from the ceiling.　Through the open small window I perceive how the sleepy cook, her wig awry, leaning with her left arm upon the big cauldron, is slowly lifting the big spoon to her lips with her right hand.　I see how the assistant cook, also sleepy, is making *Lokshen* for to-morrow, whilst the overseer is counting the tickets for dinners served at the expense of the Committee.　Perceiving no one else, I cast a look under the tables, but no trace of the boy.　I had come too late.

It is lucky, at least, I think, leaving the kitchen, that no one has noticed me.　I suddenly become aware that I have been wandering about in the streets for hours.

" What the devil is the matter with me ? " I exclaim, waxing very wroth with myself; and I begin to wend my way home.

I am glad to find that my family has gone to bed. Divesting myself of my shoes in the vestibule, I stealthily walk in and creep into bed.　I have a bad night, though. Tired, exhausted, cold, and wet, it was a long time before I had finished coughing and got warm ; but a sort of shudder was still running in my bones. I fell asleep very late, and then terrible dreams came to torture me.　I awoke bathed in a cold sweat, and jumping out of bed, rushed up to the window.

I looked out of the window and beheld the star-studded vault—the stars looking like so many diamonds set in an iron sky, wandering about so proud, so calm, and so distant.　The storm was still raging, and the house was shaking.

I quickly got into bed again, but I did not sleep any more.　I dozed off a little, still haunted by dreams, all turning round the boy.　Every time I saw him in a different place.　I saw him trudging along the muddy streets, crouching on some steps, under the protruding roof of a shop.　I saw demons tossing him about in mid-air like a ball, and later on I discovered him lying quite frozen and stiff upon a dunghill.

It was scarcely day when I impatiently rushed off to the soup-kitchen.

The boy was there! Had I not been ashamed, I would have washed off the dirt from his face with grateful tears. Had I not been afraid of my wife, I would have adopted him and taken him home. He was there, and I was not his murderer.

" Here," I said. And I handed him a coin. He took it, greatly surprised, not knowing what he had done for me. Long may he live!

The next day, when he once more begged from me, I did not give him anything, but I no longer dared to preach. I went away, thoroughly ashamed, feeling dissatisfied with myself.

I really cannot afford to give away so much in charity, but my heart is aching. Why can I not afford it?

My grandfather, peace be upon him, was right when he used to say: " A man who is not religious lives with heartache and dies without consolation."

IX

FOUR GENERATIONS—FOUR WILLS

———

1

WHEN Reb Eliezer Haikel's departed this world they found under his pillow the following will :—

" It is my will that my children remain associates in my timber trade. After my death they are to make a new enclosure round the cemetery, and repair the roof of the synagogue.

" All my books I leave to my unmarried son Benjamin, may he live. My other sons and sons-in-law have received their share of books when they married.

" My wife, may she live, should occupy my house by herself, but take in a poor orphan girl to live with her, so as not to be lonely. The ceremonies of *Kiddush* and *Habdalah* she is to perform herself. She is to have an equal share with all the other inheritors. Besides— — "

But the remaining part of the will was illegible, as it had evidently got damp under the pillow, and the letters were almost obliterated.

2

Reb Banjamin, Reb Eliezer Haikel's son, left a longer will :—

" My time is coming, and I shall soon have the advantage of returning the pledge I have received to Him to whom all pledges belong. Man is afraid of His blessed name, and of the judgment awaiting him in the next world; but I am going without any misgivings, heaven forbid. I have implicit faith in a merciful God and am firmly convinced that He will not only mete out to me strict justice, but deal with me in accordance with His great mercy and loving-kindness.

"I know, alas, that in my keeping the pledge He entrusted to me has become soiled and damaged."

We pass over the account he gave of his immortal soul, and the moral instructions he left for his children.

"And my legs," he continued in his will, "are growing colder every day, and my brain is getting more confused. Yesterday a wonderful thing happened to me. I fell asleep whilst studying, and I dreamed a dream. The book had slipped from my hand and I awoke with a start. I understood that it was not an ordinary occurrence, but that I had received a call from above.

"All that was really mine in this world, I leave behind only temporarily, and it will come back to me after a hundred and twenty years. By virtue of it I shall be permitted to witness the Majesty of the Holy *Shekhinah*. Amen, may thus be His will. And all my possessions which will not follow me have never really been mine. Heaven is my witness that I leave them behind without any pang.

"With regard to my wealth, I leave no will, for I am convinced that the members of my family will either live in peace and unity among themselves, or will divide my wealth among themselves in justice and equity, and that none of them will, heaven forbid, hide anything or keep it secret from the others.

"It is furthermore my wish that my family, that is my wife, may she live, my sons and sons-in-law, should give tithes twice—that is to say, immediately after my demise they should draw up an equitable and just account of my worldly possessions, my estate, furniture, and household affairs, of all bills and debts due to me; and from the amount take off one tenth part, as my personal share, and distribute it among the poor for the welfare of my soul.

From the remainder—that is, from their real inheritance—they should give tithes a second time on their own account, distributing the money among the poor, just as I have always been accustomed to give away a tenth part of my income, my profits, and revenues.

" In both cases—that is, when distributing the tithes—they should add three per cent, as they may have made a mistake in their accounts. They are to distribute the tithes among poor strangers, not their own relatives. As for the latter—that is, our poor relatives—my family will decide how much to give them. By no means should they help poor relatives from the amounts destined for charity. A man should not derive any personal benefit from charity, and when he gives away money to poor relatives it is just as if he had given it to himself.

" My epitaph should be very short, and the inscription on my tombstone should only contain my name, the name of my father, of blessed memory, and the day of my death, nothing more. And I beg that my sons and sons-in-law be not given too much to vanities, or too anxious to grow rich and very prosperous merchants, for the bigger the merchant the smaller the Jew in him. They should not endeavour to do business with foreign countries, and scatter money in all corners of the world. The Lord sends His blessing wherever He chooses, and there may be blessing in small enterprises as in big ones. I say this in particular for the benefit of my dear son Yehiel, because I have noticed that he is too anxious to grow very wealthy. *Sapienti sat.*

" I also beg my children to observe the custom of distributing alms ; of giving every year, on the eve of the New Year, one tenth of their profits to charity. Should it sometimes happen that the business does not show any profit at all, and even a loss, which heaven forbid, they should give charity all the same, for their losses may only be a test from His blessed name.

" And above all, I beg my children to study every day, at least one page of the *Talmud*, and to read one column of the book *Reshit-Hoshmah*. The womenfolk should read the *Kav-Hayashar* in Yiddish, and also the *Tsenoh-Urenoh* on Saturdays and high festivals. On the day of the anniversary of my death, they should study the Holy Law all day long, and the women should distribute charity, and, above all, charity given in secret, the recipients to remain unaware of the names of the givers."

3

When Maurice Benditson, a son of Benjamin, died, a will was found written in Polish. It ran as follows :—

" A wire is to be sent to Paris and my funeral must be delayed until my son arrives.

" I leave in trust ten thousand pounds to be administered by the community, the yearly income to be distributed among the poor. I leave another ten thousand for the endowment of a bed in the new hospital, this bed to be called after me. Charity should be distributed on the day of my funeral. Money gifts should be sent to all *Talmud-Torahs*, and both teachers and pupils should follow my bier. A *Dayan* or other learned and pious man should be hired to recite the *Kaddish* over me.

" My tombstone, after the model I am leaving behind, should be ordered abroad.

" A certain sum of money should be deposited with the community, and the latter is to undertake the upkeeping of my grave and tombstone.

" My business shall be known by the name of Maurice Benditson, *junior*.

" And with regard to—— " but we will pass over the figures relating to the fortune and outstanding debts, as well as the good advice and instructions given for continuing the business after the death of the testator.

4

" I, Maurice Benditson, junior, am leaving this world neither in joy nor in grief, but on account of its emptiness. Aristotle was a great philosopher, and he was right when he said that nature hates emptiness. A terrible machine is this world, every wheel having its particular work to perform, its particular purpose. And when a wheel happens to be out of gear, or when it has performed its task, it automatically disappears from the machine, going over from existence into nothingness.

"I can no longer live, because I no longer have anything to do here. I am absolutely useless, because I have outlived my life. I have drunk fully from the goblet of life. I have tasted all the joys and pleasures allotted to me. I have eaten, drunk, and loved my fill.

"I have been taught many things, but I have never been taught how to live and not to swallow up life. I have nothing in the world to keep me here, to tie me to it. I have never wanted for anything that would be of value and worth to me. I have taken everything freely, without care, worry, or labour. I have taken it as from public property. Thus have I taken both things and people—men as well as women. All have willingly met me with a friendly smile, but I have never had a real friend. All women have willingly kissed me, but I have neither needed nor yearned for one.

"I inherited a vast fortune, and it grew and increased without my help, without any effort on my part. It grew and grew until it has outgrown me. Frequently my heart wept within me, and I was desirous of *wanting* something, of having something *to do*. The doctors ordered me to take long walks, to travel, play, and take up some sport. It was not life, but a substitute for life; it was an artificial life, artificial work.

"I have visited many countries, but I could call none of them my own. I admired many sights and places, but I loved none. I spoke fluently several languages, but I cared for none. I have played with words as if with *balls*. I have changed nations and languages, as one changes gloves. The whole world was mine, but I was too small and insignificant to grasp it and get a hold on it. My arm was too short to embrace it, and I could not subdue any world. And whatever I could have subdued and acquired, I already found ready waiting for me ; it had been left to me. Everything had been done for me and on my behalf ; everything had been bought for me. My wealth did the rest. Everything had been bought for me ; the smile of a friend, the kiss of red lips, even the *Kaddish* for the soul of my father. At the utmost, I have *paid* for things, but I have never been taught to give and to bestow. The trifles, the small things, were too small for me, and the big things too big ; and I had nothing to live for.

" I am dying, because I am barren, both in body and in soul, physically and mentally. There is nothing in me that can either live or make live. It is already some time since I have been alive ; I take no pleasure in life, and now I am quite disgusted with it. I have been treated after the manner in which the peasant treats a pig : I have been stuffed. But when the pig is fat enough, the peasant kills it, whilst I am told to kill myself, and I dare not disobey.

" The arsenic is upon my table ; it is the last drink which will intoxicate me and from which I shall never awake or grow sober. Have I any instructions to leave with regard to my wealth ? What for ? My fortune has proved my misfortune. Have I to thank anybody ? No, I have paid for everything. I have paid also for my last drink."

X

THE DEVOUT CAT

———

ONCE upon a time there were three little singing birds in a house, but all three were devoured by the cat. It was not an ordinary cat, but a really, really devout cat. It was not in vain that it was arrayed in a white robe of immaculate purity, and that its eyes reflected the heavens.

It was a pious cat, a cat that scrupulously performed all its ablutions. Ten times a day would this cat wash itself; and as for food, it devoured it very quietly, lying curled up in an obscure corner. It fed all the day on a modest milk diet and only in the evening did it partake of a bit of meat, the *kosher* meat of some mouse. And then again this cat, unlike those of a grosser nature, did not hury over its food, or gorge itself like a glutton, but ate slowly, whilst playing with its victim. " Why not let the little mouse live another few minutes ? " thought the devout cat. " Let the poor mite dance a little while, tremble, and make its confession ; a really pious cat never hurries."

When the first singing bird was brought into the house, the cat at once felt great pity for the bird and its heart grew constricted.

" Such a beautiful, tiny thing," sighed the compassionate cat, " and to think that such a nice little bird will never enjoy celestial bliss." For, of course, the cat was fully

convinced that a little bird like tnat could not deserve
heaven. "First of all a bird washes itself in a vulgar
way, plunging its whole body into a basin of water. Then,
again, the very fact that it is put in a cage proves it to be
a very wicked animal. In spite of its still being very
young, gentle, and kind, this bird is already showing an
inclination towards violence rather than law and order.
And what about its song? Its song, to say the least, is
full of effrontery, and its manner of looking straight up
to heaven is quite disrespectful. And think of all its
efforts to break the cage and fly out into the impious
world, into the free air; think also of its look turned to
the open window. Have you ever seen a cat shut up in
a cage? Has a pious cat ever ventured to whistle with
such effrontery? The pity of it," sighed the tender-
hearted and devout cat, "for, after all, it is a living being,
possessed of a precious soul, a spark from above."

Tears welled up in the eyes of the pious and devout cat.

"All its misfortune is due to the fact of its possessing
such a beautiful sinful body, a body attracted to terrestrial
pleasures and joys, over which the spirit of temptation has
so much sway. How can you expect such a gentle little
bird to be able to resist the terrible spirit of temptation?
And the longer the poor thing lives," thought the
devout cat, "the greater the number of sins it will commit,
and the more terrible its punishment in the hereafter."

A sacred fire enflamed the heart of the devout cat.
Jumping upon the table where stood the cage with the
little bird, it. . . . The feathers were soon scattered over
the room.

Blows rained upon the cat, but it accepted its punishment with humility, as behoves a devout cat. Sighing
piously, it began to mew, to groan in pious resignation,
reciting a pitiable *mea culpa*. In future the cat will not
commit such an error, for being a reasonable cat, it understood why it had been beaten. Henceforth it will never
deserve such blows.

"I have been beaten," reasoned the devout cat,
"because I have scattered the feathers all over the room,

and also because I have left traces of blood all over the white and embroidered tablecloth. When executing such sentences, one ought to proceed with kindness, with gentleness, and piety ; one must never scatter the feathers nor spill a drop of blood."

When the second bird was bought and brought into the house, the pious cat acted quite differently. This time it strangled the little bird gently and delicately, and swallowed it whole, body and feathers. Nevertheless the cat was soundly thrashed.

This time the cat understood that it was not at all a question of either feathers or traces of blood left on the tablecloth. The secret of its punishment lay in the fact that it was a sin to kill. On the contrary, one must love and forgive. It is not by means of punishments and tortures that we can reform and save a world steeped in sin. What is required of us is to lead the sinful creatures upon the path of virtue, preach morals to them, and appeal to their hearts.

A repentant canary can soar to lofty summits in heaven, unattainable even for a devout cat. And the heart of the cat swelled with joy. Over were the old, hard, cruel, and wicked days. Over was the shedding of blood. Pity, was the watchword, pity, and once more pity. And it was a cat full of pity that approached the third canary.

" Don't be afraid," said the cat in the most gentle voice that ever issued from a cat's throat. " It is true thou art steeped in sin, but I will do thee no harm, for my heart is full of pity for thee.

" I will not even open thy cage, I will even refrain from touching thee.

" Thou art silent ? Excellent. It is better to be silent than to sing impudently.

" Thou art trembling ? It is better still. Tremble, my child, but not on account of me !

" May it please God that thou shouldst remain thus gently pure and trembling.

" As for me, I will help thee to tremble. From the depth of my pious soul I will breathe upon thee the spirit of calmness, of gentleness, and piety. May my pious breath instil into thy body profound faith, may divine fear penetrate into thy little bones, and may remorse and repentance fill thy little heart."

It was now only that the devout cat understood how sweet forgiveness was, what holy joy one may derive from the action of breathing into others the spirit of piety and of virtue. And the heart of the most pious and devout of white cats swelled for joy and happiness. But, alas, the canary could not breathe in the atmosphere of the cat. It was stifled.

XI

THE CABBALISTS

In bad times the finest merchandise loses its value, even the *Torah*—which is the best *Sckhorah*. And thus of the big *Jeshibah* of Lashtshivo, there remained only the principal, Reb Yekel, and one of his students.

The principal is an old, lean Jew, with a long unkempt beard and extinguished eyes. Lemech, his favourite pupil, is a tall, slight, pale-faced youth, with black curly locks, sparkling, dark-rimmed eyes, dry lips, and an emaciated throat, showing the pointed Adam's apple. Both the principal and his pupil are wearing tattered garments showing their naked breasts, as they are too poor to buy shirts. With great difficulty the principal is dragging on his feet a pair of peasant's boots, whilst the student, with stockingless feet, is shuffling along in a pair of sabots much too big for him. The two alone had remained of all the inmates of the once famous *Jeshibah*.

Since the impoverished townspeople had begun to send less and less food to the *Jeshibah* and to offer fewer *days* to the students, the latter had made tracks for other towns. Reb Yekel, however, was resolved to die and be buried at Lashtshivo, whilst his favourite pupil was anxious to close his beloved master's eyes.

Both now very frequently suffer the pangs of hunger. And when you take insufficient nourishment your nights are often sleepless, and after a good many hungry days and sleepless nights you begin to feel an inclination to study the *Cabbala*. If you are already forced to lie awake at night and go hungry during the day, then why not at least derive some benefit from such a life ? At least avail yourself of your long fasts and mortifications of the body to force open the gates of the invisible world and get a glimpse of all the mysteries it contains, of angels and spirits.

And thus the two had been studying the *Cabbala* for some time. They are now seated at a long table in the empty lecture-room. Other Jews had already finished their mid-day meal, but for these two it was still before breakfast ! They are, however, quite used to it. His eyes half-shut, the principal is talking, whilst the pupil, his head leaning on both his hands, is listening.

" There are," the principal is saying, " four degrees of perfection. One man knows only a small portion, another a half, whilst a third knows an entire melody. The *Rebbe*, of blessed memory, knew, for instance, an entire melody. And I," he added sadly, " I have only been vouchsafed the grace of knowing but a small piece, a very small piece, just as big as—— "

He measured a tiny portion of his lean and emaciated finger, and continued :

" There are melodies which require words. That is the lowest degree. There is also a higher degree ; it is a melody that requires no words, it is sung without words —as a pure melody. But even this melody requires a voice and lips to express itself. And the lips, you understand me, are appertaining to *matter*. The voice itself, though a nobler and higher form of matter, is still material in its essence. We may say that the voice is standing on the border-line between matter and spirit. Anyhow, the melody which is still dependent upon voice and lips is not yet pure, not yet entirely pure, not real spirit.

" The true, highest melody, however, is that which is sung without any voice. It resounds in the interior of man, is vibrating in his heart and in all his limbs.

" And that is how we are to understand the words of
King David, when he says in his Psalms : ' All my bones
are praising the Lord.' The melody should vibrate in the
marrow of our bones, and such is the most beautiful song
of praise addressed to the Lord, blessed be His name.
For such a melody has not been invented by a being of
flesh and blood ; it is a portion of that melody with
which the Lord once created the Universe ; it is a part
of the soul which He has breathed into His creation. It
is thus that the heavenly hosts are singing—— "

The sudden arrival of a ragged fellow, a carrier, his
loins girt with a cord, interrupted the lecture. Entering
the room, the messenger placed a dish of gruel soup and
a piece of bread upon the table before the *Rosh-Jeshibah*
and said in a rough voice :

" Reb Tevel sends this food for the *Rosh-Jeshibah.*"
Turning to the door, he added : " I will come later to
fetch the dish."

Torn away from the celestial harmonies by the sound
of the fellow's voice, the principal slowly and painfully
rose from his seat and dragged his feet in their heavy
boots to the water basin near the door, where he performed
the ritual ablution of his hands. He continued to talk
all the time, but with less enthusiasm, whilst the pupil
was following him with shining, dreamy eyes, and straining
his ears.

" I have not even been found worthy," said the principal
sadly, " to know the degree at which this can be attained,
nor do I know through which of the celestial gates it
enters. You see," he added with a smile, " I know well
enough the necessary mortifications and prayers, and I
will communicate them to you even to-day."

The eyes of the student are almost starting out of their
sockets, and his mouth is wide open ; he is literally
swallowing every word his master his uttering. But the
master interrupts himself. He performs the ritual ablution
of his hands, dries them, and recites the prescribed
benediction ; he then returns to the table and breaking
off a piece of bread, recites with trembling lips the pre-

scribed blessing. His shaking hands now seize the dish, and the moist vapour covers his emaciated face. He puts down the dish upon the table, takes the spoon into his right hand, whilst warming his left at the edge of the dish; all the time he is munching in his toothless mouth the morsel of bread over which he had said a blessing.

When his face and hands were warm enough, he wrinkled his brow and extending his thin, blue lips, began to blow. The pupil was staring at him all the time. But when the trembling lips of the old man were stretching out to meet the first spoonful of soup, something squeezed the young man's heart. Covering his face with his hands, he seemed to have shrivelled up.

A few minutes had scarcely elapsed when another man came in, also carrying a basin full of gruel soup and a piece of bread.

" Reb Joisseff sends the student his breakfast," he said.

The student never removed his hands from his face. Putting down his own spoon, the principal rose and went up to him. For a moment he looked down at the boy with eyes full of pride and love ; then touching his shoulder, he said in a friendly and affectionate voice :

" They have brought you food."

Slowly and unwillingly the student removed his hands from his face. He seemed to have grown paler still, and his dark-rimmed eyes were burning with an even more mysterious fire.

" I know, Rabbi," he said, " but I am not going to eat to-day."

" Are you going to fast the fourth day ? " asked the *Rosh-Jeshibah*, greatly surprised. " And without me ? " he added in a somewhat hurt tone.

" It is a particular fast-day," replied the student. " I am fasting to-day for penance."

" What are you talking about ? Why must you do penance ? "

" Yes, Rabbi, I must do penance, because a while ago, when you had just started to eat, I transgressed the commandment which says, ' Thou shalt not covet—— ' "

Late in the night the student woke up his master. The two were sleeping side by side on benches in the old lecture-hall.

" Rebbe, Rebbe ! " called the student in a feeble voice.

" What is the matter ? " The *Rosh-Jeshibah* woke with a start.

" Just now, I have been upon the highest summit."

" How's that ? " asked the principal, not yet quite awake.

" There was a melody, and it has been singing in me." The principal sat up.

" How's that ?   How's that ? "

" I don't know it myself, Rebbe," answered the student in an almost inaudible voice.   " As I could not find sleep I plunged myself into your lecture.   I was anxious at any cost to learn that melody.   Unable, however, to succeed, I was greatly grieved and began to weep.   Everything in me was weeping, all my members were weeping before the Creator of the Universe.   I recited the prayers and formulas you taught me ; strange to say, not with my lips, but deep down in my heart.   And suddenly I was dazzled by a great light.   I closed my eyes, yet I could not shut out the light around me, a powerful dazzling light."

" That's it," said the old man leaning over.

" And in the midst of the strange light I felt so strong, so light-hearted.   It seemed to me as if I had no weight, as if my body had lost its heaviness and that I could fly."

" That right ; that's right."

" And then I felt so merry, so happy and lively.   My face remained motionless, my lips never stirred, and yet I laughed.   I laughed so joyously, so heartily, so frankly and happily."

" That's it ; that's it.   That is right, in the intensest joy—— "

" Then something began to hum in me, as if it were the beginning of a melody."

The *Rosh-Jeshibah* jumped up from his bench and stood up by his pupil's side.

" And then ?   And then ? "

" Then I heard how it was singing in me."

" And what did you feel ? What ? What ? Tell me ! "

" I felt as if all my senses were closed and stopped ; and there was something singing in me, just as it should be, without either words or tunes, only so—— "

" How ? How ? "

" No, I can't say. At first I knew, then the song became—— "

" What did the song become ? What ?—— "

" A sort of music, as if there had been a violin in me, or as if Joyné, the musician, was sitting in my heart and playing one of the tunes he plays at the Rebbe's table. But it sounded much more beautiful, nobler and sadder, more spiritual ; and all this was voiceless and tuneless, mere spirit."

" You lucky man—— ! "

" And now it is all gone," said the pupil, growing very sad. " My senses have again woke up, and I am so tired, so terribly tired that I . . . . Rebbe ! " the student suddenly cried, beating his breast, " Rebbe, recite with me the confession of the dying. They have come to fetch me ; they require a new choir-boy in the celestial choir. There is a white-winged angel—Rebbe—Rebbe—*Shmah Yissroel, Shmah*—— "

Everybody in the town wished to die such a death, but the *Rosh-Jeshibah* found that it was not enough.

" Another few fast-days," he said, " and he would have died quite a different death. He would have died by a Divine Kiss."

XII

HE WHO GIVES LIFE GIVES ALSO THE WHEREWITHAL TO LIVE UPON

(A Story Told by Johanan the *Melamed*)

———

I

Preface : *My excuse and declaration that heresy and disbelief do not exist in the world.*

Gentlemen : I, Johanan the *Melamed*, will tell you a story, and this story will be like a wheel within a wheel —that is to say, a story within a story. None of the stories, however, have I invented, or, as the saying goes, " sucked from my finger." Thank God, I am no scribbler, neither were any of my ancestors writers. I will tell you the stories simply, without any trimmings, for I dislike high-sounding words. He who is telling the truth has no need of rhetoric, for he is speaking in his mother tongue. An introduction, however, I must give you. The stories which I am going to tell you will show you that in many things, you, gentlemen, have gone too far, relying too much upon your senses. My stories will convince you that there are many things in this world of which neither yourselves nor your great wise men have ever dreamed. Therefore I beg you not to be annoyed with me.

You may believe me, if you like ; if not, it is also well. At the same time, I will also apologize to my friends.

The latter may perhaps feel annoyed with me because I am telling tales out of school, as the saying goes ; and especially nowadays when there is so much heresy about. It may give rise, they will say, to some scandal. Heaven forbid ! I have therefore good news for these my friends —namely, that they are greatly mistaken, for there are no heresy and no disbelief at all in the world. It is all pure invention. The whole world is simply *full of faith*. Could it be otherwise ?

The universe is immense, infinite, absolutely boundless, whilst our reason or understanding is so small, so finite. We may be likened to a man who, on a dark night, is walking through a vast infinite barren desert, carrying in his hand a small candle that scarcely sheds a light over a few yards. I maintain that without faith existence is quite impossible, for intelligence alone does not suffice. Whence then, you will ask, does the legend of heresy come ? Well, I will tell you. All these futile and useless scribblers who are manufacturing books for the simple folks, for the crowds of cooks, kitchen- and parlour-maids ; who are inventing those stories of brigands and murderers, of forgers and bankrobbers, so as to frighten their readers and make their blood curdle—these authors have also invented the legend of heresy and disbelief. They have done it with the same purpose in mind—namely, that of frightening the simple folks, the crowd of servants, tailors, and bootmakers' apprentices.

The real truth is quite different. Without belief there is no will-power. In plain Yiddish it means that a man who does not believe in anything ceases to will anything, and has no yearning for anything. Such a man is nothing but a clod of clay, a log of wood. And whenever you behold men who are either swayed by passions and desires, or who are curbing these passions and desires for the sake of others, higher and stronger ; when you see men who eat and drink, enjoy family happiness, work by the sweat of their brows, and are planning commercial enter-prises, then you should know that these men *believe*, that anyhow they *believe* in their own existence and life.

For, if it comes to doubt, we may even doubt the reality of our very existence and life. If you like, you can say: "Life is naught; and what can you do?" Against such an argument we really have nothing to say.

In short, everybody *believes* in something. Only what? One man believes that at the Messianic banquet the *Leviathan* will be served before the *Shor-habor*, whilst another says that on the contrary the *Shor-habor* will be dished up first, to be followed by the *Leviathan* as a side-dish. And an enlightened young man, one who believes neither in the *Leviathan* nor in the *Shor-habor*, believes in the æther. And what is this æther? To this question one of these young men once gave me the following answer: "The æther is something that has neither body nor physical strength; it is neither spirit nor anything spiritual; it neither occupies any space nor has it any weight—in a word, it is both a *yea* and a *nay*." And when I asked him whether he had ever seen that æther, he replied, no, but that he believed in it. In short, everybody *believes*. Now where is the difference?

Everybody believes in his Rabbi and has faith in him; everybody has his faith and his belief, his little idol, so to speak. Everybody reads the words from the lips of other people. Everybody is kissing something sacred to him. Whilst, however, one is kissing the curtain in front of the *Torah* shrine, even though he knows not what is in the shrine, another is kissing the cabbalistic work *Megale Temirin* when it has fallen down from the table upon the floor. I have even seen with mine own eyes how one of the enlightened people kissed the *Mysteries of Paris*. And I have it on good authority that these mysteries relate the gruesome story of a certain Harbonah (not our Harbonah of blessed memory mentioned in the Book of Esther, chapter i. verse 10, but a certain Parisian woodcutter who used to walk about with bare feet upon broken glass), and similar lies invented by a Parisian liar which have been translated into the sacred tongue by one of the Vilna intellectuals.

Gentlemen, I have, praise be unto the Lord, seen a good deal of life and the world. I have been a *Melamed* in villages, in small towns, and also in big cities. For the last seven years I have been *Melamed* in Warsaw and, thank God, I am constantly meeting people, and I know men. I know *Missnagdim* who will jump out of their skins when they hear the *Hassidim* add the words *veyazmaeh purkoneh* in the *Kaddish*, whilst I know *Hassidim* who look upon one of their sect who visits another wonder-rabbi than themselves, as a heretic. I also know many enlightened people, intellectuals, big authors, bookmakers and scribblers—plenty of them. I know also many dissolute people and apostates. All these I know, but I have never met a man who absolutely did not believe in anything.

I even make so bold as to maintain that in all the crowd of the so-called enlightened ones, there is not one who follows his own mode of thought, his own system, his own way. I have never met one who looked at things from his own point of view. With the exception of perhaps two or three really big fishes, all the rest of the company are not worth as much as an empty eggshell. They, too, are merely fanatic *Hassidim*, only of a different stamp. They believe in *their* wonder-rabbi and are following in the footsteps of the great man of their age, as we are following in the footsteps of our Rabbis. I could even take an oath that not one of these enlightened ones has ever had, even for one short hour, a theory of his own. They are all clinging to their belief in the great man of their age. And they are in the habit of repeating everything that he says, without making any selection. They care not whether the words they are repeating have been spoken after reflection, seriously, and with a clear intelligence, or whethe rthey were uttered in haste, in a moment of anger, or simply out of a spirit of contradiction. I tell you it is all just as among the people of our own mode of thought. There is hardly any difference.

And when one of these gentry comes up to me and says that he does not believe in anything, I simply shrug my shoulders and think that he is a fool; although, of course, I am not going to put him to shame by telling him what I am thinking of him.   In my heart of hearts, however, I know that he is either having his joke with me, or is simply boasting.   As a matter of fact I know that it is usually one of these boasters who is afraid to go out alone late at night.   It is also possible, I reflect, that his man is compelled to speak like that for professional or business reasons.   What will not a man do for the sake of his business or his profession?   It is also possible that he is merely an ignorant man, one who does not even know what he is ignorant of and what he ought to believe.

And if such be the case, why should we be ashamed of our beliefs?   Why should the people of our mode of thinking be worse than the crowd of so-called enlightened people, who are merely repeating grandmothers' tales and wonders for the glory of their great men?   Is it because our stories are not fiction?   Is it because we are not telling gruesome stories about brigands and murderers, forgers and bankrobbers, to frighten people?   Is it really indispensable to tell only such stories which are pure invention and fiction, without rhyme or reason?

Besides, I have no intention whatever of telling you a story which happened beyond the seas or in most remote times.   I am going to tell you something which has actually occurred here in Warsaw, and only very recently too.   But someone might come and say: " It is not true, you are telling lies."

Well, say I, let him come, let him have the insolence. I am, thank God, only a *Melamed* and not a scribbler or writer of fiction, heaven forbid!   It is neither my business nor my profession to tell lies, and my living does not depend upon story-telling or fiction-writing.   In short, my story is true.   Should, however, someone come forward and try to suggest a different interpretation, we can only say that we are ready to listen to him.   Thus far goes our Introduction, and now for the story.

2

*A saying by the Taciturn, of blessed memory. The virtues of
my brother, may he rest in peace. A good beginning.*

I have been told that the *Taciturn*,[1] of blessed memory,
upon being once asked why he, unlike all the other
Rabbis, never expounded the *Torah*, vouchsafed no reply,
but, as was his custom, simply remained silent. Another
time, however, when he was more favourably disposed
and his followers again insisted upon putting the question,
he smilingly made the following reply :

People wonder why I am not expounding the wisdom
of the *Torah*. Well, I, in my turn, am wondering at those
who are able to do so. How can a man begin and end
in the *Torah*, the *Torah* which has neither beginning nor
end and which is infinity itself ?

But the answer to my question is very simple : People
who have no notion of the *Torah* and yet are preaching
whatever comes into their mouths, begin and end where
and whenever they like. For the *Torah* which they are
expounding is not the infinite *Torah*, the *Torah* of the
Master of the Universe, but one of their own making and
invention. He, however, who really knows the *Torah*
refrains from expounding it, because he does not know
where to begin and where to end. This remark also
applies to worldly things. Take, for instance, a legal
action when witnesses are being called. The really truthful
man who is neither able nor willing to tell lies begins
his declaration with the creation of the world and never
touches the point at issue. As for the conclusion, he
never reaches it. But the witness who is drawing upon
his imagination has everything quite pat, nicely arranged
in his mind, and he talks like a man who knows both
the beginning and the end of what he is going to say.
His words are flowing as smoothly as oil.

This rule also applies to all sorts of stories. The fiction-
writer who draws merely upon his imagination, is
able to begin his story when and wherever he likes. The
story is his thing, his own creation, and he can do with it

as he pleases. At will he can either make it long or cut it short. But I, who am about to relate a true occurrence, and not fiction, am really at a loss where to begin and how to end.

" There is nothing new under the sun," and every event is connected with and depends upon another thing or event that has preceded it ; which, in its turn, depends upon another. The latter event, however, we also fail to understand unless we know what has preceded it, and thus we arrive at the six days of creation.

In honour, however, of my late beloved brother, Zeinvel-Yehiel, may his soul rest in peace, I will begin with him. It is a well-known fact, the whole Franciscan Street can attest the truth, that my brother of blessed memory was a great scholar, and a profoundly pious and God-fearing man. He was a widower, and in his old age he remained alone, having only his daughter, Broche-Leah, with him. He lived in very straitened circumstances. Unable, by reason of his weakness, to continue his profession of teacher, there was literally not a crust of bread in his house—may the Lord preserve you and all other Jews from such misery. In the meantime, however, Broche-Leah was growing up, *unberufen*, as if upon yeast. In a word, there was misery in every way.

Now what did the Lord do ? A few inhabitants of the town, all very decent and highly respected men, whose children my brother had formerly taught, made up their minds to save the situation. They took it upon themselves to marry off Broche-Leah and to provide my brother, peace be upon him, with means to travel to the Holy Land, there to pass his last days.

My brother never really reached his destination, for he died on the way of heart disease—may you be preserved from such a fate. It was, nevertheless, vouchsafed unto him to see the town of Safed in the Holy Land. It was there that he breathed his last and was buried in the Jewish cemetery with great honours. Over his grave the Rabbi of Safed pronounced a fiery funeral oration, which he subsequently printed in his work entitled *Precious Pearls*.

Readers of this work will be delighted with it, will literally lick their fingers and smack their lips. And now, since I have been able to find a beginning, I will continue my story.

3

*The story itself. A bad choice. Misery. Broche-Leah
abandoned by her husband.*

Charity is a fine thing, but only for those who are giving it. I do not envy the poor wretches who are receiving alms and are compelled to address themselves to the president of some charitable institution. I envy, however, my late brother, may he rest in peace, who died at the right moment and was spared much subsequent misery. The respectable inhabitants of our town who had provided Broche-Leah with a dowry had forgotten one thing— namely, that she was the daughter of a scholar and herself a pious and pure soul. When choosing a fiancé for my niece they were thinking but little of the girl's virtues and much less of her father's merits. What interested them solely was to provide Broche-Leah with a husband who would be able to keep her. They were merely anxious to marry her off, and be rid of her. They acted in a hurry, without careful consideration. They discovered somewhere a young man and got him cheaply. He was sometimes employed by a lawyer, and from time to time earned something. As he was not very hard to please and said that he could keep a wife, they snatched him up and concluded the bargain. Quickly the trousseau was acquired, the dowry deposited, musicians were hired, and the wedding was celebrated ; *Mazoltov.*

To tell the truth, I, for my part, did not at all care for the young man. My wife Feige, may the Lord send her health, said that he was not the pick of the basket. But as my brother, may he rest in peace, had said nothing, we kept our peace. Future events, however, proved that our silence had not been wise. Scarcely had my brother, of blessed memory, left the town, than the storm broke out and it became evident that all was not well in the new household.

I soon learned that the domestic peace was gravely disturbed, that there were frequent scenes and quarrels, and that the neighbours were knocking at the walls to impose silence. I also heard that the young man, Moishe-Yisroel was his name, was not a model of piety, and that Broche-Leah was greatly distressed on that account. He, in his turn, was constantly threatening his wife that he would dress in European fashion, that he would even study to become a lawyer.

Moishe-Yisroel further maintained that the charitable matchmakers had shamefully deceived him; they had shown him before the wedding another girl, much more beautiful than Broche-Leah, and he would never have consented to marry the latter. He also turned up his nose at her trousseau. Old rags, he said, that was all they had given her. Besides, they had promised him board for a couple of years, as was the custom, but soon after the wedding they had given him a fig. His last grievance was that the charitable gentlemen who had done their best to marry Broche-Leah ought to have done their best to advance his prospects in life, as he had hoped they would. And what was the result? After having banqueted, fed and feasted and danced at this marriage of the poor, they now refused even to see him.

Of course, I had no intention of meddling in this business. Neither Broche-Leah's protectors nor my wife Feige, may she live long, would let me. Besides, such things are neither new nor unusual. It happens often enough that in the first years of married life, before husband and wife have had time to grow accustomed to each other, there are quarrels. And yet, in later years, habit becomes second nature, and they manage to live quite peacefully together. To tell the truth, even between myself and my wife Feige, may the Lord send her health, there used to be friction in the first years after our marriage. Later, however, when the children began to arrive, we gave up all that nonsense. I tried to find some business, did not

6

succeed, and became a teacher. And it is really not so bad ; we live—may our life last for a hundred and twenty years. Well, the long and short of it was that I kept my peace, especially when, after some time, my wife Feige, may she live long, conveyed to me by hints and allusions the glad news about Broche-Leah. Of course, I understand things without having the *i*'*s* dotted. That is the best proof, I said, that things are going well.

But, alas, things did not go well at all ! The fellow did not mend his ways or improve his conduct, which, on the contrary, became worse. He evidently possessed the virtue of our father Abraham—namely, of talking little but doing much. Not only did he now dress in European fashion, but he also began to pass his nights playing cards. Every evening he invited his boon-companions to his house and forced Broche-Leah to make tea for them, and to serve them brandy and herrings ; and the herring had to be served with vinegar and oil, if you please ; he would not have it otherwise. And then there were alto to be white rolls ; he turned up his nose at brown bread. And should it happen that one of these delicacies was missing, then there would be a terrible scene. To crown all, he began to ridicule his wife, to abuse her and make a laughing-stock of her in the presence of his guests. He heaped abuse upon her head, using the most vile language and swearing at her.

I saw, now, that it was wrong to remain silent any longer. I therefore mustered up all my courage and went to see the couple. I came in and began, of course, by speaking kindly and nicely, even interspersing my remarks with a joke, as is my habit. I endeavoured to look at things in a friendly manner, telling him that though he was a great sinner before the Lord, his case was not quite hopeless as yet. I then described unto him the great respect which repentant sinners enjoyed in heaven. I told him also that if he repented, the merits of Broche-Leah's pious ancestors would certainly be of great assistance to him in heaven. All he had to do was to repent, seriously and sincerely. I also promised him to take a friendly interest in him socially. I would introduce him into my own synagogue, and should I one day, please God, undertake the pious journey and go on a visit to my wonderrabbi then I would take him with me. Such and other kind words did I speak unto him.

And what do you think he did ? He burst out into loud laughter. Gladly, he said, would he forgo all these joys, if I would only deliver him from Broche-Leah. And he made use of language which no God-fearing man can repeat. I was then compelled to change my attitude and to speak to him in a different, more severe, tone. I told him that though he was dressing in European fashion, he was after all an ignoramus and a fool. I then told him, quite fearlessly, that if he wanted to repent of his sins it was well, but if he refused to do so then he would pass many black and miserable years in hell.

Again he laughed at me. " What hell ? " he asked ; " where is hell ? " He denied its very existence, as if he had already been there and seen with his own eyes that there was no hell—heaven forbid ! And then the insolent fellow had the audacity to show me the door. What could I do but leave him ? I looked at Broche-Leah and saw that she was green and yellow, that tears were flowing like rivers from her eyes. I went away and summoned the impudent fellow to appear before the ecclesiastical court. He did not come, of course, and I waited a long while.

Then for some time I heard nothing from the couple. You see, I did not hear from them because the wicked fellow had forbidden Broche-Leah to cross the threshold of my house, threatening to beat her to pulp should she disobey him. As it behoves an honest and pious woman, Broche-Leah did what her husband told her. She thus remained at home, shedding tears in secret. And since I heard nothing, I, of course, knew nothing.

In the meantime I had my own troubles. My wife Feige had fallen ill ; the doctor said it was fever, the neighbours were of another opinion ; whilst I myself attributed her sickness to the " evil eye." Anyhow there was no mistress in the house, and the children were deprived both of their mother and of their father. For, you see, it was just before the beginning of a new school term and I had to run about to find another two pupils to complete my class. That was not all, however; I myself did not feel quite well. The steep staircases in Warsaw had taken all the strength out of me. Besides, I was being harassed on all sides. There was the landlord, who was claiming his rent—I owed him already for two quarters—and then there was the school inspector. The latter insisted on my enlarging my school premises. I should hire another room, he said, so that my pupils might have more space and more air.

Heaven forgive me, but I had entirely forgotten Broche-Leah. And whenever I did remember her, I said unto myself: "As I am not hearing from her, the wicked fellow, her husband, must surely have mended his ways and they are now living happily together, kissing and hugging each other. In her happiness, as is quite natural, she has forgotten her poor relations."

Then one evening, when I came home, terribly tired and exhausted—may heaven preserve you from such a state—with swollen feet, and was just about to perform the ritual ablution of my hands, thinking of getting a bite of something, that I might quickly say grace and then throw myself upon the bed, my wife Feige conveyed unto me the glad tidings. Broche-Leah, she told me, had been here and shed bitter tears. She had called us murderers, because we did not care a rap for her and had no pity for her in her misfortune. She was a poor abandoned orphan, miserable and lonely like a stone. My wife also told me that Broche-Leah's husband was torturing her and was her deadly enemy; he was beating her mercilessly, so that many a time blood had spurted out from her nose and ears.

I asked my wife Feige: "How can that be? Is it possible that a Jew should beat his wife, and especially a wife who is *enceinte*?" My wife replied that it must be the effect of his insane wickedness. Moishe-Yisroel, she said, had already long ago deviated from the right path.

He had lost all faith and trust in the Almighty, and was
crying that he had nothing to live upon.   And he insisted
—may his name and the remembrance of him be extinguished and wiped out from the memory of men—he
insisted that Broche-Leah should destroy the child to be
born.   Everybody, he said, was doing it, even the finest
ladies.   And as the poor woman refused to obey him, he
was beating her mercilessly, insulting and cursing, not
only herself, but also her departed father.

When I heard that the fellow was cursing my brother
of blessed memory, I waxed mightily wroth.   I forgot
everything, seized my walking stick and cried out, " His
death or mine, I will kill the dog ! "   And breathlessly I
ran out of the house.   When I reached my niece's house
I beheld a terrible, heart-rending spectacle.

The door was open and the house was dark.   The
fellow had bolted, and all the furniture had disappeared.
The blackguard had carried away even the very bed linen.
And where was Broche-Leah ?   She was lying on the
floor in a terrible agony, writhing in pains.

4

*A miracle.   My wife Feige and her deeds.   I am thrown out
of the house and whither I go.*

It was a miracle that my wife Feige—*unberufen*—
possesses a good deal of common sense.   When I had
seized my walking stick and cried out that I was going to
kill the dog, my wife Feige had remained quite undisturbed.
She knew quite well that I was not a murderer, heaven
forbid, and that I was incapable of killing even a fly on
the wall.   She is quite aware of the fact that when my
fury is at its highest, I simply break out in tears.   Such
is my nature ; anger makes me shed tears.

My wife Feige also knows that I never even beat my
pupils as they deserve to be beaten.   The fathers of the
boys are rather dissatisfied with me on this account, and
I myself am sometimes afraid that I am not doing my
duty to God and men.   A good thrashing is sometimes

necessary ; and especially since one of my pupils had got into bad company and taken the wrong turning, I became firmly convinced of the necessity of a good leathering. But let us not digress.

And thus my wife Feige, having no misgivings with regard to the fellow's safety, and knowing full well that I would do him no harm, calmly remained seated upon her bed. When, however, an hour and two passed and I did not return, she grew rather frightened, saying unto herself that I had perhaps, after all, cut the fellow into pieces and was now in jail. She was in a terrible state. Forgetting her own pains, forgetting the children in their beds and our scanty furniture, forgetting even to lock the door behind her, she snatched up a shawl and rushed out in search of me.

I looked round—and there she was. And scarcely had she come in when she took in the scene at one glance. First of all, seeing me standing there like a log of wood, she contemptuously shouted at me one word," Lazy-bones ! " then swiftly opening the door, she loudly called for help. The neighbours immediately came in, my wife took command of the situation, and the others followed her instructions. At Feige's command one of the women actually pushed me out of the house.

Where should I go ? Wet snow was falling, and the wind was lashing my face and stealing in through the holes of my torn garments. I therefore made up my mind to go to the *Beth-Hamidrash*. There were still a few people there who are in the habit of studying the *Talmud* after the evening prayers. I, too, took up a *Talmud* folio, and all was over. I require nothing more ! Scarcely did I open the *Talmud* when Broche-Leah was entirely forgotten. Forgotten also was Broche-Leah's husband, the arch-wicked fellow ; forgotten was the whole world. Who had been abandoned by her husband ? Who had run away ? Who was being delivered ? Nothing existed for me.

5

My pupils. Who is my teacher? The Torah and its reward.
The parable of the bird. Wicked thoughts and doubts.

Sometimes, when I am myself studying with such ardour
and joy, my wealthy pupils fail to understand the reason.
They ask me whether I have still need of studying and who
my teacher was. The dunces ! They evidently ignore
the fact that the world is a very good teacher, and that
cares and worries about daily bread are excellent masters.
Suffering and misfortune, too, are good *melamdim*. The
wasp which is constantly gnawing the brains with the
question : " What shall we eat ? " is also a very energetic
master. And my pupils themselves and their respective
fathers, my bread-providers, they are all very good,
excellent masters.

Everything impels me to study. But study, like the
Torah, is its own reward. As soon as I open the *Talmud*
folio I become a different man, and none is my equal. I
feel as if the heavens had opened before me, as if the
Master of the Universe had, in His everlasting mercy,
lent me wings, broad, large wings, and I am flying with
these wings. I am an eagle, soaring up to dizzy heights,
into distant regions. I am not flying beyond the seas,
but out of, and away from, the world. I am flying away
from the world of lies, of hypocrisy, meanness, and suffering. In my flight I soar up and escape into quite another
world, a new world, a world where goodness reigns
supreme. It is a world where neither stout landlords nor
ignorant fine gentlemen enjoy any consideration ; it is a
world where money is unknown, where worries about
earning a living do not exist, a world where there are
neither painful delivery and childbed, nor hungry children
or scolding wives.

And it is in the midst of this world that I am now, I
the poor, sick, oppressed, hungry *Melamed*. I, the poorest
among the poor beggars, dumb like a fish and trodden
down by everybody like a worm. I am a *man* in the new
world, a gentleman whose opinion carries weight. And

I am free, too, and my will is free.   I am master and can
issue commands.   Worlds do I create and worlds do I
destroy, raising up new ones upon the ruins of the old.   I
build new worlds, more beautiful and better worlds.   And
in these worlds I live and fly to and fro.   I am in Paradise,
in the real Paradise.   And I am aware that I know more
than I can or care to communicate to my pupils, more
than I dare admit to myself.   I guess things which cannot
be expressed in speech, which neither eye can behold nor
ear perceive, things which only grow in the heart, live
there, and make it beat.

The two men mentioned in the *Talmud* who have
simultaneously found a garment and are grasping it, and
whose quarrel the sages of the *Talmud* are discussing,
are not men of the street, not an ordinary Simeon and
Reuben, as I am explaining it to my pupils.   Nor is the
garment over which the two finders are quarrelling an
ordinary garment, one that you might buy in the shop of
Yossel Peshes.   I go more deeply into the subject.   I
absorb all the sparks and rays *between* the lines, between the
words and letters, and my soul sucks them in like a sponge.
I feel how the hidden light reserved for the pious in the
next world is penetrating and filling my whole being, my
very soul.   Ah, what joy it is only to sit and study, only
to study !   I must also tell you this :—

Whenever I am visiting the houses of the rich and see
the people therein playing cards all through the night or
idling away their time with women and other frivolities ;
whenever I am walking in the street and through the
open door of some public house perceive a working man
wrapt up in a cloud of smoke, drinking and uttering
stupidities—whenever I see these things, I tell you frankly
that I do not at all grow angry.   I never accuse these
people, but, on the contrary, I am exceedingly sorry for
them ; my heart aches for them and is full of compassion.

For, after all, what can they do without the *Torah* ?
As I have already mentioned above, I once taught also
in a village.   Towards the end of the summer my pupil
once showed me how the birds were all forgathering and

preparing to leave our cold climate before the approach of winter. I saw how they were assembling in flocks and then taking their flight into distant lands. The little birds cannot and will not remain here throughout the days of frost and snow, for they can find no nourishment. The little birds know and feel when winter is approaching ; they know that their angel of death is coming. One day, however, I saw how a poor mite of a bird, crippled, with a broken wing, was hopping about on the moist, cold ground. It was chirping, but was unable to rise from the ground to join and follow the big birds. It was really heart-rending to watch this little bird hopping about so restlessly, and casting longing glances at the other free birds, soaring high in the air and flying away. It was then that I said unto myself : " The soul of an ignorant man may be likened unto this wounded little bird. These ignorant men are unable to fly, because they have no wings—that is, no *Torah*."

Give them the *Torah*, give them wings, and they, too, will soar high up in the air and fly away into distant superior worlds. But their wings have been broken, and they are for ever hopping in the cold mud. That is the reason why they are indulging in shameless and frivolous conversations or are playing cards, the rich in their drawing-rooms, and the poor in the public houses.

But let us return to our subject. Thus I was sitting and studying the *Talmud*. The few people who had remained had now all left the *Beth-Hamidrash*. The beadle was the last to go, and I remained alone. But what did I care ? I scarcely noticed it. A lighted candle in front of me, in the warm *Beth-Hamidrash*, an open *Talmud* folio before me, I fear nothing. I was deeply plunged in my studies, as was right and proper. The *Torah*, as you well know, is likened unto the ocean, and the waves are constantly rising up. They are threatening to submerge me, but I am able to swim. I dive, but the next instant I am once more on the foam-crested waves. Sometimes the sea grows calm, lying there as beautiful, pure, and clear as the sky, and my soul is bathing in fresh, vivifying waters; in beauty and delight it is gliding as if over a mirror. And the waters are washing my soul, cleansing it of all its impurities, washing away the black, earthly dust-spots. And pure and holy my soul becomes.

Suddenly I felt a burning pain on my fingers—and I was in darkness. The candle-end had gone out between my fingers. Alone in the darkness, I felt afraid, and an immense terror seized me. When there is light around me, be it day or night, I fear nothing. I can see the world and I feel myself master of the universe, *above* the world. I can behold the world, and the world can behold me. And I know that I am a part of the world, and that its Master is also my Master, and that without His will not a hair on my head will be harmed. He will not permit it, nor will the world itself permit it. Why should they allow it? But when I am surrounded by darkness and cannot see the world, ah, then I cease to be a man. Wicked thoughts then crowd my brain, and it seems to me—heaven forgive me—that I have no connection whatever with the world, that I have been torn out of it and led away from it. I have nothing in common with the world, neither I myself nor my wife and children. None of us has anything to do with the world. Soon either myself or one of mine will be quietly taken away from the world, and no one will see it; no one will know it, and certainly no one will feel it.

Scarcely had the light gone out when my festive and superior soul at once left me, that festive superior soul which only dwells in my body during the hours of study. And once more I was aware only of my trembling, frightened, ordinary soul, the soul of a poor beggarly *Melamed*. Once more I am a mere nothing, a worm, a lost thing. And my trembling lips are muttering: " Heaven help me! Heaven help me! " My heart is wrung and is lamenting, and I am thinking: Broche-Leah will give birth to a child, of course she will. She will even give birth to twins, for her mother was quite famous for bearing twins. You have not enough worry, as it seems, trying to find sustenance for your own children;

now you will have to keep Broche-Leah with a child, with two children, or perhaps even three.   Zeinvil-Yehiel is resting in his grave; he is dwelling in Paradise and studying the *Torah*, and you will now have to work and keep his daughter.

My trembling lips were uttering: " Heaven help me ! Heaven help me!" And my wicked thoughts were whispering: If God wishes to manifest His pity, there is only one way for Him to do it—by sending His angel of death to me—to the woman on the point of being delivered.   Merciful heaven !   Merciful heaven !

I know that I am committing a sin before God, that I am blaspheming.   I know it, but I lack the strength to drive away my evil thoughts; for, alone, I am weak and feeble, and the more so when I am in darkness.   I know that the only remedy against such thoughts is to study the *Torah*, and I am endeavouring to repeat by heart passages from the *Talmud*.   I am trying to remember some of the talmudical problems, but I fail to do so.   I have forgotten everything; I have forgotten all the *Torah*.   And in my agony I cried with all my strength:

" Lord of the Universe, help me ! help me ! "

And then a miracle happened.

6

The miracle. The hidden light. The redemption of a soul. The angel of death who came because he had been called.

When I afterwards told the story to one of the " enlightened " people, one of my former pupils, he laughed at me, and how he laughed ! It was no miracle at all, he said, but merely an incident, an outcome of my lively imagination, or perhaps nothing but a dream.

" Jethro the father-in-law of Moses," I said, " had seven names, and yet there was only one Jethro." But what matters it ? Call it whatever you like, miracle, incident, imagination, the story remains a story.

All that I know is that when I thought that I was going down into the lowest pit of hell, heaven forbid, a great light had suddenly filled the whole *Beth-Hamidrash*. It was one of those wonderfully soft, blue lights, similar to the luminous columns which in summer sometimes emanate from the sun and enter a room by way of the window. On such occasions one may notice, quite clearly and distinctly, that the column of light consists of small luminous partices, rotating one around the other. And it was such a column that now penetrated into the *Beth-Hamidrash*.

I had suddenly grown calm, and ceased to think. The *Beth-Hamidrash* was filled with a soft light, while a luminous comforting faith in God penetrated my entire being. Everything in me became so clear, so pure, and so crystalline. Looking up to the east from which the light was emanating, I beheld some one. Whom do you think I beheld? I beheld my brother of blessed memory. He was sitting in the very place which he used to occupy during his lifetime whilst studying the *Talmud*. An open folio was in front of him. I could not distinguish his face, because he was leaning his head upon his hand. My heart, however, told me that it was my brother, Zeinvil-Yehiel. And I was not at all frightened.

As a rule those who fear not the living tremble before the dead. But, I, miserable poor worm that I am, who am always trembling before everything that lives and moves, why should I be afraid of the dead? And of whom? Of my own brother Zeinvil-Yehiel who, even when alive, was of such a gentle disposition? I therefore simply asked him:

" Is it you, Zeinvil-Yehiel? "

" Yes," he replied, " it is I," and he removed his hand from his eyes.

And then I saw his face. A wonderful, brilliant, loveliness emanated from it; and a peculiar gentleness was mirrored in his eyes. I asked him again:

" And what are you doing here, my brother? "

" What am I doing? " he asked. " I am doing a great deal. When I was alive and sitting in this place studying, Satan often came to disturb and confuse me; then there were also my daily worries about earning a living. The result was that I used to skip many passages and to study many others with but little concentration of mind. I am now doing what I have been commanded from above to do, in order to redeem my soul. I am repeating."

"And are you doing this with fervour?"

He nodded his head in the affirmative, and I said:

"Zeinvil-Yehiel, you are studying with such fervour because you do not know that——"

In his gentle voice he interrupted me.

"You foolish one," he said, "it is just the contrary; I can study with such fervour because I *do* know. When alive, I used to skip over many passages because I knew but little, and doubted much. For it is only our ignorance and our doubts that confuse us. At present, I know; no doubts are troubling me, and I can thus study with fervour and concentration of mind."

"Do you also know, Zeinvil-Yehiel, that Moishe-Yisroel——"

"Has run away to America? Of course I know it. I even know which vessel he boarded. I also know that he is eating forbidden food on board of ship."

"Do you also know that Broche-Leah——"

"Is being delivered? Of course I know it. I even know that she will give birth to a son."

"Not twins?"

"No, not twins. But she will deserve great pity, because the child she is about to bear will be a cripple. That blackguard had knocked her about and beaten her too often, and thus injured the child."

And I asked him again:

"Do you perhaps also know what she will live upon?"

"This, too, I know," he replied in a gentle voice. He then went up to me and placing his hand upon my shoulder said, "Look out of the window."

I obeyed.

"And what do you see?"

"I see someone passing, someone dressed all in white, and his countenance is shining as if the Glory of God was resting upon it. He is walking slowly. Methinks that I can hear a sweet and delightful melody, a melody played by some walking musician. Now he has passed—the man."

" It was no man—but an angel."

" An angel ? "

" A good, a very good angel."

" The angel of death ? " I exclaimed, greatly frightened.

" Why are you trembling so much ? Would you like to run away from him ? "

" But whither did this angel go ? "

" Whither he went ? He went to the wealthy Reb Simhe. His daughter, too, is lying in travail."

" I know it. This very morning I and many others recited the Psalms for her and the child."[1]

" Prayers only help halfways. The child will live."

" And the mother ? "

" Have you not seen ? "

" Then it is to her that the angel of death went ? And he was walking so listlessly and so slowly ; is it because he has pity for her ? "

" Perhaps. But he need not hurry, because in the present case he is not a divine messenger."

" What are you saying ? " I exclaimed in great fright. " Who else has a right to command ? "

" Man has his own will. It was she herself who had called the angel of death."

" She herself ? "

" She did not want to have a child, did not want to become a mother. She, too, tried to injure her child."

" Lord of the Universe ! " I exclaimed in great agony. " She will die for her sins ! But what crime has the innocent child committed ? It will remain a motherless orphan ! Lord of the Universe ! "

" Don't cry," said Zeinvil-Yehiel, taking me by the hand. " Don't cry ! Broche-Leah will be engaged as the child's nurse. And henceforth you should know that He who gives life gives also the wherewithal to live upon."

Saying this, my brother evaporated in the air, and the

luminous column disappeared.   Through the window the
grey dawn was looking in.

7
He who gives life gives also the wherewithal to live upon.

You cannot imagine what I felt in that moment.   I fell
down upon the ground like a log, the fountains of my eyes
opened and tears began to flow abundantly.   Methought
they were not tears I was shedding, but ſtones ; ſtones
seemed to come up from my heart and to roll out of my
eyes.   And the more tears I shed the less ſtones there
remained upon my heart, and the freer and less oppressed
I became.

And here is the end of my ſtory.   I went home.   The
door of my house was open.   I entered the house and
by the pale morning light I saw that thieves had passed
here and carried away our scanty furniture.

" Never mind," I say unto myself.   The children are
coughing in their sleep, but again I say : " Never mind,
it will be nothing."   And now my wife Feige comes
home and greets me with a *Masoltov.*

I reply, " A boy, a cripple ? "

She looks at me in aſtonishment.

" Are you a prophet, or what ? "   She does not seem
to hear how the children are coughing nor to notice that
the house is empty.   " How did you know it ? " she asks.

And I tell her : " I know this and much more, Feige,
I know that Reb Simhe's daughter has passed away "—
I could not bring the word *died* to my lips—" and that
her child, a boy, is alive.   And I also know that Broche-
Leah will be the nurse."

" Who has told you all that ? "

" He who gives life gives also the wherewithal to **live**
upon," I replied.

And then I told her everything.

XIII

MOONPEARLS AND OLD WARES

———

ONCE upon a time there was a princess. But I am not going to deceive you : she was not a real princess. Her father, whose fatherhood was somewhat doubtful, had been a melancholy cobbler, and her mother, a market-woman, loved a drop of something strong. She had, however, the eyes of a real princess, and that is how people made the mistake. And two poor young men had looked deeply into those eyes and fallen in love with them. Both took her to be a real princess, and both said, " Either she or a rope round the neck." Neither of the two young men knew that the other had uttered these words ; it is possible that they did not even know one another.

And each of the two young men had made up his mind to woo and marry the princess. But how ? You can't visit a princess—and particularly a real princess, as they believed her to be—empty-handed. Therefore both began to think of ways and means to find favour in her eyes.

And both were searching, each in his own way. One of them began to walk about all the day long with eyes looking down upon the ground, whilst the other was walking all night with eyes raised to the skies. The one with eyes lifted up to the skies was of a romantic nature, not caring to pick up his luck in the mud of the streets. He was searching for his luck in the star-studded vault of dreamy nights. He passed his nights in the outskirts of

the town, in woods and fields, or at the riverside. Sometimes he would ſtand for hours at the little window in his
garret under the roof, looking up to the skies, to the blue
immensity above, to the moon and the stars. With eyes
moiſt and pleading, he was complaining of his misfortune ;
with trembling lips he was telling the moon and the ſtars
of his love. He was conſtantly imploring the heavenly
bodies for help.

" Grant me," he would say, " some heavenly gift,
something pure and noble that I may offer it as a present
to the beautiful princess and thus find favour in her eyes.
Help me to win her love, for what is my life without her ? "

The firſt young man, with his gaze lowered to earth,
aſted quite differently. He knew that many caſt-off or
loſt objeſts scattered upon the earth could be had for
nothing. Old wares are often thrown out of houses ;
a slippery coin is often loſt in the mud ; and horses
frequently caſt off their shoes. Broken nails may be picked
up in the ſtreets, and sometimes one may even make a
lucky find. With patience, a good eye, and persiſtence in
the business of searching, it is quite possible to get on in
the world. A few trifles make something, and a couple
of such somethings realize a few coppers ; the greateſt
fortunes have been amassed by taking care of coppers.
And when you are able to boaſt of a fortune—then even
the hearts of princesses become as soft as wax. Thus
thought the firſt young man, and he began to search in
the mud of the ſtreets.

Such were the different means employed by the two
fortune-seeking lovers.

Of which of these lovers shall I tell you firſt ? In daily
life, in business, or when you are trying to marry one of
your daughters, you are, no doubt, praſtical people, and
would be much more intereſted in the young man who is
walking about with his eyes fixed upon the ground. But
when, in the hour of twilight, you take to reading, you
become idealiſts, souls and spirits, and then your sympathy
certainly goes out to him who is walking about with eyes
lifted up to heaven and gazing upon the ſtars. I will,

therefore, leave for a moment the lover with eyes fixed upon the ground and tell you first how the star-gazing lover had fared.

For a long time he kept his eyes fixed upon heaven and gazed upon the stars ; for a long time he poured out his heart to the heavenly bodies, telling them in touching accents of his fate, describing unto them in moving words his poor life and his rich love. He poured out so many beautiful and passionate words when speaking of his loneliness, of his yearning and the flame that was burning in his heart, that at last the kind and soft-hearted little stars were moved to great pity and pleaded his cause before the cold moon. More than one little star said that its heart was grieving for the poor star-gazing lover.

And at last the proud and cold moon, too, was moved to pity. One beautifully clear night, just before dawn, the moon cast a favourable eye upon him. Through the little window she cast into the garret a silvery ray, and with it neither more nor less than a " string of moon pearls." The poor lover nearly went out of his mind for sheer joy. He immediately rushed out and went to knock at the door of the princess.

" Who is there ? " he heard the sweet voice of his princess, perhaps a trifle sleepy and frightened. " Who is disturbing me in my slumbers, who is it that is chasing away my lovely doves, my winged dreams ? "

" It is I, it is I," answers the young man in a trembling voice. " It is I, princess. I have brought you a gift from heaven, a gift which no prince has ever offered to his wife, not even to his sweetheart or mistress, a gift which the richest do not possess in their treasure stores. I have received it straight from heaven, and I have come to claim your love as my reward for this gift."

" From heaven ! " exclaims the princess in amazement. Jumping out of bed, she unlocks her door and through a narrow aperture extends her marble white hand to receive the heavenly gift. When the lover reminded her of the reward he was expecting to receive for his gift, she told him to come for his answer at sunset.

The lover with eyes fixed upon the stars was mad for joy. Singing and dancing, he hurried away to the meadows, the woods, and the river. Before his eyes was flitting the marble white hand, and in his ears resounded the sweet voice of the princess. He was not walking, but flying, and it seemed to him that the rustling sheaves in the cornfields were all wishing him joy, that the river was murmuring *Masoltov*. It seemed to him that the flowers were nodding their heads as if to say: "Yes, yes, you deserve your luck, you favoured of the moon," and that the birds in the air were singing the praises of his beloved!

Neither food nor drink did he taste all day long, but whiled away his time in song and dance. The flaming orb of the sun was setting; soft, cool shadows began to hover over field and river, and the tree trunks grew golden. A calm wind spread out its wings, and a strange bird was beating with its beak against the tree, calling aloud, *tick, tick*. The lover rushed back to town to fetch his answer.

Once more he knocks at the princess's door; this time, however, with more assurance.

"Who is there?" asks the princess, a little sharply and impatiently.

"It is I, your lover who brought you a string of moon-pearls. I have come for my answer."

Light steps are heard, and once more the door is opened, and just as in the morning an alabaster white arm becomes visible, but this time not naked.

"I took your pearls to all the goldsmiths in the town, but no one would touch them, neither buy nor barter them. They are strange, foreign stones, they say, absolutely valueless. I went into a draper's shop, hoping to get at least a few yards of cloth for a dress, but they simply laughed at me. Tired out and exhausted, I went into a food-shop and asked for some refreshment in exchange for your pearls, but not even a bit of cheese would they give me. They thought I was mad and showed me the door."

The marble white hand cast the pearls at the lover's

feet, withdrew and slammed the door. And the lover could hear the key turning in the lock.

Quite different was the fate of the other lover, he with his eyes fixed upon the ground. He collected and amassed for days, months, and years. In a short time he had a roomful of odds and ends, rags, old wares and such like things which he sold to a rag-merchant. He put his money in the savings bank and continued his pursuit. Again he collected and again he sold. Once he made a lucky hit, because when you are searching you usually find, and God also helps you. Nothing and nothing sometimes make a trifle ; a couple of trifles realize a few pence, and it is out of pennies, as the saying goes, that the biggest fortunes have been built. He amassed a fortune and also came to great honours. At first the people used to turn up their noses at him. " The man is searching in the mud," they said. But soon they began to favour him with a friendly smile, to take him seriously ; and when at last he had succeeded and grown rich, they openly admired him, even quoting him as a model. And when he had grown rich, the lover bought a palace from the mistress of some prince, and filled it with old but wonderful and costly furniture. The finest room of the palace he furnished as a bedroom with a golden bed, with bedding and hangings of silk and velvet.

And one day he put the golden key of his palace into his pocket, went to the princess and asked her whether she would like to live with him in the beautiful palace and sleep in the golden bed ? And the princess graciously answered, " Yes." On his wedding day he offered a feast to the poor, and among the guests was also the lover with eyes lifted up to the sky. He ate and got drunk, and in the night, when the newly married couple were speeding to some distant land there to spend their honeymoon, he went out into the wood and hanged himself on a tree.

XIV

DEVIATING FROM THE RIGHT PATH

In the calm star-studded immensity, between two courses of heavenly bodies, a sigh is heard from among the silvery and golden little stars.

" Who is sighing there, children ? " asked the gliding moon in a voice full of pity.   She asks, but does not stop in her course, nor does she turn round to look whence the sigh is coming.

" It is I," a little star beneath the moon replies, flickering up red.

" What ails thee, child ? "

" Mother, I can no longer stand it, I cannot, indeed. To run eternally, for ever and ever, in the same course, to continue on the same path ! "

" It is the right path," says the moon by way of consolation.

" Between what points ?   Whence and whither ? Where is the beginning and where is the end of our eternal wandering ?   Are we perchance going from nothing to nothing, from bad to bad ?   Whither is our path leading ? Dost thou know it, mother ? "

" *He* knows it."

" And why does He not reveal His secrets unto us ? Why does He refuse to tell us what He is expecting from us ?   Why does He refuse to tell us what we are actually doing, and for what purpose we are shedding our light ?

" The old story.   We are sending light to those who

are below us and who are consoling themselves with our light. We are pathfinders for those who are wandering in steppes or are entrusting themselves to the waves of the ocean, but what about ourselves?

" We are shedding light, whilst our own souls are veiled, wrapt up in shadow. Others can see by our light, whilst we ourselves are being driven like blind sheep. And we are not allowed to stop in out courses, to stand still and reflect for one minute, to ask: What for? For what purpose? We are not allowed to go either slower or faster. We have to run once for all in our fixed courses, to confine ourselves to a fixed time. We are not allowed either to wait for one star or to catch up another. We are not allowed to turn aside, to talk to someone on our way.

" And always, always, we are lonely. Every star has its own course, every star is lonesome in its particular course. Thousands of thy unhappy sisters are crossing thy own path, but none ever comes up to thee. Thou art never allowed to greet one of them, to ask her: ' How do you do, sister?' None of them ever smiles at thee, nor dost thou ever smile at one of them. We are all so near and yet so far, such strangers. Our hearts are yearning and longing all the time, and we are feeling so humiliated."

" Are we not high up?" consoles the moon. " Those below us are envying us."

" The fools! They are allowed to meet, to embrace, to kiss and console each other, and their lives are so short! The fools, they are envying us, us miserable, lonesome orphans, condemned to live eternally, or almost eternally! Look, they are pointing at us with their fingers from below, look, they are saying, ' A little star has dissolved in liquid gold,' but they know not that it is the soul of a star that is pouring itself out for great yearning.

" ' The stars are singing hymns,' they are saying below, ' the happy stars,' and they never dream that between one *Hallelujah* and another we here above are crying and yearning."

" Be silent, child, thou wilt be heard, run along on thy right path."

" I cannot, mother."

" Child, *His* will must be obeyed. A little star deviating from the right path is immediately hurled down."

" Whither, mother ? To those who are below ? "

" No, child, deeper still, where it is punished, punished in all eternity. He who has thought out worlds has also thought out the punishment. Terrible must His punishment be, for heavy is His hand ! Thousands and thousands of my children have I thus lost, and none has ever returned to tell us at least what is happening there, what tortures one suffers there in the deep. Terrible must the tortures be, His hand is so heavy, but no sigh from yonder has ever reached us. In the darkness there everything is being stifled, and no ray of the punished sinners has ever reached our heights, for already during the fall their light is extinguished. Take care, beware, my child ; repent of thy sins."

" No, mother, I would sooner be hurled down, I would sooner suffer ; I would sooner suffer tortures in all eternity and know that they are tortures which I alone have chosen to undergo ; that they are *my* tortures, that it is *my* own will that is being done."

Thus spoke the little star, and burning like gold it moved aside from its path.

Swift as lightning the little star is hurled down into the bottomless deep, and in its fall its light is extinguished. And the moon sighs, gliding along in her course. She is not permitted even to look round.

XV

JOCHANAN THE GABBAY

(President of the Community and Communal Worker)

———

Tired and exhausted from his communal work, Jochanan the Gabbay came home. The smell of food, of meat and boiled apples coming from the kitchen, greeted his nostrils. Hastily he entered the house, where, however, he met with a scarcely friendly welcome from his wife Soshye.

" Idler ! " she scolded in an angry voice, as soon as he had stepped over the threshold.

" And why are you scolding ? " asked Jochanan, sitting down upon a chair to get his breath.

" Why am I scolding, he asks ! You are always busy with your communal work, and when, I ask you, you idler, will you do something for yourself ? "

" For myself ? " asked the Gabbay greatly astonished. " What have I to do for myself ? Our children, thank God, are all independent, and we are suffering no want whatever. What have I to do ? " Casting a look round the room he added : " The beds are made without me, the dishes are washed without my help. I have not touched the walls and yet there is no trace of cobweb upon them. I see that the table is already laid ; a snow-white tablecloth is spread, and the knives and forks and spoons are sparkling like gold. I see that there are already on the table dishes of raddish and horse-raddish, and also a small flask of brandy."

" Have done with your speeches and go and perform the ritual ablution of your hands."

" No, Soshye, I will not perfom the ritual ablution of my hands until you yourself have admitted that I am right. Here, in my home, I have nothing to look after ; but a lot of work awaits me in the synagogue. For who is there to look after everything if not I ? Who ? I ask. Yosske the shopkeeper, perhaps, who scarcely finds time even for his meals ? Or perchance Yehiel the pedlar, who leaves his house immediately after the *Habdala* to return only with sunset on Friday ? Ruben the money-lender, who is busy running about to squeeze a few more *groschen* of interest out of the poor borrowers ? One of the poor artisans, perhaps, they who are working so hard to earn a miserable pittance ? "

" All right, all right, I am not angry any more. Never mind."

" I know that you are not angry any more, but I am going to prove to you that I am working for myself. Look at me, Soshye, look at my white beard and my grey earlocks. I am no longer young, and I must prepare for a long journey."

" A journey ? What journey ? " asks Soshye, greatly astonished. Soon, however, she guesses the meaning of his words, and greatly frightened she exclaims : " For heaven's sake, do not talk about it, heaven forbid ! "

" You need not be so afraid, Soshye. You, too, are no longer twenty years old. And what shall we say for ourselves when we are asked above how we spent our time in this world ? That we ate and drank ? And what will the Lord say to this ? *You* will at least be able to say that you were a member of a society providing poor brides with trousseaux."

" Don't talk of it," begs Soshye, afraid lest the boasting of her good deeds lessen her reward in the next world.

" And therefore, I, too, am anxious to perform some good actions."

" Very good, very good. Do whatever you like, only go and perform your ablutions."

" One thing more, Soshye," continues the Gabbay.
" Do you remember your wedding dress, a silken one with
silver stripes ? "

" If I remember it ! "

" Now, would you like to present this dress to the
synagogue to make a curtain out of it for the *Torah*
shrine ? "

" With the greatest of pleasure. I will go at once and
find it."

" One moment, Soshye, I have taken it myself, and it
has already been turned into a curtain for the *Torah* shrine."

" You thief ! " says Soshye, smiling.

And now Reb Jochanan performed his ablutions and
took his seat at the table. He ate with a good appetite,
said grace after his meal, and went to bed.

Reb Jochanan the Gabbay fell asleep almost immediately,
and during his sleep his soul soared up to heaven and
inscribed his merits in the book of records, and that is
what his soul wrote :

" I, Jochanan, the son of Sarah, have been busy all this
day with sacred communal work. I said unto myself : I
and my wife Soshye are living in a fine house, whilst the
house of God is falling in ruins and needs repairs. Therefore have I hired workmen and instructed them to make the
necessary repairs. To-day two new benches and a new
table have been brought into the synagogue. I have also
had the floor cleaned, the walls, furniture, and utensils
dusted and polished. I have bought a new candlestick for
the reader's desk in the east side. There were only
forty-five roubles in the cash box, and I had to lay out of
my own pocket six roubles and eighty-four copecks. On
behalf of my wife Soshye, I have presented the synagogue
with a silken curtain for the *Torah* shrine ; my wife is also
a member of the society for providing poor brides with
trousseaux. May the Lord of the Universe take all this
into account for the salvation of our souls.

" The repairs of the synagogue have been completed
to-day, and I have given strict instructions to the beadle
henceforth never to allow any beggar to pass the night

in the synagogue.   The synagogue should no longer serve as a dormitory for strange beggars.   Henceforth the beadle will have to lock up the house of God every evening."

Reb Jochanan's soul was still writing, when another soul flew up to heaven and began to inscribe as follows in the book of records :

" I, Berl, the son of Judith, am seventy years old.   So long as I had the strength, I earned my living with the work of my hands and in the sweat of my brow.   But now that I am old and feeble and no longer able to work, I am compelled to beg from strangers.   At first I did not fare so badly.   People in my native town knew me, and I always obtained sufficient to eat.   But gradually the people became tired of me and gave me less and less alms.   Sometimes I was given a dry crust which I could scarcely bite with my old teeth.   I saw that I should soon die of hunger if I remained any longer in my native town, and so I left it and came here.   It is bitter cold to-day, and I wended my way to the synagogue, with the intention of passing the night there, as is the custom in all Jewish towns.   But the beadle shut and locked the door in my face and would not let me in.   The Gabbay had given instructions not to allow anybody to pass the night in the synagogue, the synagogue not being a lodging-house. And now I am sleeping under the open sky, and the frost is eating up the marrow in my old bones.   I am hungry and I am freezing.   And now I ask Thee, Lord of the Universe, who needs the synagogue more, Thou or I ? "

And a voice resounded in heaven :

" Both shall immediately be summoned before the Supreme Tribunal."

And on the following morning were found dead—Reb Jochanan the Gabbay in his bed, and an old beggar, frozen stiff in the street, in front of the synagogue.

XVI

YENKEL THE PESSIMIST

―――――

ONE day Yenkel pushed away *The Duty of Hearts*, and leaning his head against the back of his bench, stared at the ceiling. His expression was so sour and so bored, he made such a wry face, that one might have thought life was speedily oozing out of all his pores.

" The whole misfortune," says Yenkel, " is that we are living against our will."

" Yenkel, what is the matter with you ? Which *day*[1] are you still wanting, a Monday or a Thursday ? "

" He is trying to prove to me," replies Yenkel, pointing to the open book ; " he is trying to prove to me that I am the crown of creation, that everything has been called into existence for my sake. I am living in the most beautiful apartment, the earth being my floor, the sun and the moon my chandeliers, the stars my lights, the beasts, birds and animals and even the worms so many of my servants. Well, what more can I want ? "

" Which *day* is it you are still wanting ? "

" Nonsense," says Yenkel, " it is not a question of days. On Saturdays I am the guest of Berl the butcher, and my food is worth as much as the food I could get elsewhere during a whole week. Berl's wife, stout Shprinze, is constantly urging me to eat ! ' Eat, young man,' she says, ' eat as much as you can, so that you may gather strength to study, and the merit of your studies will benefit us too

and be counted in our favour.' And so I am compelled
to devote my attention to hot sausage and *kuggel*, and do
my duty, so that the merit of my studies may save my
hosts from the punishments of hell whither they are afraid
of being condemned, for the sins of giving false weight,
of substituting a bone for meat, and even for casting a
covetous look—for I have noticed that Shprinze sometimes—— "

"But what is it you really want, after all, Yenkel?
God be with you."

"I don't want anything, I am only disgusted with life."

"Well, who prevents you from making an end to it,
Yenkel?"

"We are living against our own will, that is what I am
telling you," says Yenkel, not taking his eyes from the
ceiling.

"What do you mean by 'against our own will'? And
what about knives, razors, rivers, and ropes? If you are
anxious to have a sweet death, then buy a sugar cord; if
you want to die a pious death, then hang yourself upon the
chandelier, facing the holy ark."

Yenkel burst out into loud laughter.

"Listen," he said, "I have already been thinking of all
this. When I was at home I had made up my mind to
divorce myself from the world once for all. Why? I
will tell you this some other time. The question I am
trying to solve is how to do it? The best thing, I thought,
would be to shoot myself. I used to know a Jewish
soldier, but whenever he took the gun into his hand, my
legs began to shake so violently that I could not persuade
myself to go near him. It seemed to me as if someone
was pulling me back by my hair. Our next-door neighbour was the ritual slaughterer. One day I tried to steal
his slaughtering knife, but I cut my finger and nearly
fainted. I am terribly afraid of cold water, as you well
know. And so I made up my mind to hang myself. I
found a rope, went up to the garret of the synagogue, and
had already put the noose round my neck, when I suddenly
felt so thirsty that I was absolutely compelled to go down

and have a drink first. In the meantime mother sent me out to take a fowl to the slaughterer, and until this day I have not yet found a favourable opportunity to hang myself."

We all burst out into loud laughter.

"Whose fault is it?" we asked, "if you are such a coward?"

"Who is a coward? I? Is it my fault perhaps? Do I wish to be afraid of death? Don't I know that the sooner the better? I am firmly convinced that the best thing a man can do in the world is to commit suicide! I am trying with all my might *not* to be afraid, but this ' to live against our will ' is deeply rooted in my heart, and whenever I am ready to do something, this instinct comes to the surface. It is this instinct that causes my legs to shake; it is this instinct that pulls me back by the hair; it is this instinct that whispers into my ear and informs me of my thirstiness. It is not I that am to be blamed!

"And sometimes," Yenkel continued, "another fear seizes me. I am thinking—who knows, but I might be condemned to live over again in another world, to be once more a poor student and feed once a week on hot sausages and *kuggel* to last me six days, so that Berl the butcher's wife might benefit by my merits. Who knows? My soul may even migrate into an ox or a calf, and I shall be led hungry and thirsty by a rope to the slaughter-house. I shall reach out my tongue to every blade of grass, to every drop of muddy water, and some other Berl butcher will follow me with a stick in his hand, driving and beating me. Later on some pious Jew will come, will roll his eyes, recite a blessing and—cut my throat."

Yenkel grew terribly pale, and beads of cold perspiration covered his brow.

"You are laughing," he said in a hoarse voice, "you are laughing because Maimonides denies the transmigration of souls? But Luria[1] believes in it. And King Solomon, the truly wise man, merely says : ' Who knows? Who indeed knows? Who can know?'"

7

XVII

ORMUZD AND AHRIMAN

———

THE Persians believe in the existence of a dual divinity, in two gods. One god, our spirit of good, *lehavdil,* is a good, benevolent god. He creates light, pity, benevolence, intelligence, and other good things—for the use of mankind. The other god, Ahriman, our spirit of temptation—heaven forgive me for the comparison—is a wicked god who loves darkness, like a bat or a mole. He is as cruel as a Torquemada. May heaven preserve us from such a god.

You understand—that had it not been for Ahriman, the world would have been a veritable Paradise. People would have lived here like twin-brothers, and even husband and wife would never have quarrelled. Men would have run about in the streets, not on the look-out for business or swindling, but for pious deeds and good actions. They would have called out: "Whoever is naked we will clothe him; whoever is hungry we will feed him; whoever is thirsty we will provide him with water, nay, with wine and rum, whatever he likes—whole barrels of Carmel wine." Had it not been for Ahriman, then the famous Heidelberg cask would have borne the following inscription: "Whoever is thirsty let him come and drink," just as in our *Passover-Haggada.* Women would never have worn upon their hats the wings of birds shot for the purpose. It would have been a question rather whether it was permissible to massage the human body in the vapour-baths.

And on the contrary, had there only existed Ahriman alone, then the world would have been a veritable hell. It would have resembled a ship tossed about on an ocean of human blood. The smell of burnt, roasted, and smoked human flesh would have risen and spread over the seven heavens.

The world, however, is neither all heaven nor all hell. From time to time *auto-da-fés* are extinguished, the clanging of chains ceases, and even the roaring cannons are silent for a while. Not all the milestones are gallows, and there are meetings at the Hague where people actually talk of peace. Both prisons and hospitals exist in the world, both societies against cruelty to animals and anti-Semites, chauvinism and International Congresses. The Boers send the English New Year greetings and a Christmas pudding in a shell. All this is due to the fact that both Ormuzd and Ahriman are equally busy, one undoing what the other is accomplishing.

I have learned all this, not so much from old Persian books and various translations, as from the lips of an old Persian. He is a neighbour of mine, and one day I made his acquaintance. We now often meet, and like two long-nosed gentlemen who both dislike to listen to the barking of dogs, we often indulge in a friendly chat. Whenever the Persian and myself meet, we greet each other very cordially.

" How is your old one ? " he asks smilingly. And I

" Quiet for the present ; and Ormuzd, how is he ? "

" Oh, he will conquer." The Persian is quite sure that Ormuzd must conquer in the end. The old optimist then blows his nose loudly and confidently, and wipes his face with a red silk handkerchief, large enough to serve Ormuzd as a banner. Once, though, the old Persian did not feel quite so sure.

" Who knows," he said, " who knows ? You see, Ahriman is crafty ; he is as smart and clever as you make them. As long as he was waging open warfare against

Ormuzd, I felt quite sure that Ormuzd's everlasting day would soon dawn, and that night would have disappeared for ever. But, alas, I have noticed—— "

" What have you noticed ? "

We sat down upon a bench—it was summer and we were walking in a garden—and the old Persian sighed.

" I have noticed that Ahriman has changed his tactics and is growing really dangerous. He is swindling, is pretending, and disguising himself. He pretends to be submissive to Ormuzd, and honeyed is his speech. He is cheating poor Ormuzd, and simple and kind-hearted as he is, Ormuzd allows himself to be cheated."

" Really ? Is it possible ? "

" Listen," said the Persian ; " I will quote you a few examples which will give you an adequate idea of Ahriman's new policy and tactics.

" Thus, for instance, in olden days, when Ormuzd was anxious to spring some pleasant surprise upon the world, to bestow a glorious gift and give it a great pleasure, he created a wonderfully beautiful woman. Then Ahriman used to come and touch the cheek of the beauty. That was enough : the peerless beauty suddenly had a scar upon her cheek, or her face was suddenly covered with pimples. But what was the good of it ? Ormuzd saw it at once, sent a ray of his grace and, lo ! the scar or pimples disappeared, and the beauty became even more beautiful and dazzling. Nowadays Ahriman is adopting quite a different method. He pretends to be content with everything that Ormuzd is doing. Quickly he dons evening dress and top hat, appears before the beautiful woman and, smiling sweetly, thus addresses her :

" ' Gracious lady, Madame or Mademoiselle, I congratulate you upon the boon vouchsafed unto you by my Lord Ormuzd. You fully deserve the gift of beauty bestowed upon you. The whole mortal world will bend its knee before your immortal beauty.'

" And the mischief is done ! The beauty becomes a flirt, a cold and heartless ensnarer of men, a devourer of hearts.

" Another instance. Ormuzd wakes up and perceives a poor man toiling hard in the sweat of his brow, and yet scarcely earning a miserable pittance. He is kind-hearted, is Ormuzd, and there is plenty of money in his treasury. Quickly he takes a few coins from a money bag and throws them down to the poor man. In former days Ahriman was wont to send robbers and thieves, or cause a fire to break out. The divine gift was taken away from the poor man or destroyed. It was, however, of no avail. Ormuzd continued to pour wealth upon the poor man and even to put luck at his door, so that the man grew rich and happy. Nowadays Ahriman acts quite differently. Ormuzd, he thinks, has made a present of a few coins to a poor man— well and good. He does not make any effort to outwit the elder brother. On the contrary, he is anxious to learn from him, to imitate him and to become kind-hearted in his turn. He consequently hurls into the poor man's lap a bag full of gold. The once poor man becomes a million-aire, his wealth grows and increases, and the more it grows the greater its attraction. It absorbs entirely the new rich. He cannot live happily among the poor surrounding him. His nights are restless, and even more so are the nights of his poor fellow-men.

" Ormuzd used to give someone a good thing, strength, for instance, a lion's heart. Such men often arise in every nation, at all times. In former days Ahriman did his best to destroy such men, to kill them. He used to send hosts of evil spirits and demons, commanding them to seize the strong man, destroy him, and wipe out his memory. But Ormuzd frustrated the efforts of Ahriman. Against the hosts of evil spirits and demons he sent hosts of angels who put to flight the former, driving them back to hell whence they came. The hero remained a hero. Nowadays Ahriman acts differently. When Ormuzd gives strength to someone, Ahriman adds a little more, and he that had been favoured by Ormuzd becomes an adventurer, a savage, because his strength is overwhelming. Instead of being useful to the world, he only brings harm in his wake."

The sun was setting and it was high time for my Persian to go home. He took leave of me. Rising from his seat, he thus concluded :

" I will tell you one more thing. A man must eat and enjoy his food. Ormuzd therefore gave him a stomach. It is a very necessary organ, for without it a man could not exist. Now what does Ahriman do ? He cannot very well cut out all men's stomachs, so he adds a blind process, called appendix, another piece. And it is this additional piece that proves dangerous, causing illness and disease."

The Persian left me, and I began to think about his words, wondering whether he was right after all.

Ormuzd, or the good spirit, instils in us a feeling of love, prompting us to love those who are dear and near to us—our nation, for instance, our poor nation, for which we are ready to work and sacrifice ourselves. What does Ahriman or the tempter do ? He adds a little more sentiment, and, lo ! the feeling of love becomes nationalism, chauvinism, Jingoism. The rich feeling of real love is turned into the disgusting fanaticism of charlatans ; neither light nor warmth emanates from it ; it glows and burns in the darkness, threatening to consume us altogether.

A poor homeless wanderer is anxious to find a roof to shelter his head, a resting-place for his weary limbs, where he can lie down and rise up again in the morning, like his fellow-men, refreshed and fit for renewed labour ! All for all ! What does Ahriman do ? He turns the roof and the resting-place into some sort of eternal, sublime goal, into an ideal, and we . . .

We have put the clock back for a hundred and twenty years. It is a sheer waste of time.

XVIII

IF NOT HIGHER

―――――

EVERY morning during the *Selichot* period[1] the Rabbi
of Nemirov used to disappear. He was nowhere to be
found, neither in the synagogue or the smaller places of
worship, nor in the *Beth-Hamidrash*, and certainly not in
his own house. The Rabbi's house always stood open,
and anybody could enter it freely. Nothing had ever been
stolen from the Rabbi's house. But no one was to be
found in the house during Selichot time.

Then where could the Rabbi be ? In heaven, of course.
During the awful days[2] such a Rabbi has his work cut out
for him. Jews, *unberufen*, require many things. They
want sustenance, peace, health, good matches for their
children. They are anxious to be good and pious ; but,
alas, their sins are many, and Satan, with a thousand eyes,
is watching from one end of the world to the other,
noticing everything, slandering and accusing Israel. And
who should help at such a moment if not the Rabbi ?

Thus thought the whole community. One day, however, a *Litvak* came to the town, and when he heard
the story he simply laughed. You know what a Litvak
is. He does not care a rap about devotional books, but
stuffs his head with the *Talmud* and the Bible ; and this
Litvak actually endeavoured to prove from the Bible and
the *Talmud* that even Moses, when alive, had never really
ascended to heaven but remained a good distance beneath

it. Well, now, how can you discuss such a matter with a Litvak ?

" Then where is the Rabbi ? " we ask.

" Much do I care," he replies, shrugging his shoulders. Whilst saying this, however, the Litvak already makes up his mind—fancy what a Litvak is capable of—to investigate the matter.

On that very evening, immediately after prayers, the Litvak steals into the Rabbi's bedroom and hides under the bed. He has decided to pass the night there and to see what the Rabbi was doing at dawn, when all the people went out to recite the Selichot. Another man in the Litvak's place would certainly have fallen asleep and thus missed the right moment, but a Litvak is never embarrassed. In order to keep awake, he repeated in his head a whole tractate of the *Talmud*. I do not know exactly whether it was the tractate dealing with *Slaughtering* or with *Vows*.

At dawn he heard the beadle rapping at the shutters and calling the inmates of the house to prayers. The Rabbi had been awake for some time, and for over an hour the Litvak had heard him sighing. Now anybody who had ever heard the Rabbi of Nemirov sigh knew how much grief over the whole people of Israel, how much agony of soul, there lay in each of his sighs. It simply gripped one's heart to hear the Rabbi of Nemirov sigh. But a Litvak has a heart of iron. He listened—and remained. And thus they were both lying, the Rabbi—long may he live—on the bed, and the Litvak under it.

A little later the house began to stir. The Litvak heard beds creak and people get up. Now and then a word in Yiddish was uttered, water began to flow into basins, doors were opened and shut. Then all the inmates left ; and the house once more became quiet.

The Rebbe's room was wrapt in darkness, illumined only by a pale ray of the moon entering through a chink in the shutters.

The Litvak afterwards admitted that when he had remained alone in the room with the Rebbe, terror had

seized him. He had felt hot and cold all over, and the
roots of his earlocks had pricked his temples like needles.
It is no joke to be alone in a room with the Rebbe at
dawn during the Selichot period. But a Litvak is
obstinate. He was trembling like a fish in water, but—he
ramained.

At last the Rebbe got up. First of all he performed the
ritual ablution of his hands and face, and did everything
that a pious Jew is expected to do in the morning. Then
he went up to a wardrobe and took out a bundle containing a peasant's dress. There was a pair of linen
breeches, long boots, a peasant's smock, a big fur cap, and
a wide belt ornamented with brass nails. And the Rebbe
arrayed himself in the peasant garments. From his coat
pocket the end of a stout rope, a peasant's rope, was
peeping out.

The Rebbe left the room, and the Litvak followed him.
Passing through the vestibule, the Rebbe entered the
kitchen and from underneath a bed he fetched an axe.
Sticking it into his belt, he left the house. The Litvak
was trembling, but did not remain behind. A gruesome
stillness, the gruesome stillness of the awful days, was
hovering over the dark streets. Here and there one might
hear the loud voices of the worshippers in one of the
smaller places of worship, or a groan uttered by a sick
man. The Rebbe is creeping along the walls, always
keeping in the shadow. He thus glides from one house
to another—and the Litvak is gliding in his wake. The
Litvak could hear the beating of his own heart, mingling
with the sounds of the Rebbe's heavy footsteps, but he
did not remain behind, and together with the Rebbe he
reached the outskirts of the town.

There was a small wood, and the Rebbe—long may he
live—entered it. He walked thirty or forty paces and then
stopped in front of a young tree. With amazement the
Litvak saw how the Rebbe took out the axe from his belt
and began to fell the tree. He saw the Rebbe repeating
his efforts and he heard the tree groan and creak. At last
the tree was down, and the Rebbe split it into logs and

the logs into splinters.   Then he made a bundle of wood, and tied it up with the rope he had taken out of his pocket. He then took the bundle upon his back, put the axe back into his belt and returned to town.   In one of the back streets in the slums, the Rebbe stopped in front of a poor, half-ruined, dilapidated house and knocked at the window pane.

"Who is knocking?" asked a frightened voice.   The Litvak recognized the voice as that of a poor sick Jewess.

"It is I," replied the Rebbe in the language of the peasants.

"Who art thou?" again queried the voice.

"Vassil," replied the Rebbe in Little Russian.

"What Vassil?   And what dost thou want?"

"I have wood to sell," said the disguised Vassil. "Very cheap, almost for nothing."

And without awaiting the reply, the Rebbe entered the house.   Creeping after the Rebbe, the Litvak beheld in the pale light of dawn a miserable room with broken furniture in it.   Upon the bed lay a sick Jewess covered with rags, and in a petulant, bitter voice she said:

"To buy?   What shall I buy it with?   Where dost thou expect a poor widow like myself to find the money?"

"I will give thee credit for the money," replied the pseudo-Vassil.   "It will only be six *groschen*."

"But how can I ever pay thee?" groaned the poor Jewess.

"Foolish woman," said the Rebbe reproachfully. "Look here!   Thou art a poor and sick Jewess, and I trust thee with the money for this bundle of wood.   I have faith in thee that thou wilt pay me, and thou who hast such a great and mighty God, thou hast no faith in Him?   Thou dost give Him no credit to the extent of six paltry *groschen*!"

"But who is going to light the fire?" groaned the widow.   "Have I the strength to get up?   And my son is already out at work."

"I will light the fire," said the Rebbe.

And whilst he was putting the wood in the stove, the

Rebbe, with many groans, recited the first section of the *Selichot*.   And when he had lit the fire and the wood had begun to crackle lustily he recited, a little more cheerfully, the second section of the *Selichot*.   He recited the third section of the *Selichot* when the wood was burning properly and he had closed the stove.   The Litvak, who had witnessed all this, went away and became a follower of the Rebbe of Nemirov.

And afterwards, whenever people told him that every year, during the Selichot period, the Rebbe ascended to heaven every morning, the Litvak no longer laughed. Under his breath, however, he added:

"If not higher."

XIX

THE CRAZY BEGGAR-STUDENT

———

1

HE was pacing up and down the hall of the *Beth-Hamidrash* and suddenly stood still.

Lord of the Universe! Who am I? Who am I? They call me Berl Hanzè's. *Nu*, am I really Berl Hanzè's? Am I really that? The signboard is not yet the shop. The house where our Minister is living is called *Pod-Karpiem*, and I am called *Berl Hanzè's*.

In *Zikhanovka*, our town, they know me; they know who Berl Hanzè's is. But what about America? Suppose someone in the *Beth-Hamidrash* in America were suddenly to call out, " Berl Hanzè's," would people know that he meant me? Here it is different. Here everybody smiles, nods his head, as if to say: " Oh, yes, we know him, he is a familiar figure, is Berl Hanzè's." One thinks: " Oh, yes, the *batlen* "; the other: " The madman "; whilst a third thinks heaven knows what. A fourth might remember that I am called after my uncle Berl. It is true that Taybele, when she remembers it, heaves a sigh, because she knows that I am an orphan, but what about America? There they know not Hannah, the street-hawker, and are also unaware of the fact that there had once existed a Berl the seeker, critic, and philosopher, my mother's brother. What impression, I ask you, would the words Berl Hanzè's produce in America where they know not that I am what they call me—namely, a madman, a *batlen*, an orphan, and perhaps also a seeker; for it seems that I am taking after my uncle. And after all I *do* know

who I am.   Don't I say myself : " A madman, a *batlen* " ?
Well, that is what I am.

Am I *not* crazy ?   Have you ever heard of anyone
suddenly beginning to ask himself who he was ?   A man
is a man !   I am a man, and my name is Berl Hanzè's.
Had I been a house, I might have been named *Pod-Karpiem* ;
had I been a prisoner, I might have had a patch upon my
shoulder and a number ;   had my father, instead of my
mother, been the provider, the bread-winner, and not a
batlen, then I might have been called Berl-Shmerl's.   It
might perhaps have been somewhat difficult for people to
pronounce the words Berl-Shmerl's, but they would have
had to do it.   And who knows, I might have been less
talked about by people, had it not been so easy for them to
pronounce my name ?   But whatever my name, I am a
man.   Yes, of course, a man, only a *batlen* into the bargain.
Plenty of men remain orphans, but do they all live in
the *Beth-Hamidrash* ?   Am I not able to do something ?
Could I not go on errands, chop wood, be a servant, wear
a decent garment, instead of going about in rags ?   Could
I not earn my bread, instead of being a beggar-student until
the age of thirty, being short of two *days* in the week,
and pacing up and down the room, wondering who I am ?

If I only knew where my gaberdine comes from !
Heaven is my witness that I know it not.   It has various
origins, this gaberdine, it is a piece of Bendit, a piece of
Hayim, a piece of Jonah, and three-quarters from the
dustbin.   It is lucky that Taybele can sew and managed
to put the pieces together, otherwise I would have had
to walk about stark naked.

Is not this alone madness ?   To be such a *batlen* ?   I
can remember how many dwellers in this *Beth-Hamidrash* I
have already outlived, Shmerl, Hayim, Jonah, and numerous others.   One is a merchant by now, another a carrier,
a third a public-house keeper.   One has had time to
become a widower, and even Shmerl has already married
for the third time.   But all of them have children,
businesses, occupations.   Whether they are doing well or
not does not matter : anyhow, they are busy, they do not

eat *days*, are not *batlonim*. They are men—and I, too, want to be a man! What is a man? As I am a Jew, I am not a man! As I am a Jew! I *am* a Jew, of course, I am a *Jew*. All the inhabitants of the town of *Zikhanovka* are also Jews, but they are not *I*. Look, for instance, I am a male (although woe unto such a male); *nu*, all individuals who are not females are males, but are they all also Berl Hanzè's? No, brother Berl, don't you fool yourself. You are a male, you are a Jew, it is quite true, but it is not *you*, the real *you*, who is the male, who is the Jew! You yourself are something else. All these things are an addition, a supplement, but they are not the real *you*.

I persuade myself that I am a *batlen*, a madman, an orphan, an unhappy male, but there are plenty of *batlonim*, madmen, and orphans in the world. There are also some unhappy males, like myself; no matter where—maybe in in other towns, maybe in America. Well, are they all *one*? Heaven forbid, each for himself. Then who am I, in the name of hell?

Some demon must have entered my body, some outsider must be sitting in me, thinking and wondering about me, whilst it seems to me that it is I who am thinking. The best proof of this is that during the whole week, except on Mondays and Tuesdays (when I have nothing to eat), when I have strength and am not faint from fasting, that outsider has no power over me, and then I think and search much less. In truth, philosophically speaking, no man in the world can really analyse himself. What does it mean? I want to expel my own ego? I want to tear myself out of myself, put this *I* or this *He* somewhere else, and bid him look at me! The *I-He* should look at the *He-I*. Ha, ha, ha! What does it mean? Let us go deeper into the matter. Ah, I feel quite warm in my head.

He rushes up to the brass water-basin, pours cold water over his head, produces a rag from behind the stove and wraps it round his head.

Now it will be all right; now let us see once more, I want to know who I am. Where shall I look, downwards or upwards? To the right or to the left? Methinks

that *I* am in myself.   Suppose that I climb up to the
top of the holy ark, then I shall be entirely on the top, I
shall not have left any part of me upon the floor; or
suppose that I run down into the cellar, then I
shall be entirely there, and leave no part of me
behind.   Then how can *I* look upon my own self ?   How
can that be ?

Then who is it that is sitting in *me* and doing the thinking
for me ?   And yet there *is* something in me.   What is it ?
I know, for instance, that when the beadle's wife once had
in her possession a lot of cakes which she had not counted,
and I had tasted no food for three days, I felt greatly
tempted to steal a cake.   I told myself, however, " No,
thou must not, the cake is not thine."   Afterwards I found
a thousand excuses for doing so.   " The beadle's wife," I
told myself, " has made a good deal of money out of you,
and she might make you a present of one extra cake.   Had
I asked her for one, she would surely have given it to me
herself.   Besides, one day, when God will help me, I will
pay her for it."   But again I told myself : " No, you must
not," and I did not steal the cake.   At first the questions,
answers and arguments followed each other quite regularly.
It seemed to me that it was I myself who was asking the
questions and answering them, but suddenly it all became
mixed up.   Questions were raised and answers given all
at once, the yeas and nays were uttered simultaneously,
and a discussion seemed to be going on in me.   I did not
steal the cake, not because I did not want to, not because
I had lost the inclination for it, but simply because my
hand would not budge.   My hand was wavering because
it did not know whom to obey.   The best proof that there
was a discussion going on in me is the fact that I felt very
tired and exhausted afterwards, as if after some long
discussion or a heated argument with Jonah Loksh.
The fellow is always endeavouring to persuade me that
the Gaon of Vilna[1] was condemned to sit in the vestibule
of Paradise, because he had refused to adopt the doctrines
and theories of the Hassidim.

What a silly ass !   Anyhow, I felt very tired ;   I

remember it perfectly well. I also recollect another instance. It happened on the feast of *Purim*, and I was sent on an errand to carry *Shlach-Manuth* from the rich Mr. Peretz Feinholz to our minister. It was a plateful of delicacies : sponge cake, macaroons, and some other good things. My mouth was watering, the tongue in my mouth was moving about in a mad fashion, just as I am now running about in the *Beth-Hamidrash*, and my hand was shaking. The gourmand in me wanted to steal a piece of cake, but the honest man in me said, " *No*." They say that it is the good inclination—well, let it be thus. But then I am only a dwelling, an apartment inhabited by two neighbours, one of whom is called the good angel or inclination—and the other the evil spirit, the tempter. Is it not so ? Then it is the story with the names all over again. But who are they, these two ? And who am I ? I am an apartment and I am both the good neighbour and the bad neighbour ; it is always I, and it is also I who am anxious to know who I am. Ha, ha, ha ! Hush, wait a minute ! It was only yesterday that the people were laughing at me because I had stood rooted to the same spot for an hour at least. I know quite well why I stood still. I did it because I could not move. They were just chopping wood in the synagogue yard, and it occurred to me to go out and try whether I, too, could chop wood, whether I, too, was able to work. I was already wending my way to the door and was passing between two benches. On one bench people were sitting and talking, saying that the vapour-bath was open to-day. I suddenly felt an itching all over me and felt inclined to go to the vapour-bath at once. On the other bench sat Zorah the schoolmaster. He was telling his cronies, among them Yenkel Ketzl, that the work called *Baal-Akkeda* contained a wonderful, a simply marvellous, explanation of the section of the Law read this week. I suddenly felt curious to know why Zorah the Melamed was so greatly delighted with the passage in the *Baal-Akkeda*, and I felt inclined to rush to the bookcase, take out the work in question, and read up the passage. *Nu*, what was the result ? I stood

still as if rooted to the spot.   My feet did not know whom
to obey, whether the Berl Hanzè's who was anxious to go
out and chop wood, or the Berl Hanzè's who wanted to
rush to the vapour-bath, or the third Berl Hanzè's who was
curious to know why Zorah the Melamed liked the passage
in the *Baal-Akkeda* so much.   I stood still for a long time
until I suddenly remembered that I had not yet recited my
afternoon prayers.

Well ?   What does it prove ?   It proves that there are
four people living in me :   There is the woodchopper, the
reader of the *Baal-Akkeda*, the bather, and last, but not
least, the afternoon-prayer reciter.   It was the latter who
ultimately subdued all the others, ordering them to keep
quiet and not utter a sound ;   he alone was master of the
house, and my feet were forced to obey him and to do his
bidding.   The best proof of this is that I actually walked
up to the wall and recited my prayers.   I have another
proof for the existence of these four individuals, for they
did not utterly disappear.   They were hiding in some
corner, stealthily looking round, winking at me and trying
to disturb me in my devotions.   All through the prayer of
Shmoneh-Essreh thoughts were   crossing   my brain about
woodchopping, perspiring in the vapour-bath, and the
explanations of the *Baal-Akkeda*.   Well, then, what is the
use of the explanation of a good and an evil spirit, if I am
sometimes three and sometimes four individuals ?

At the present moment, for instance, I feel that *I* alone
am a mere nothing, that *I* alone would not even be alive,
and even if I were alive, I should never get up from my
couch in the morning, but lie there like a log of wood for
ever and ever.   And, after all, I *am* only a log of wood
and have no soul.   How do I live ?   All things around me
live ;   they have souls, and from their souls emanate long,
thin, pointed threads, rays one might say, entering into
me, penetrating and creeping into me ;   they are pulling me
up, putting me upon my legs and commanding me to
walk ;   to do, to run . . . but I alone am nothing.   Then
who is it after all that is thinking ?   What ?   Who is it
that is sitting in me and is thinking ?   Again a stranger ?

Not I ? Well, let it be a stranger ! Who is he ? How did he come to get into me ? Am I perhaps a cage and he a bird ? King David speaks in his Psalms of a little dove. Is it the dove that is anxious to chop wood, to go to the vapour-bath, to steal a piece of cake from the *Shlach-Manuth*, to sneak a cake from the beadle's wife, and at the same time to study the *Baal-Akkeda* ? Fie, little dove ; it is not nice. If it is really you, then you ought to be ashamed of yourself. Ha, ha, ha ! Berl Hanzè's is a dove, a little bird ; Berl Hanzè's has a tiny beak and a pair of wings ; Berl Hanzè's will one day escape from the cage.

Well, Berl Hanzè's, will you then also wonder who you were ? Will you then, too, be an orphan, a *batlen*, or crazy ? Of course you will, who else ? Surely the *cage* is not crazy, the *cage* is not an orphan. Lord of the Universe, who am I after all ?

2

Wolf the Merchant enters the *Beth-Hamidrash*. Berl Hanzè's perceives him and hastily retires into a corner. Wolf the Merchant washes his hands, wipes them on the skirt of his coat, takes a book out from the book-case and sits down to study. Berl Hanzè's never takes his eyes off him.

" Who is he ? " he asks himself and immediately answers : " He is Wolf the Merchant," he says, pinching his own cheek. " Animal ! Ass ! Wolf the Merchant is just like Berl Hanzè's ! That is his name, but who is he in reality ? Is he one, two or three ? How many birds are chirping in *his* cage ? You understand, you dunce ? "

Berl took his head into his hands. " Let us think," he said.

At present Wolf is *one*, one Wolf the Merchant. He is studying, deeply engrossed in his folio, and does not even see me. He is no doubt studying the Talmudical tractate of *Vows*, because it is the only one that he knows. I know what he is at the present moment. He is the tractate *Vows*. And afterwards ? Afterwards Wolf the Merchant will go back to his shop, will give false weight in selling wheat, will deceive and cheat everybody and then go home to his wife, the poor, long-suffering, kind-hearted Taybele. He will box her ears and slap her face, not once but a dozen times. Do you see him now, Berl Hanzè's, do you see that innocent lambkin of a Wolf, that lamb ? Do you see, Berl Hanzè's, how he is wrinkling his brow, do you notice his pious glance, do you see it, do you see it all ? And you fool of a Berl Hanzè's, you ass, you want to persuade me that the this Wolf is the same as the other, the thief in the shop, the same as the ruffian at home ? Berl Hanzè's, you are talking sheer nonsense ; you won't persuade me to believe such rubbish. No and no. That is not the look of a thief, the look of an assassin, of a murderer. You fool !

I tell you, Berl Hanzè's, that there are *three* Wolfs : one is a lambkin, a pious lambkin who is studying the *Talmud*-tractate of *Vows*, and who will also study it in the next world with a commentary written by God Almighty Himself ; the second is a thief, and even in the next world he will steal from the plates ; the third Wolf is a murderer who beats his wife mercilessly. Oh, how I pity her ; my heart is aching for her ! She often appears to me in my dreams, imploring me to help her. That is to say, she is not imploring me in words, because a Jewish daughter, heaven forbid, will not talk to a strange man, but she is imploring me with her eyes, with such a pitiful look. Lord of the Universe ! She may look at me ! She may look at a male !

He, ha, ha ! I, a male ! Wolf the merchant is a male, may he rot, Wolf the Merchant ! I hate him with all my heart, I hate him like death. I have a meal in his house one day in the week, but I hate him. I should be happy to stab him : not Wolf the Merchant who is sitting here and studying, not even Wolf the thief, but Wolf the murderer. But I alone cannot do it, I have nothing to say, I am only a cage. I have a penknife, of course ; it is a small knife but very sharp ; you can cut your nails with it and even shave your head. I even refrain from making a lantern for fear of blunting the knife. But I alone cannot stab Wolf, someone must command me to do it, some mysterious voice fron heaven, even Zorah the Melamed. If he were to tell me to do it, or, better still, if *she* herself were to command me at night, in my dreams. But she won't do it, of course ; a Jewish daughter won't do it, heaven forbid. Besides, I would hate her, were she to talk to me.

It is better so ; let her look at me, always, and only during the night ; by day someone night notice it, heaven forbid. It is quite enough if she looks at me all night. Ah, how glorious it would have been ! I should have taken out my penknife, sharpened it on my bootleg, once, twice, three, four times, and *bukh*. Ha, ha, ha ! Out would come his bowels and entrails and blood ; red blood, ha, ha, ha !

No, no, Wolf the Merchant, you *Talmud*-student, I do not mean you, I mean the other Wolf, the murderer, not you. Listen, Berl Hanzè's, had you been a man, not an orphan, a *batlen*, a crazy beggar-student, a dreamer and a philosopher, it would have been all right. Of course, Taybele would have cried, for she would have remained a widow, but I would have told her in my dream to console herself. " Taybele," I would have said, " have you not enough with two husbands ? One is a thief and the other a *Talmud*-student, what do you want a third husband for ? Are you so anxious to have the third who beats you, Taybele, and makes you cry all day and all night ? "

And after all, he is perhaps only one ? Berl Hanzè's, I tell you, there are three of them, I swear, there are three. Come, let us purposely go out into the street, whilst he is sitting here and studying, and you shall see how the other Wolf is first cheating in his shop, and then goes home and beats his wife. Come along and you shall see for yourself.

The crazy student runs on tiptoe to the door, takes out the key, and locks the door from the outside.

3

He comes back pale and furious. The thieves ! They are hiding. They have nothing to do to-day ; there is no business going on, it being some sort of holiday ; flags are seen everywhere. They have no opportunity for cheating to-day. Taybele herself is not at home, she must have gone to a neighbour, for the door is locked. I peeped through the window, peered under the bed, and it seemed to me that something was moving there ; the shadow was playing and struggling on the floor. Who knows ? *He* is sitting here and studying, whilst the other two Wolfs are hiding under the beds—where else could they be ? And Wolf the simpleton, the student of the tractate of *Vows*, did not even hear me lock the door. He is deeply engrossed in his studies. And who knows ? He is perhaps not studying at all ! It is perhaps Wolf the thief who is sitting here, pretending to study, cheating both me and the Lord of the Universe !

" Wolf," he suddenly calls.

" What is the matter ? "

" Nothing."

" *Batlen.*"

A minute later :

" Wolf ! "

" Well ? "

" I have a penknife ! "

" Much good may it do you."

" Would you like to see it ? "

" No."

" Please yourself."

A few minutes elapse.

" Wolf ! "

" What *is* it ? "

" Are you really studying or merely pretending to ? "

" What business is this of yours ? "

" I must know ; it is very necessary that I should know."

" Be quiet, you madman."

A few minutes later :

" Wolf ! "

" Oh, *what* is it ? "

" How many are you ? "

Wolf grows angry, shuts the book, and leaves the *Beth-Hamidrash* ; Berl Hanzè's remains alone.

" Have I really been talking to Wolf ? What did I tell him ? Why did he run away ? How did I go out ? Ha ! Why am I holding the penknife in my hands ? "
He wonders greatly and grows angry when he suddenly notices that he had cut his bootleg.

" *Nu*, Berl *batlen* ! you yourself have cut your bootleg. You have many other bootlegs ? Do you imagine that Taybele will make you a present of another pair of boots ? Has she not suffered enough on account of the last pair of boots she gave you ? You see, you *batlen*, you see, you crazy beggar, that there *is* someone within you, someone who is not the *real* you, you see it ? Let me see how you really look, you ass, who allows his bootlegs to be cut, let me have a look at you ! "
He runs to the brass water basin, snatches up the rag he had wrapt round his head, and hurriedly begins to rub and polish the brass.

" Ah, I can see you a little, you *batlen* ! Wait, wait a minute, I shall soon be able to see you more clearly. I shall soon see your damned phiz, your ass's head."
Kneeling down, he begins to rub and polish with all his might. Suddenly he stops.

" Who is polishing the water basin ? Who ? I ? Have I any strength left in me ? Have I had any food to-day or yesterday ? What day is it ? Tuesday ! On Mondays and Tuesdays I have nowhere to eat. Who, then, is it that is rubbing and polishing ? " Once more he continues his labours.

" Well, no matter who it is that is rubbing, let it be the bird or the dove, the good spirit or the tempter, but I must behold your damned *batlen's* countenance. I must see it soon and see it all at once."
He shuts his eyes, continues to rub with all his strength and then suddenly opens his eyes again.

" Ha, ha, ha ! That is how I look ! A corpse ! Quite a corpse, ready to be laid in the coffin ! You see, Taybele, how I look ? And that is how I must always look when you give me a morsel of bread ! How should I look if you had given me no bread ? "

He grows pensive, then recollects himself.

"A corpse, that is what I am! Yes, yes, that is Berl the *batlen*, Berl the orphan, Berl the crazy—that—that—and who, after all, am I?"

He looks upon the water basin and then upon himself.

"In the brass I see no torn bootlegs," he wonders, growing angry. "A plague upon thee," he suddenly exclaims; "a plague upon thee, thou water-basin-image; thou, too, must needs have torn bootlegs? Because I have them, must thou also have them?"

He crouches on the floor, leaning his head on it, pushing with his feet against the water-basin.

"I cannot see, but you *do* have torn bootlegs, you see!"

He finds it difficult to rise up from the ground; it seemed to him that the man in the water-basin was holding him fast by his feet. He tore himself away, nevertheless, and rose up, a little surprised, a little frightened.

"You water-basin-man, you *batlen*," he called defiantly, afraid, however, to look upon his image in the brass. Rushing up to the stove he took up a handful of chalk and quickly dirtied the polished brass.

"Rot where you are, don't look out!"

His head was aching terribly, and his legs were shaking; again he grew pensive.

"Let me remember something! My head aches now; when the murderer beats Taybele, my head aches and I feel pains in my legs; when I pinch my cheek, my cheek flames. It is all because I have a cheek, have hands and feet, a head and a heart, and perhaps also a soul. I have everything; but I myself, what am I? I am neither the heart, nor the head, or the soul. Then what am I? Nothing. If I could commit suicide and watch what would remain of me, when the head, the hands, the feet, the cheek and the torn bootlegs will have come away, then I might be able to know something. Why not try it? If *she* were only to command me to do it. Why not try it first on him?"

XX

DURING THE EPIDEMIC

———

I

IT is coming, it is coming, alas, it is quite near. In the neighbouring villages it is something awful. Lord of the Universe, what is to be done ? One must not paint the devil on the wall, and even the name of the epidemic must not be mentioned, but nevertheless the people are feeling the alarm like a heavy stone upon their hearts.

And every day the news is growing more and more terrible. In Apte, it seemed, a water-carrier suddenly dropped down in the street with his water cans ; and in Ostrovtse the corpses of two Jews had been submitted to a post-mortem examination ; a doctor and a medical student had been sent down from Warsaw to Bratkov, whilst Rakhev is now completely isolated, no one being allowed either to enter or to leave the town.

A cordon of Cossacks was surrounding the town of Radom, whilst at Zosmir men were dropping in the streets like flies, heaven have mercy upon us. It was simply terrible. Business was becoming slack, whilst piety was increasing. Grain-merchants were afraid to budge, and big Jossel had already sold his horse and cart—a pity to waste money on oats for the animal. The agents in the grain-trade were daily tightening their belts by a notch over their empty stomachs. The houses were growing emptier every day, and every Friday another article of furniture was taken out to the pawnshop, to provide the necessary money for the oncoming Sabbath. Working-men, and sometimes even respectable house-holders, were indulging in an extra drop of brandy to gain courage. As far as the public-house keeper, however, was concerned, these occasional visits of Jews were bringing in but small profit, and the peasants were coming to town less and less frequently. In return, the wife of the barber discarded her wig and took to wearing a hairband ; a young man, secretly inclined to be an intellectual, publicly burned the novel *Love of Zion*, and took to reading the Psalms ; the servant at the vapour-baths confessed her sins to the local Rabbi because on Fridays she had sometimes peeped through a chink in the wall into the men's compartment. A young man, whose name people refused to divulge, was already fasting for a whole month and declared his intention of becoming an anchorite. Heaven alone knows what sins he had committed. Many tailors were voluntarily handing back the *cabbage*, or remnants appropriated by tailors to their own use, to their customers ; while butchers were giving better weight. Only one man, Jeruchem the money-lender, still remained adamant, refusing to lend money at any lower interest than ten per cent per month, insisting on a note of hand and good security ; the fellow had a stone in the place of a heart. Faces were growing yellow and livid, lips blue, and eyes hollow ; the streets grew more and more empty and silent. Here and there one could see small groups of people, men and women, conversing in whispers with an air of mystery, nodding their heads, gesticulating and raising their moist eyes to a leaden sky spread over the town. Silence reigned even in the *Beth-Hamidrash*, in the interval between the afternoon and the evening prayers, but on the other hand, the women's gallery was now crowded even during the after-noon and evening prayers. From time to time some woman burst out in loud and pitiful sobbing, and the men's hair stood on end. It seemed always to be Kol-Nidrei night, the night of the Day of Atonement, to judge from the lamentations and the shedding of tears.

What was to be done ?   What remedy could be found ?

People were saying that in Warsaw the inhabitants were very active, doing their best in the way of charity, and thus fighting the enemy, the terrible epidemic. They had opened tea-shops for the poor, and also a cheap kitchen ; they were distributing coal, food, and clothing among the poor. All these were remedies borrowed from the Gentiles and adopted with a view to pleasing the head of the police. Here, in this town, people said, they had other and better charities, such as a penny in the box of Rabbi Meir the miracle-worker. They also had the wonder-rabbis. We have excellent remedies against the epidemic, said the inhabitants, such as kindling the Sabbath candles immediately after sunset on Friday night and placing them on the window sill. We can marry an orphan boy and an orphan girl,[1] or besiege the holy ark and the graves in the cemetery with prayers. Of course, nothing would be left undone. All these remedies date from time immemorial, and yet during the epidemic in the year 5590 (1830) the grass had grown all over the whole market place, and was only trodden down in one or two places by the members of the burial confraternity.

Worse even than the epidemic itself were many incidents accompanying it and following in its wake. Among these terrible things were disinfection, isolation, and, heaven preserve us, post-mortem examinations and autopsies. A man does not live for ever and dies only once, but both death and life are in the hands of the merciful Lord. Tears, prayers, and repentance can do a great deal ; charity, too, is a good remedy, but, unfortunately, all the sanitary institutions are in the hands of the Gentiles. All their institutions cost a great deal of money ; they literally suck the marrow out of one's bones, and the end is a post-mortem examination. They cut up a corpse into tiny bits, heaven preserve us, and then bury it without any shroud, in a grave laid out inside with pitch. As for hospitals, they are simply poisoning people there. They are also burning innocent bedding, surrounding the private houses with a cordon of Cossacks, isolating them, and letting the inmates either die of hunger or devour one another. Well, something will have to be done, to prevent the enemy from penetrating into the town.

The Sabbath candles were already burning on the window-sills, and there was serious talk of marrying an orphan boy and an orphan girl ; the terror was increasing daily. People had hoped that together with the summer and the terrible heat, the danger would have passed, but, alas, their hopes had been vain. Summer had passed ; the awful days, the Day of Atonement, and even the Feast of Tabernacles, were over ; it was bitterly cold and snow had made its appearance, and yet the epidemic was creeping nearer and nearer. Heaven alone, said the people, can preserve and save us.

2

Two Who Were Not Afraid

There were, however, two individuals in the town who were not afraid of the epidemic ; on the contrary, they hoped to derive some benefit from it. These two individuals were the young medical practitioner Savitzky, a Christian ; and, *lehavdil*, Jossel the *Talmud*-student. Savitzky had come to the town three and a half years ago, immediately on finishing his studies at the University and obtaining his degree as a qualified doctor. When he first came to the town he was a kind-hearted Christian, as good as gold, a real philo-Semite. People were wishing that the head of the municipality had been as kind-hearted as Savitzky. There was not an atom of pride in him. He answered everybody in the street who greeted him, even children and Jewish women. He would step aside to let old folks pass and was very fond of fish as prepared in the Jewish manner. The inhabitants consequently honoured him greatly ; they bowed to him in the street, they even took off their hats, sent him a *Halah* on Sabbath, often invited him to their houses to taste a bit of fish, and so on. They wished him every possible happiness—but they never called him to a patient. Who wanted a doctor ? Was not the barber-surgeon enough ? And especially

such a barber-surgeon as the town could boast of. He
had only to cast one glance at the patient and immediately
he knew what ailed him. No wonder that the apothecary
consented to make up his prescriptions. It is possible, of
course, that another doctor in Savitzky's place might have
managed to build up a practice. Had it, for instance, been
an old doctor, rich and with a great experience behind him,
people might have called him in. But here was a green-
horn, a youngster who could not manage to let a moustache
grow on his upper lip, a pale-faced youth looking like a girl,
dressed up like a dandy ; in short, a boy who had just left
school. And as the eggs always pretend to be cleverer
than the chickens, he needs must go and contradict the old
barber-surgeon who had grown grey in his profession.
He needs must tell the latter that his patients were absorb-
ing too much castor oil, that scarified cupping was dangerous, especially for a woman in child-bed. Leeches, he
said, should be put on the window pane, then they would
cause no harm. As for dry-cupping, he made fun of it,
and he did not have any faith in ointments. Have you
ever seen a doctor without an ointment, a little blood
letting, and absolutely without cupping ? Now how
could one call in such a doctor ? The apothecary himself
turned up his nose at Savitzky's prescriptions worth a
paltry twenty coppers.

Thus Savitzky had been behaving for six months ; at
war both with the barber-surgeon and the apothecary ;
openly with the former and in an underhand way with the
latter. He was still, however, on good terms with the
inhabitants. Thus things went on until he had spent the
little money he had brought with him. He began to get
into debt, was owing his landlord, the butcher, the grocer,
and the tailor. In a word, he was in debt to everybody,
and his creditors were growing more impatient every day.

One day, when the butcher had refused to serve
Savitzky's maid with any more meat, the doctor pocketed
his pride and began to admit that blood-letting was very
necessary and that castor oil could be taken at any moment.
This, however, helped him but little, because in the first

place, people did not believe that he really meant what he asserted, and, secondly, since he had himself now admitted that the barber-surgeon was right after all, then what the dickens did they want with the doctor?

Savitzky once more procured a little money from somewhere (Christians, you see, frequently inherit money from rich uncles and aunts) and managed to exist for another six months ; but his position did not improve. At last he conceived the idea of turning anti-Semite, a really fanatic anti-Semite. He gave up greeting people in the street, even going so far as to draw back and openly spit, when meeting a Jew in the street.

He persuaded the Mayor to expel a few Jewish families from land which was peasant-property. When a new police sergeant was appointed (the old one had constantly been bribed and kept his mouth shut), the doctor immediately took him round all over the town and showed him the Jewish courtyards where dirt was accumulating. He once told the apothecary that, in his place, he would long ago have poisoned all the Jews in the town. Such, and other, terrible things did he do and say.

This helped him a little, a few Jewish inhabitants began to call him in to their patients and to pay him for his visits ; although, of course, they immediately tore up his prescriptions or threw away his concoctions and his ointments. It was only a question of shutting the enemy's mouth ; it was merely a sort of bribery to which they had consented, not sufficient, however, to keep the practitioner going.

Savitzky's bag of tricks was now exhausted, and he had no prospect of ever improving his desperate position. As his ill-luck would have it, he had a few unfortunate cases. A boy had pushed a pea into his ear, and Savitzky failed to get it out ; a patient, who at the risk of his life had actually swallowed the doctor's medicine, had died a week afterwards. The worst came when one day he could not refrain from declaring that temperature was not a disease in itself, but, on the contrary, a remedy ; it was so to speak, the weapon the body was employing against the disease. Those who heard him saying this could not refrain their loud laughter. And how they laughed when he was once called to a woman in child-bed! The local midwife happened to be away in a neighbouring village, and the family was compelled to have recourse to the doctor. You ought to have seen his stupid preparations! First of all he asked for a basin of water and a cake of soap. Then he took out a small bottle he had brought with him and poured some of its contents into the water. The family stood round, watching his preparations, and thought that he had himself prepared the medicine out of spite against the apothecary. But they were mistaken; he simply washed his hands in the water. Fancy it! And his hands were really as clean as can be, as is the fashion among Christians. That was not all, however. He took out a pen-knife and cleaned his nails with it, just like a pious woman before taking her ritual bath. Then he turned up his sleeves and again washed his hands. Who could enumerate all his stupid preparations, resembling the tricks of a conjurer? It is true, of course, that the patient herself who had borne other children said afterwards that his hands were much smaller than those of the midwife, and that, apart from his foolish hocus-pocus, he had performed the operation much more quickly than the midwife ever did. But who could stand all his silly legerdemain? And besides, suppose there had been no soap in the house? Luckily it happened to be washing-day.

The result was that Savitzky fared like the wicked in hell. Two years and a half had thus passed, and it soon became clear to him that he would not be able to hold out any longer. It is a shame to confess it, but his trousers became too large for him, for he was growing thinner every day. Feeling that he would fall ill, he had at last made up his mind to run away from the town, when suddenly came the news of the approaching epidemic.

Now, thought Savitzky, this is not the right moment to leave such a town, because a golden harvest was now in store for him. Instructions had already been received from the authorities to build barracks for the cholera patients, and to isolate a house for the families of the sick. The heads of the community had, of course, spent a lot of money, bribed the mayor and the police-sergeant and persuaded them to put down the expenses, but not to frighten the inhabitants. But everybody felt sure now that the epidemic was really near, that it was creeping along and would soon be in the town. What seemed to be fraught with danger as far as the inhabitants were concerned, presented the prospect of a fair fortune for the doctor. He would get three or four roubles a day from the Government; the patients would pay, and so would those who, though not infected, would be anxious not to be declared sick, heaven forbid. All these dear little Jews will now have to fork out; some will have to pay for disinfection and others for non-disinfection; some for isolation and others for non-isolation; they will have to pay for talking and for being silent, for the right of going in and out of their houses. The principal source of the doctor's revenue will be the burials. People will have to pay if they wish to escape a post-mortem examination and a grave with pitch in it.

Savitzky revives; his heart is bounding for joy. He is walking about in the streets, joyously whistling a song; with a cheerful glance he is scanning the faces of the passers-by; peeping into houses through open doors and windows. Jews are fond of hiding themselves, but they will have to pay him for all his years of misery. He will now get his own back! Then he would shake the dust off his feet, leave this God-forsaken town and go somewhere else, where he would marry; for whom could he marry here? The apothecary's ugly daughter?

3
THE SECOND WHO WAS NOT AFRAID

Jossel the poor *Talmud*-student is also anxious to get married, and he, too, has placed his hopes on the epidemic. You see, he is the only orphan boy in the town. Even if it wanted, the community could not find another orphan boy. They will thus be compelled to get him married.

Jossel is very anxious to get married, and no wonder too. It is in the family. His father and his grandfather before him at his age had long ago been married, and even buried children. And Jossel is already eighteen and the laughing-stock of the town. They called him an old bachelor, an old maid. During the day he had no respite in the *Beth-Hamidrash*, where the jokes made at his expense pricked him like so many needles ; but when night came it was even worse. Alone, on his hard bench, he was either passing sleepless nights, or being tortured by bad dreams. It was driving him mad. He was constantly begging and imploring his neighbours to find him a wife, to marry him, but always the same answer was vouchsafed unto him : " With whom ? With the Queen of Saba ? For who would have thee, such a mangy dog ? "

To tell the truth, Jossel was not afflicted with the itch, but, to make up for it, he enjoyed some advantages. Fourteen years ago he came to this town with his father, an itinerant bookseller, who had suddenly fallen ill and—heaven preserve you from such a fate—had died. Jossel had never known his mother, and had therefore been constantly wandering about with his father. The community had pity on the orphan ; the inhabitants bought up all the books and gave the deceased a decent burial with the money thus realized. The boy was sent to the free-school, and given permission to sleep in the *Beth-Hamidrash*. Charitable people took turns to give him his food one day in the week.

Six months afterwards Jossel had the measles in the *Beth-Hamidrash*. He then fell ill with small-pox, which left his face pock-marked, making it look like a grater. A year later he met with another misfortune. There was an old broken stove in the *Beth-Hamidrash*, and Jossel had been promoted to the function of regular stoker. The stove was an old invalid, giving out but little heat. During the day it was bearable, but during the night he used to freeze nearly to death. The rags which the charitable inhabitants used to give him on the eve of festivals were just sufficient to hide his nakedness, but he never had anything to cover himself up at nights.   One day, there-fore, Jossel conceived the idea of purloining the key of the woodshed.   Henceforth he began to steal logs of wood every night to make up a big fire and warm himself. Once, as people said, God punished him for this theft ; the stove suddenly burst, one of the bricks hit him and broke his leg.   The barber-surgeon patched him up, but Jossel could only walk with a limp.

Besides, he was neither a genius nor a very industrious student, and there was no one anxious to secure him as a husband for his daughter.   Even a water-carrier would not have him as a son-in-law.   And, as if to spite him, his eyes often burnt like two glimmering coals, his heart was oppressed with yearning for something.   He often suffered from headaches and giddiness, felt a ringing in his ears, and hot and cold all over ; he was frequently shaken by fever.   But who could pay any attention to a poor orphan ?   The inhabitants thought that they had done their duty towards him by giving him his food every day. To tell the truth, it was rather miserable food he got, because they did not think it worth while to spend much on him, as the reward in the next world for their good action would certainly not be great.   Why should it ? The fellow never studied assiduously, but was always sitting over his folio and dreaming.   When people talked to him he never heard them ; he would suddenly jump up from his seat, run about like mad over the *Beth-Hamidrash*, upset reading-desks and jostle people, as if he had been possessed by the devil.

A madman, an abnormal fellow.   It was a sheer waste to give him even tendons, bones, musty bread, or buck-wheat porridge that had remained over from yesterday. There was no benefit to be derived from him ; it was only lucky for him that he was an orphan.

When parents happen to have such a fellow as a son, they put him to an apprenticeship and let him become an artisan ; but no one dared to dispose of other people's children ; no one ventured to take the responsibility upon himself.   The boy's father had been a *Talmud*-scholar, had discussed the subject with the people till his last moment; and had died like a pious man, in the month Nissan,[1] after a very remarkable recitation of the confession of sins. Well, how could you go and make an artisan of his son? Who would like to be responsible to the deceased for such a deed? And so Jossel grew up alone in the *Beth-Hamidrash*. During the day his life was made as bitter as gall through the jokes made at his expense, whilst at night the evil dreams sucked the very blood from his veins. It was already two or three years since he had had any respite and had lost his peace of mind.

In the beginning he tried to defend himself; he knew they were evil thoughts that were torturing him, wicked thoughts. Alas! the evil thoughts became stronger, and his will-power grew weaker and weaker. He tried to fight them by means of fasting, but it was useless; he recited the Psalms, but it was of no avail; he tried to study, but it was no good; he could not distinguish the letters and only saw wheels of fire dancing before his eyes. Seeing that the evil one, the tempter, was after all stronger than himself, he let fall his wings and ceased to defend himself. He consoled himself with the thought that one day he would after all be able to marry, and began to wait for the matchmakers. As they did not come to him, he put aside all bashfulness and decided to go to them. It took him, of course, some time before he was able to get rid of his bashfulness. It took him months before he could muster courage enough to broach the subject to a marriage broker. He spoke about the matter first to one, then to another, in short, to all the *shadhanim* in town; and when the last had given him the same reply as all the others—that the Queen of Saba alone would marry him, he grew melancholy. He felt disgusted with life.

One night the thought flashed through his brain that sooner than live such a life, it would be better to die. And now a struggle began within him with the new sinful thought; and once more he failed to conquer. The first time the thought had flashed as swift as lightning across his brain, vanishing immediately. The second day the idea returned and lingered a little longer, and on the third day he began to harbour the thought and to examine it carefully. He remembered that last week there had been a storm. No doubt, he thought, somebody must have hung himself. A Gentile, perhaps ? No, no strong wind would blow on account of a Gentile committing suicide ; it must have been a Jew. He recalled to his mind the fact that last year a Jew, Hayim the tailor, had been drowned in the ritual swimming bath. He may have committed suicide ; for why should a tailor visit the ritual swimming bath in the middle of the year ? Had it happened on the eve of the Day of Atonement, it would have been a different matter, for on that day everybody visited the swimming bath to purify himself, but on an ordinary day ? It was rather strange. A few days later the swimming bath began to fascinate him, to draw him irresistibly like a magnet. " There is no harm," thought Yossel, " in visiting the swimming bath." He went, but never even undressed himself. He felt that once he entered the water he would never leave it again alive, but remain there for ever. For an hour he stood there looking down into the water, unable to tear himself away. He looked down into the dirty water, contemplating his feebly reflected image. Then it seemed to him that it was not at all his own image he was looking at, but that of Hayim the tailor, who was smiling at him, winking and calling : " Come down, it is so nice here, so quiet, so fresh and cool, so pleasant."

He felt hot all over and ran away in a great fright. In the street he came to himself again. Passing the shop of a rope-maker, he noticed how the goods exposed there were lying about without anybody keeping watch ; the rope-maker must have gone somewhere. Why had he left his shop ? Whither had he gone ? Such silly questions were crowding his brain, whilst his hand mechanically, without his being aware of the fact, was stealing a rope which happened to be lying on the threshold. It was only when he found himself again in the *Beth-Hamidrash* that he became aware of the theft he had committed. He was greatly amazed, unable to make out how the rope had come to be in his pocket.

" It is the will of the Almighty," he thought, tears welling up in his eyes. " God alone wills it that I should commit suicide, should hang myself." A great pity for himself filled his heart. God alone, he thought, who had created him, who had rendered him an orphan, who had afflicted him with small-pox, who had hurled the hot stove against his leg, God alone now wanted him to commit suicide. He had refused him this world, and now He wanted him to lose the next world too. Why? Was it because he had not conquered the evil thoughts, the tempter, the evil spirit?

How could he? He was alone, had neither parents nor comrades, whilst the tempter was after all an angel, an expert in his profession, exercising it since the six days of creation. And Jossel feels terribly miserable and unhappy. God Himself is being unjust to him if He wanted him to hang himself. It was clear, of course, there could be no doubt about it, that such was the will of God. And what was the use of his struggling? If such was the will of the Almighty, what could he do? He a worm, an orphan? He was unable to conquer the tempter, then how could he dare be so presumptuous as even to think of acting against the will of God? No, he dare not even attempt to oppose the will of God.

Taking up the rope he climbed into the garret. He would not soil the *Beth-Hamidrash* by committing suicide there, he would not hang himself in face of the holy ark. In the garret, he found a hook, evidently put there purposely. For, otherwise, why should there be an iron hook? Who knows how long the hook had been waiting for him? God Himself had perhaps prepared the hook even before He had fashioned him, Jossel. Thus reflecting, he fastened the rope to the hook. But suddenly a new thought came to his mind.

" And after all," he thought, " this may be the work of Satan. It is perhaps the same Satan who tormented me with the other thoughts who is now putting these ideas into my mind ? "

He let fall the rope. He would not do things in a hurry, but must first think the matter over. It is no joke to lose both this world and the next !

In the meantime the *Beth-Hamidrash* clock had struck the hour of four. It was the time of his daily meal, and Jossel suddenly felt acute pains and cramps in his stomach, for he was very hungry. Leaving the rope fastened to the hook, he descended from the garret.

Nightly now the rope was drawing him ; he was trying to save himself as well as he could. He rushed to the holy ark, put his head inside, close to the holy scrolls, weeping bitterly, imploring them to save him. Sometimes he would take hold of a reading-desk, clinging to it like grim death, so as to have some difficulty in moving from his place ; or he would seek a refuge by the side of the stove, leaning against it with all his might. And heaven knows how this struggle would have ended, had it not been for the epidemic. Oh, now Jossel could breathe again. No more hanging himself, no more melancholy : all this was now over, over. The community will have to marry him, for, after all, he was the one and only orphan in the town.

4

SAVITZKY GIVES WAY, JOSSEL IS SEEKING SOLITUDE

Since the fear of the epidemic has begun to increase, the inhabitants are avoiding Savitzky. They are all afraid of him. You never know ; a man is only mortal after all ; he may suddenly feel somewhat unwell, and in these days such a Savitzky is wielding unlimited power and authority. He may immediately give instructions to the policemen to put the patient to bed, rub him, make him swallow medicine, expel the family from the house, burn the furniture, then poison the poor man and make a post-mortem examination. It is murderous ! When doctors are anxious to know the nature of a certain disease, what do they do ? They poison the first patients and then search for little worms in their entrails.   Well, what can you do when you are in exile ?

At Apte the barber-surgeon had given away the secret ; the doctor, he had said, was poisoning the patients.   They sent him to prison for three months, putting him on bread and water.   You think the doctor ?   Heaven forbid, the barber-surgeon.

And therefore whenever Savitzky showed his face in the street, it suddenly became empty ;   whenever he tried to peep through a window-pane, a curtain was immediately lowered, a bed sheet hung up, or a pillow placed in front of it.

One fine morning the side street where Savitzky was living was empty.   All the inhabitants, landlords, and tenants, had quietly left.   They would not live in the doctor's neighbourhood.   That is the true meaning of the Talmudical dictum :   " Woe unto the wicked, and woe unto his neighbour."   Savitzky, of course, noticed this exodus, but he kept silent.   He did more ;   he pretended to give in to the town.   Thus a cat sometimes draws back from the little mouse, for it knows that it cannot escape.

The whole day Savitzky either remained at home or went out for long walks to the outskirts of the town, in the mud.   He was quite sure of his ultimate victory, then why should he annoy the people and try to find out ?   He would know immediately, as soon as something happened. " The news," he thought, " will rush out through door and window.   There will be cries and lamentations as on the Day of Atonement.   These dear little Jews," thought the doctor, " cannot restrain themselves.   That nation is very much afraid of death and is quite helpless when confronted by disease."   He had already witnessed an outbreak of typhoid fever in the town, and had heard their cries of despair and their lamentations.   It had seemed to him then than he was drowning in a sea of tears, of misery and lamentations.   No, they won't be able to keep still, to keep anything secret.   He therefore yielded the street to them.   As for Jossel, he had given up both the *Beth-Hamidrash* and the street.   Savitzky did it of his own free

will, Jossel was compelled to do it.   Ever since they had
begun to talk more often about the epidemic, his melancholy had entirely left him.   On the contrary, he was
growing more cheerful and joyous every day, and against
his will he often burst out into loud laughter, unable to
restrain himself.   He could not keep it back, he simply
had to laugh, it was tickling him.   The paler the inhabitants
of the town grew, the more flushed and animated became
his countenance ;   the lower the people drooped their
heads, the higher did his own rise up ;   the more muffled
their voices, the louder his own ;   the more the *Beth-
Hamidrash* was sighing, the more he laughed—Ha, ha, ha !
And it was not really Jossel's fault ;   something was
laughing and jubilating within him.

When the eyes of all the inhabitants were sad and moist,
his own sparkled brightly ;   when small groups of men
were standing about agape, afraid to move, his hands and
feet were restless ;   he wanted to dance.   He felt that he
could embrace the very reading-desks for sheer joy, hug
the stove, kiss the walls.

" Was he mad ? " people were asking.   " What the
dickens was the matter with him ? "   He must certainly
be mad.   For sure, he ought to be sent to a lunatic asylum.

Jossel was not afraid of the lunatic asylum ;   for he
knew quite well that the community would not go to the
expense.   Last year a mad woman had been frozen to
death in the street, after having danced about in the snow
all the winter.   Everybody had pity on her, but no one
ever thought of hiring a cart and sending her to the
poor-house.   Another woman might at least have been
possessed, tramped from town to town, and collected
some money ;   but that poor woman had not enough
intelligence even for that.

Well, what had happened ?   The inhabitants had sighed
and groaned, but that was all.   Now why should he,
Jossel, be more favoured ?   However, he did not care to
annoy the influential men of the community.   True, there
was no other orphan in the town, but you never can tell.
The community might grow angry and import an orphan

from some other town. Besides, someone might in the meantime lose his parents, who could tell? Then again, the townspeople would have to give him a wedding-present and it was better to be on good terms with them. He was also afraid that they might think he was really mad and be compelled to procure another orphan; for, after all, you can't marry a real madman. All these reasons, however, would not have sufficed to compel Jossel to avoid people. The fact was that he was really craving for solitude, that he needed it greatly. He had to be alone with his thoughts; he had to think, to consider, to dream both by day and by night.

At night he was all right. When everybody had left the *Beth-Hamidrash* and he remained alone in the company of the benches and the reading-desks, he immediately ran up to the window, pressed his burning brow to the cool window pane; and his brain being refreshed, his thoughts unrolled in perfect order. Sometimes, on a starry night, it seemed to him that Joshua, the son of Nun[1], was answering him in gestures; *yes* or *no* according to circumstances.

During the day, however, he would wander about alone behind the town. He felt neither the bitter cold, which penetrated through every hole of his tattered garments, nor the water, which was entering freely and unimpeded through his half-open boots. He gesticulated with his hands, talked to himself, to the leaden clouds, or to the cold, pale wintry sun. He had such a lot to think about, such a lot to discuss with himself. He was the only orphan boy in the town, but there were *three* orphan girls, and Jossel was anxious to know which of the three was destined to become his wife.

In the first place there was Dvoshe, the daughter of Jeremiah the cobbler. Jeremiah, before his death during the last epidemic, had often befriended Jossel. He used to invite him to his house and mend his boots; once even he made him a present of a pair of old shoes. He used often to treat him to a slice of bread with fat, and even to an onion. During his visits to the cobbler's house,

Jossel never took his eyes off Dvoshe. Oh, he remembered her quite well, and she now stood before his mind's eye. She was a stout, buxom girl, red like an apple, and so strong. When she took up the axe to chop wood the splinters would fly up in the air. Had not Jeremiah died, Jossel would himself have asked for her hand. He loved a healthy girl like Dvoshe, and whenever he thought of her his mouth literally began to water. One day—he will never forget it—he met her on the staircase. She attracted him like a magnet ; he approached and touched her dress. She gave him a slight push and he nearly tumbled downstairs ; it was lucky he had taken hold of the railing. For a long time Jossel had felt ashamed to show his face ; he was afraid that she might have informed her father of the incident. Later, when he was ready to risk it and go to the cobbler's house, Jeremiah was lying ill. He suffered for twenty days and died. Soon afterwards the cobbler's wife fell ill in her turn and also died. Dvoshe was now a domestic servant in the house of Saul the usurer. Jossel had an occasional meal there, and often met Dvoshe alone in the house. Never, however, did he dare to lift his eyes to her, or address a word ; her gaze was so severe. But when the leaders of the community command her to marry Jossel she will not dare refuse ; the community is, after all, the community.

" Dvoshe," thought Jossel, and his mouth literally watered, " Dvoshe would be an excellent wife," he could not wish for a better. Of course, she would sometimes " caress his cheek," but what of it ? Such things were of daily occurrence in married life, and he will gladly submit to her treatment of him. On the contrary, he will repay her with kisses, will wash the dust off her feet, will follow her about and obey her like a little child. He will caress her, pamper her, press her to his heart, firmly, oh, very firmly, were his heart to beat even faster than it was beating now, were it even to burst, were he to die, to die at her feet.

Ah, thought Jossel, if only the community were to think of Dvoshe as his wife ! Her little finger was worth more than the entire body of another wife. For the present he would be perfectly content with her little finger ; how he would squeeze it, squeeze it with all his might, to persuade her to marry him, to prove to her that she wanted a husband.

But suppose the choice of the community were to fall upon another orphan girl ? There was, for instance, an orphan girl at the cemetery. Yes, there was one, although he did not know her name. To tell the truth, she was only half an orphan. She still had a father, although it were better for her she had none. A fine fellow was that Berl the grave-digger ! The whole day he would go about in town from one public house to the other, leaving his daughter alone among the tombs. Sometimes he came home completely drunk and beat the girl. People said that he dragged her about by her hair all over the graves. The whole town was sure of it, but no one ever dared to interfere, as they were all afraid of Berl. He was a drunkard and a giant into the bargain. Last year, being in a playful mood, he dealt Moses the glazier a friendly blow in his ribs, and the poor fellow has ever since been suffering from his lungs ; every day he is growing more yellow, he is consumptive and has hardly strength enough to draw his breath. The poor girl must have an iron constitution to be able to stand such treatment at the hands of her terrible father. He had sent her mother to an early grave, and what does he now want of his daughter ? When Jossel thinks of the poor girl his heart begins to ache within him. He had seen her only once, but has never forgotten her. It happened at Jeremiah the cobbler's funeral. Jossel had been afraid to go near the grave for fear of meeting Dvoshe. The girl, he knew, would be crying, and her tears would be like molten lead poured upon his heart. He therefore kept at a distance, near the mortuary. Passing the window of Berl's little house, he saw his daughter through the window. She was standing, her eyes lowered to the ground, peeling potatoes. She was pale and frail, but she looked so kind-hearted. What eyes she had, what a look ! Once only she had lifted her eyebrows, and immediately Jossel had forgotten Dvoshe and the funeral. There was such a world of kindness reflected in her blue eyes, such sweetness and grace in her pale countenance. Only Queen Esther could have possessed such sweet grace, but Queen Esther, tradition said, was of a greenish pallor,[1] whilst the grave-digger's daughter was as white as alabaster. Her hair was jet black, although, of course, it would be shaved off immediately after her marriage. Oh, how beautiful she was, appealing to one's heart!

The grave-digger's daughter attracted Jossel in a different manner. When he saw Dvoshe his blood began to course faster in his veins, to boil, so to speak; but when he looked at the grave-digger's daughter he felt light-hearted, with such a pleasant warm feeling over his whole frame. Ever since Jossel had caught a glimpse of the pale-faced beautiful girl, he assiduously followed all the funerals in the town, never omitting to take a peep through the little window.

Yes, he would gladly consent to take the grave-digger's daughter to wife. On the contrary, he would even prefer her to Dvoshe. He would cherish her like a toy, a precious plaything, would pamper her all day long and do everything for her; never allow her to put a finger into cold water or do any work. He would chop the wood, cook the meals, bake the bread, do the washing—in a word, do all the housework; on one condition only, and that was that she should always be at his side, look at him and smile. He would carry her about in his arms like a little baby. He would get up with dawn; light the stove in winter, set the kettle to boil for tea in summer. He would walk about on tiptoe, brush her dress, clean her boots, and quietly place her garments at her bedside. Then he would approach her, quietly, very quietly, bend over her, look at her in silence for a long time, a very long time, until the sun had risen in the sky and the rays had entered through the window. Then, only then, would he wake her up with a kiss. Oh, it would be a life in the sun!

It would be a good match, too, *oy*, *oy*—what an excellent match it would be ! Dvoshe, it is true, must have a bit of money, she is constantly saving. The grave-digger's daughter would, on the other hand, bring as her dowry a claim to a permanent post. Everybody knew that Berl's constitution had been ruined by drink. The barber-surgeon maintained that the grave-digger never tasted any food, his entrails being perforated, heaven preserve us. After Berl's death, therefore, Jossel, as the girl's husband, would take up the function of grave-digger. Why not ? In the beginning, of course, he would be somewhat afraid of the dead bodies, but he would soon grow accustomed to them. In the girl's company he would grow accustomed even to hell itself. It was not a nice business that of a grave-digger, but it had its advantages. He would live out of town, far away from everybody, and people would not come to poke their noses into his life. It would be a fine life, a veritable Paradise within the precincts of the cemetery.

But suppose the choice fell upon *Lapai*. Lapai was the nickname of the third orphan girl, a town girl this one ! At the very thought of this third orphan Jossel felt cold all over. She had been an orphan ever since he could remember her. She was sickly, bald-headed, with a big head and strangely distorted legs. She never walked upon the soles of her feet but upon her toes, her heels never touching the ground ; and whilst walking she balanced her body to and fro, walking in zig-zag like a man who is drunk. Jossel often met her in the street, for she had no corner she could call her own. She dragged herself from house to house, doing odd jobs for the servants and housemaids, carrying in water, chopping wood, cleaning cupboards, or filling baths. When she could find no job, she went about begging. Once a year she cleaned the floor in the *Beth-Hamidrash*. Jossel had no idea where the woman slept at night. Lapai, Lapai ! Before his mind's eye her image appeared, and he shivered. He felt cold all over. She must be about forty ; as long as he could remember her she had looked as she did now.

"Lord of the Universe ! " cried Jossel in his fright, "this would be worse even than hanging myself." He raised his frightened, supplicating eyes to heaven, and beads of perspiration, as big as peas, appeared upon his pale brow. Suddenly pity for the poor girl filled his heart. She, too, deserved to be pitied like himself ; she, too, no doubt, would like to get married ; she, too, was a wandering sheep, an orphan ; she, too, had only God in heaven to whom to turn. And Jossel was ready to weep over both their destinies.

After some reflection he resigned himself, decided to submit to the will of God Almighty. If God, heaven preserve the thought, willed it that Lapai become his wife, let it be so. He put his trust first in God and then in the leaders of the community. He will live with the girl whom God has destined to be his wife, and the community selects. He will treat her well, respect her, and be faithful to her ; he will be a husband unto her like other husbands —and he will forget the others.

Another anxiety, however, suddenly begins to worry him. Suppose Lapai fell to his lot, where will they live ? What will they do ? She had not a red cent to bless herself with, and went about in rags ; the maids for whom she did odd jobs paid her with a few cold potatoes ; whilst for cleaning the floor in the *Beth-Hamidrash* she got two gulden. All her earnings were not sufficient even for dry bread. And what could he do ? What was he good for ? Had he not been lame, he could have gone on errands and become a messenger, since he knew neither trade nor handicraft. "Of course," Jossel consoled himself, "I can always be a Melamed." All the rich inhabitants would give him a wedding present. With the money he would buy himself some hut and start teaching. Why not ? He knew as much as any other Melamed, and particularly a Melamed for beginners, a teacher in a primary school. Happen what might, he would anyway have a wife. There were plenty of Jews who had even uglier wives, even greater cripples, and yet they lived with them. A wife is a wife ; only not to be alone any more, not to eat *days*.

But he might be lucky enough, after all, to get one of the two other orphans ; and once more Jossel begins to picture his Paradise to himself. Again he smiles upon the mud and talks to the leaden clouds above.

Hush ! An idea suddenly strikes him, an idea based upon his sense of justice. If he were quite sure that it was the destiny of the poor Lapai to die, heaven forbid, during the epidemic, then he would quite willingly marry her, so that the poor girl might have at least a taste of married life before her death, have a husband for, say, one month. Why not ? She was a daughter of Israel, after all. It would make no difference to him, but it would be a deed of justice on the part of the Almighty. Heaven forbid that he should wish the poor girl to die ; on the contrary, he felt great pity for her. He knew what misery and suffering meant, what it meant to be lonely, always lonely.

5

SAVITZKY MEETS JOSSEL

One day, when Jossel, plunged in meditation, was strolling about in the quagmire, he suddenly felt that someone was pulling him by the sleeve. Turning round in great fright, he grew even more alarmed when he saw Doctor Savitzky stand in front of him. Savitzky and Jossel had been meeting quite frequently in the outskirts of the town, and every time the *Talmud*-student had met the Christian he had hurriedly taken off his ragged cap and bent very low. The first time Savitzky spat out, the second time he cast an ugly anti-Semitic look upon the Jew. The third time he looked Jossel straight in the eyes and at last smiled lightly. To-day, for the first time, he pulled him be the sleeve.

As they looked at each other, they both understood that they had something in common. Each read in the other's eyes that they had business together, that some hope was binding one to the other. Savitzky was now feeling quite lonely in the town. Formerly he used to call on the apothecary for a chat, but the latter had recently given the doctor to understand that his visits were driving away customers. On account of Savitzky, the inhabitants were afraid to come and buy bitter-water and castor oil, the apothecary's principal source of revenue. Even the Christians had begun to avoid the apothecary's shop. They, too, believed that the doctors were poisoning the patients, and why should Savitzky be better than his colleagues ? There was, also, a rumour that, in another town, the populace had burned down some hospital barrack and stoned the doctor. A strange little fire now often appeared in the eyes of the farmers which boded no good.

Jossel could do without company, but Savitzky was feeling lonely and yearning for society. He was himself surprised to find something almost pleasant in the pock-marked face of the halting little Jew. Besides, he had to talk to the fellow. It was quite possible that the epidemic had already made its appearance in the town, and that the people were hiding the fact. He would be able to find out something from the little Jew.

Feeling himself pulled by the sleeve, Jossel was startled ; but he soon collected himself. He did not notice how quickly Savitzky had taken away his hand from the dirty sleeve ; all he saw was that Savitzky was not cross, that he was even smiling.

" Well," asked the doctor in Polish, " there is no cholera in the town ? "

Jossel had several times accompanied the *Dayan* of the town on his visits to a mill in a neighbouring village, to watch over the grinding of wheat for the Passover-cakes, and he had picked up a few words of Polish. He understood Savitzky's question, but in spite of the hopes he had placed in the epidemic, the very word " cholera " sent a tremor through his bones. He made a grimace, but soon grew calmer and replied :

" No, my Lord, it has not come." Involuntarily his voice sounded sad.

The two separated, but met again on the following day. Jossel stood to attention, like a soldier presenting arms, without, however, lifting his hand to his cap. Savitzky stopped a moment and asked :

" Well, no more has it come to-day ? "

" No, my Lord, no," was Jossel's reply.

The third day the two met again, and this time remained together a little longer. Savitzky tried to find out from the *Talmud*-student whether he had heard of any looseness of bowels, vomiting, cholerine diarrhœa, or simply stomach ache. Jossel did not understand all that Savitzky said to him ; but he guessed, rightly, that the doctor was asking about diseases and symptoms which were, so to speak, a sort of preface to the epidemic.

" There are none, my Lord, there are none," was Jossel's constant reply. He knew that all was quiet in the town.

" There are none, but there soon will be," said Savitzky, by way of consolation, and left him.

Some time passed. At their subsequent meetings they even used to walk a little way side by side, Savitzky always asking questions, and Jossel invariably replying, " No, my Lord, no." Savitzky continued to console both himself and Jossel with the words : " But there soon will be." " It must come," he said in a tone of conviction ; words which Jossel translated into Hebrew, " And even if he tarries, I still hope for his coming." His heart swelled for joy. Heaven forbid that he should wish the town any ill.

Savitzky was perhaps anxious to see a big epidemic, but he, Jossel, would be quite content with a small one, quite a tiny one, as big as a mouthful. He did not even wish any of the inhabitants to die, heaven forbid. If only a few of the better-off people were to fall sick, it would be quite sufficient, so far as he was concerned. He did not ask for more ; for even his worst enemy, he did not wish such a death. A month thus passed. Savitzky was beginning to grow impatient and even went so far as to suggeſt that Jossel should do something. He knew, he said, that something had happened in the town, but the people were hushing it up. They were keeping the epidemic secret, for Jews were always afraid. He therefore proposed that Jossel should make inquiries, find out, and let him know whether there had been at leaſt one case, no matter what ; he would be very grateful to Jossel for the information.

Savitzky was talking too quickly, and in too refined Polish, for Jossel to underſtand him. The *Talmud*-ſtudent, however, guessed that the doctor intended to employ him as a spy, as an informer, to give away Jewish patients.

" No," he thought within himself, " no, Jossel will not be an informer ; he will not say a word to Savitzky." Involuntarily, however, out of politeness, he nodded his head in the affirmative, and Savitzky left him. Jossel was firmly decided not to tell Savitzky anything, but he would nevertheless make inquiries for himself. He muſt know whether the people were, after all, keeping something secret.

Jossel ſtarted his inquiries by making the round of the places of worship, visiting them during morning and evening prayers, to see whether anybody was missing. When he saw that someone was conspicuous by his absence, he immediately set about to find out the cause. His inquiries, however, led to no results. One, he learned, had risked his life and gone to a village to buy something ; another had had a quarrel with his wife and was ashamed to show himself in the synagogue with a swollen cheek ; a third had had a tooth pulled out, and the barber-surgeon could not stop the hæmorrhage. Such and other things did Jossel learn, all having no reference whatever to the matter in queſtion, and of little intereſt to him. Every time he quite faithfully brought Savitzky the same nega- tive report :

" There is no cholera, my Lord."

They were now waiting for each other, and every day their conversation laſted longer. Jossel had to use his hands and feet so as to make himself underſtood by the doctor. He worked hard, gesticulating with his hands, making all sorts of movements with his feet, and very frequently, although he had grown accustomed to this manner of speaking, Savitzky had to draw back, out of the way of Jossel's hand.

Savitzky still failed to understand Jossel and why *he* was so interested in the epidemic, why he was keeping away from the community, why he was anxious that the epidemic should really visit the town. But the doctor had no time to occupy himself with the riddle. He had no leisure to find out a Jew's secret. No doubt, thought he, the latter hoped to derive some business advantage from the epidemic. Perhaps he was dealing in linen required for shrouds, or manufacturing coffins. He noticed, however, that Jossel was losing heart, was wavering in his faith, not being so certain as Savitzky that the epidemic would come to-day or to-morrow, that it was even bound to come at all. He therefore encouraged Jossel, assuring him that the community could not escape, and that the epidemic would certainly come. For Savitzky it was clear as day. Was it not creeping nearer every day ? The Press was asserting it.

Thus another month, six weeks, had passed. The sharp frost which the community had hoped for did not come, but neither had the epidemic, for which Savitzky and Jossel were hoping, made its appearance.

Savitzky himself was beginning to be doubtful, but whilst consoling Jossel, he was also reassuring himself. No, it was impossible that the epidemic should not come. Was there any town that was dirtier ? Where else did the inhabitants consume so many cucumbers, raw fruit, and onions ? Where was the water, when not boiled, less safe ? In the whole town there were perhaps only three samovars, and only in three or four houses was tea ever made ; the majority of the inhabitants drinking cold water. after the *tsholent*, or Sabbath mid-day meal. Rotten fish was being sold everywhere, openly, publicly. It was inevitable, the epidemic was bound to come. Of course, there are many towns over which the epidemic had no hold, as for instance, Aix or Birmingham, and many others the name of which Jossel could not catch. But then in those towns people did not eat *tsholent* and drank tea made with distilled water. It was quite different therefore.

In the meantime another week passed, and still nothing happened. On the contrary, news came that " it " had abated considerably in Apte, whilst the town of Rakhev had once more been opened. In Zosmir they had even gone so far as to close the tea-shop, which they had recently opened for the poor to please the governor. Jossel was beginning to believe that it would be just his ill-luck if all his hopes were to fizzle out. Or was his town, perhaps, another Aix or Birmingham over which the epidemic could have no hold ? Anyhow, Jossel was once more passing sleepless nights, he was even restless during the day. His fiancées began to recede into the dim distance, and except during the half hour he was conversing with Savitzky, he knew no peace.

He clearly noticed that the inhabitants of the town were growing more and more calm. Recently news had come that all danger had disappeared in the neighbouring villages. The town literally revived ; women ceased to weep and lament in the synagogue, the younger ones even abstaining altogether from visiting the places of worship, except on Saturdays. The wife of the barber-surgeon had again taken to wearing her wig, and rumour would have it that the servant at the baths was again guilty of indiscretion. The grain merchants once more began to make the round of the villages, agents and middlemen were once more earning money ; on Sundays the market was full of peasants, and the public-house keepers were coining money Salt, petrol, and other commodities were being sold, and the town was regaining its former appearance. The curtains disappeared from the windows, and Savitzky's street returned to life.

Jossel was feeling worse every day. His old melancholy mood now frequently returned, and in the place of the fiancées, he once more had visions of the rope in the synagogue garret. He distinctly saw the rope, swinging,

beckoning to him, calling him. " Come, come," the rope
was saying, " make an end of it, free yourself of the
community, of your miserable orphan's life." But Jossel
was still struggling and fighting against the alluring rope.
" Savitzky," he thought, " is after all a doctor, he ought
to know, and he is still sticking to his conviction."

One day Jossel did not meet Savitzky in the usual place,
and it happened to be one of the poor fellow's worst
days. Very early, on the morning of that day—just as
he woke from a troubled sleep—the beadle came in and
joyfully exclaimed :

" You hear Jossel ? The doctor and the medical
student have already left Rakhev ! And during the night,
you hear, at the new moon, a heavy frost has come, a
bitter frost. That's finished the epidemic," concluded the
beadle triumphantly ; and went out to carry the glad
tidings over the town and call the people to morning
prayers.

Jossel dressed in a hurry—that is to say, he put on the
gaberdine which had served him as a blanket during the
night, and began to pace up and down the *Beth-Hamidrash*.
From time to time he rushed up to the window to see
whether it was already day, so that he could go and meet
Savitzky. Scarcely had the sun risen when Jossel quickly
recited his morning prayers and without tasting any food—
except a morsel of bread—rushed out and hurried to the
place where he was wont to meet Savitzky. He felt that
without the latter's consolation, his heart would burst
within him.

In spite of his hunger, he waited till noon. Savitzky
had not come, but he had to wait for him. It often
happened that the doctor only came in the afternoon.
Jossel was hungry, very hungry, but it never occurred to
him to return to the town and get something to eat. He
had to wait for Savitzky, for without him, without his
consolation, the morsel of food would choke him. He
will have another terrible night, the rope will again lure
him. No, he could fast to-day. Another hour passed, it
was growing darker, and the dull reflection of a wintry

sun, hidden behind clouds, was descending lower and lower ; it soon disappeared entirely behind Vassil's mill. Jossel was shivering for cold, walking up and down, stamping his feet, tapping one hand against the other, so as to get warm ; but still no Savitzky. He had never been so late. Jossel began to think that Savitzky must have met with an accident, must be ill. " It is also possible," he thought, growing angry at the thought, " that he is playing cards. You never know with these Gentiles." And in the meantime the shadow was descending lower and lower, whilst on the other side, where the sky was clear, appeared a white, thin spot, in the shape of a sickle. It was the new moon, and it was the hour of afternoon prayers.

He saw no one in the street. The men were all in the synagogue, but through the glass doors of some small shops his ear caught the joyful sound of women's voices, and the sound pursued him until he reached the steps of the *Beth-Hamidrash*. His legs were still shaking with fright and fatigue. Glad news must have spread in the town, since the women were talking and laughing so loudly. With great difficulty he ascended the *Beth-Hamidrash* steps, but stood still in front of the door. He had not the courage to turn the door-handle. Prayers had not yet begun, but he could hear the worshippers conversing loudly and with great animation. God knows what joy had fallen to their lot. He suddenly grew angry and hastily opened the door.

" And Savitzky, too," were the first words that his ear caught. " Savitzky, too, has bolted, praised be the Lord."

" Is it certain ? " someone asked.

" I saw him go away myself, saw him go with my own eyes."

Jossel heard no more. His legs began to shake and give way under him. With great difficulty, he dragged himself to a bench and flopped down. Thus he remained, almost turned to stone, his eyes wide open.

6

THE END

The happy congregation never noticed the beggar-student. Prayers over, they all hurried away, with the exception of a few worshippers who stayed on for a little while to peruse a page of the *Talmud*, and Jossel remained alone. Even the householder, whose turn it was to furnish the student with his meals on that day, never thought of asking him why he had failed to turn up for his mid-day meal and why he was not coming now for his supper. This gentleman, too, had hurried home, anxious to bring to his wife and family the glad news of Savitzky's departure. They were now rid of the doctor.

It was only two days afterwards that Jossel's absence was noticed. On the third day, when people began to inquire after Jossel, someone replied that the devil had surely not taken him away. The beadle had to light the stove which began to emit smoke. The whole day people talked about Jossel, who had become an expert in lighting the stove. They were now wondering whether the beggar-student had left for Palestine or Argentine. Of course, he had not a penny for expenses, but he would, no doubt, beg his way. On the sixth day news came that an inspector of trade licences was on his way to visit the town. A merchant going up to the *Beth-Hamidrash* garret for the purpose of hiding a piece of foreign velvet, found the hanging Jossel. The body was already rigid.

XXI

THE MIRACLE OF HANOUKA

On the point of putting on my overcoat, I suddenly stood still.

To go or not to go out to give my lesson? It is so unpleasant to go out, the weather is so vile, and I have more than half a mile to walk. And what for? Once more to teach my pupil the elements of Hebrew grammar: *I carried, he carried.* Once more to meet the old gentleman who had managed to live without grammar more than three score years, who had been ten times to Lapsk, twice to Dantzig, and had even gone almost as far as Constantinople. He still fails to understand how people can spend money on such a silly thing as grammar. Then there is the son, the young master. He knows that it would have been more practical to wear earlocks, a *shtraymel*, and a caftan, to visit the wonder-rabbi, and to ignore Hebrew grammar. But what can he do? He is, *nebbich*, a victim of circumstances. As a merchant, he is compelled to mix with people, to wear a hat, instead of a cap, and a starched shirt, to allow his wife to go to the theatre and to indulge in other frivolities; to allow his daughter to read books, and also to keep a master for his boy to teach him grammar.

"Is not my father right?" he asks. "But what can I do? The world requires such things."

And he never can withstand the world.

"At least," he says to me, "do me a favour and do not spoil the boy, that is to say, do not make him deviate from the right path of piety."

"I am paying you," he says, "such a lot of money for a little Hebrew grammar, let him at least not learn from you that the earth is turning round the sun."

And I promised the father that the boy will never learn these things from me, because—because this was my only lesson, and at home I had an invalid mother.

To go or not to go?

Whilst I am giving the lesson the whole household is present, keeping watch over me. And she too? She is always seated at a distance, always deeply plunged in her books, her reading. Sometimes she raises her long, silken eyelashes, then the room is suddenly inundated by a dazzling light. But this happens only so rarely, so very rarely. And what will be the result? Nothing, nothing but heartache.

"You hear?" The feeble voice of my mother coming from the bed suddenly wakes me up from my dreams. "You hear? The doctor says that if I had a pair of warm, woollen socks, then I might be allowed to get out of bed."

And so I must go out to give my lesson. With the exception of the lady of the house, who, as usual, had slipped out unbeknown to her father-in-law and gone to the theatre, I met the whole household round the boiling, brass *samovar*.

To my "good-evening" the young master answered with a half-loud "good-year," never ceasing to turn the pack of cards in his hand, evidently waiting for guests. A pointed velvet cap upon his head, wrapped in a wide Turkish bathgown, the old man did not think it worth while to go to the trouble of taking his pipe with the amber mouthpiece out of his mouth, or even raise his eyes from his old prayer book. Scarcely nodding his head, he once more plunged himself in the reading of the commentary upon the Hanouka melodies. She, too, is deeply plunged in her reading, a novel, as usual. Upon my pupil, however, my arrival produced a rather unpleasant impression.

" What ? " he cried, jumping up and impudently throwing back his dark curly head, " what, even to-night there is a lesson ? "

" Why not ? " smiles his father.

" But it is the Hanouka-festival to-night," the boy exclaims, stamping his foot. Thus saying he points with his finger to the first Hanouka light, burning upon the window sill.

" Quite right," murmurs the old man.

" *Nu, nu,* let him off," says the young master in a tone of indifference. It seemed to me that she had grown paler, bending her head even lower upon her book. I say good-night and am about to leave the house, but the young master will not let me go.

" You must stay and have tea with us," he says.

" And partake of Hanouka-cakes," adds the boy in a joyful voice. We should have been great friends, he and I, had it not been for the grammar, the *I carry, thou carriest.* I try to refuse, but the scamp seized me by the hand and with an impudent smile upon his mobile face advanced a chair for me just facing his sister.

Has he noticed anything ? He could only have noticed something as far as I was concerned, for she is always so deeply plunged in her reading. She looks upon me as a poor student, perhaps even worse. . . . She does not know that I have an invalid mother at home.

" The tea must be ready now," impatiently exclaims the father.

" In a minute, father, dear," she answers hastily, a flush suffusing her pale countenance.

The young master is again plunged in his meditations, the boy lets a top spin over the table, whilst the old man, laying aside his prayer book, gets ready for his tea.

Involuntarily I turn my gaze in the direction of the Hanouka-light burning upon the window facing me. It is burning so sadly, so melancholily, as if ashamed before the silver lamp hanging over the dining-table and casting such a dazzling light upon the table with its white napery. I grow sadder still, and do not notice that she is offering me a cup of tea.

" With lemon ? " The sound of her melancholy voice wakes me up.

" Perhaps with milk ? " asks the father.

" *No, no*, don't have milk, the milk is burnt," my pupil warns me.

" Unbearable ! " The word escapes her lips.

Silence fell upon us again, and one could only hear the ticking of the clock on the wall, the bubbling of the tea and the jingling of tea-spoons. Suddenly my pupil had the fancy to ask me :

" Master, tell me, what is the meaning of the Hanouka-festival ? "

" You will ask your *Rebbe* in the *Cheder* to-morrow morning," says the old man impatiently.

" Eh," obstinately retorts the boy, " I imagine that the teacher knows better than the *Rebbe*."

The old man casts an angry look at his son, as if to say : You see ! What did I tell you ?

" I would also like to know the meaning of the Hanouka-festival," says the girl softly.

" Well," says the young master, " let us hear *your* explanation of Hanouka."

" It happened in the time," I began, " when the Greeks were oppressing us in Palestine."

" The Greeks—— "

But the old man interrupted me with a sour mien : " In the *Shmoneh-Essreh* prayer it is said : ' the wicked power of Yavan ! ' "

" I suppose it is all the same," observes the young master of the house ; " what we are calling Yavan, they, no doubt, mean by Greeks."

" The Greeks," I began again, " were terribly oppressing us—and it was the worst time for the Jews. It seemed as if the whole nation was going to be wiped out and would soon disappear. The last spark of hope had been extinguished, for in our own country they were treading us down under their heel as if we had been so many worms."

The young master of the house was no longer following my words, but, bending his head in the direction of the door, was intently listening, to catch the sound of the doorbell, announcing the arrival of some of his guests. The old man, however, never took his eyes off me, and when I once more made use of the word " oppressed," he could no longer refrain himself and burst out :

" Why can't you talk plain language ? ' Oppressed,' ' oppressed '—fiddlesticks ! Say plainly that they would not allow us to keep our Sabbaths and festivals, to study the Law or to perform the rite of circumcision."

" Do you play the game of preference, or, perhaps, Oko ? " suddenly asked the young master.

Again a silence had fallen upon us, and I continued my explanation.

" Our position had grown worse, because the Jewish gentry of that period and all the rich people had themselves begun to feel ashamed of their race. Gradually they began to adopt Greek manners, to visit the gymnasia."

Both the girl and her grandfather looked at me in amazement.

" In the gymnasia of those days," I explained, " they were not teaching as in our modern colleges ; the Greek gymnasia had been established only for the purpose of physical exercises and gymnastics ; the pupils, men and women, appearing naked."

Two pairs of eyes were lowered, but those of the young master suddenly began to sparkle.

" What are you saying ? " he asked.

I paid no attention to his question, but continued to tell them about the Greek theatres, where men were seen fighting against wild beasts and bulls, and also about other Greek customs, which must have shocked the Jews.

" The Greeks, however," I continued, " were not yet satisfied, being intent upon stamping out the Jewish spirit and wiping the Jews out of existence. In the open square they erected an idol and compelled the Jews to worship it and offer sacrifices unto it."

"What does it mean?" she asked in Polish. I explained it to her. The old man grew enthusiastic.

"A pig," he added. "They commanded the Jews to offer a pig, an unclean animal, as a sacrifice to the idol."

"And one day," I continued, "a Jew came along and prepared to offer up a sacrifice upon the heathen altar . . . at that moment the old Maccabean, accompanied by his five sons, came down from the hills. Before the Greek soldiers knew what was happening, the renegade Jew was already bathing in his own blood. The altar was smashed, and the insurrection broke out. With a small company of their followers the Maccabeans conquered the Greeks, who were a hundred times stronger. The Greeks were expelled from the land of Israel, and our nation was delivered from the foreign yoke. In memory of the glorious victory," I concluded my narrative, "we are now celebrating the festival of Hanouka, or the Feast of Dedication, and are kindling these lights, a modest and poor illumination."

"What?" cried the old man, jumping up from his seat and trembling all over in his fury. "What? Was that the whole miracle?"

"Shmerke," he called the boy, "come here, at once!" The frightened boy drew back. Beating upon the table with his fists so that the plates danced, he shouted:

"The miracle was that when they had expelled the unclean *Yavanim* there only remained *one* jug with sacred oil in the Sanctuary—— " Seized with a fit of coughing, the old man could not catch his breath. The son rushed up and led his father into the next room. I wanted to take my leave, but she detained me.

"Are you against assimilation?" she asked.

"What is assimilation?" I asked in my turn.

"To assimilate means to *consume*, to eat up something and digest it. With our digestive system we assimilate meat and bread, but the others are anxious to assimilate ourselves, to swallow us up even as we swallow and assimilate meat and bread."

She was silent for a few moments, and then she asked in a frightened voice :

" Will wars and quarrels among nations continue for ever ? "

" Oh no," I replied. " There is a point in which one day all nations *must* meet and unite."

" And that is ? "

" Humanity. If every nation were only to walk along the path of righteousness—then all would soon be in agreement."

Again she grew pensive. I was going to say something, but was interrupted by the shutting of a door.

" Mother is coming," she whispered, and rushed out of the room. For the first time, however, she gave me her hand.

On the following morning, when I was still in bed, a letter, brought by hand was delivered to me. The envelope bore *her* father's business address—Jacob Berenhole—and my heart began to beat furiously. Hastily I tore it open, but found only a ten-rouble note—my fee for one month which was not yet over.

I had lost my lesson.

XXII

THE SICK BOY

"*Mummeshi*, I will tell you a secret; but above all, father must not know about it. You are asking why? Because father loves me less. . . . No, Mummeshi, I am committing a sin with my words, he does not love me less, he merely loves me differently. He is father, and has to be severe.

"Father has a long beard, and when I caress his face it does not feel smooth and soft like mother's, which is as soft as velvet. He also has different eyes and a different look. Whenever you, Mummeshi, look at me, your eyes are so laughing and moist, both kind and sad. You are mother and playmate in one. I can have no secrets from you. With your eyes you draw every secret out of my heart. Father looks at me in a quite different way; seriously, almost coldly. . . . No, Mummeshi, his eyes are really quite other eyes, different from yours.

"When I was still quite small I used to be less afraid of father. I remember how I used to jump on to his knees; I pulled his hair, divided his beard, twisting it into pig-tails, and pressed his lips together. And when he made angry faces at me, I simply pressed down his eyelids and closed his eyes. I could not do it *now*.

"Once, you hear, Mummeshi, once when I was ill, I awoke and saw you both standing at my bed. You were weeping so silently and so quietly—whilst father,

9a

Mummeshi, father had a terrible face then. I saw that he was angry with God. I grew frightened and shut my eyes. And ever since I can't approach father as I used to before. Something is holding me back. Sometimes my heart goes out to him and I would like to throw myself into his arms, but I can't do it.

"Do you think that I love father less? Heaven forbid! I love father very much and I am growing fonder of him every day and every minute. Whenever he comes up to me, my heart dances for joy, and my soul within me trembles with hope. He will take me by the hand and press me to his heart! But I do not tremble before you, for you always love me in the same way. You have always time for me and you hug and kiss me every instant. You are always, always mine, whilst father has a lot of business to attend to. I know—he is anxious for me to be wealthy one day.

"Now Mummeshi, would you like to hear my secret? I am ashamed. . . . What? You say one should never be ashamed before one's mother? That's quite true, but do you know what, Mummeshi, sit down upon this chair before the window. That's right. Oh, how beautiful the sunset is. How lovely are the reddish rays of the sun falling upon your noble, pale face. Oh, Mummeshi, how beautiful, how lovely and noble your face is!

"Wait a moment. I will just sit down at your feet. And whilst I am telling you, you must not look into my face. I will sit down on the footstool and look out of the window whilst I am telling you the secret.

"No! That won't do, I shall feel ashamed before the sun. You see, during the day the sun shines so brightly, but towards evening he takes leave of us so sadly that I feel ashamed to be talking of myself. I will lay my head in your lap—will shut my eyes—and you, you will put your hand upon my forehead. I am not too heavy, Mummeshi, when I am thus leaning on you? No?

"Sixteen years old is your child, and his head is so very light and so very small—and I am altogether. . . . Don't sigh, Mummeshi, God has not been so parsimonious with me. It is true, He has given me only a small body, but He has bestowed many other gifts upon me. He has given me you and father. He has given me days and nights with wonderful dreams—and to-day He has sent me a secret. Now I can see nothing. With my eyes shut—I shall after all be able to tell you. I will try to do so. . . . It is rather difficult, though.

" When I now think it over—it is really nothing : a net of a few wonderful rays—and yet it is weighing as heavy as a stone upon my heart. It is not an ordinary stone, it is not a stone one finds in the street or in the fields. It is a precious stone, brilliant and shining. Deep down in my breast it is lying, filling my whole being, casting its rays into my innermost being, shedding its mysterious, warm, living light. If only it were not to go out, this light, Mummeshi. So many lights go out !

" Listen, Mummeshi. No, wait a moment, I can't begin my secret so simply. But listen ! You remember, Mummeshi, how you gave me some money yesterday ? You remember it ? I have not yet spent anything of that money, and yet some of it is already missing. I have one silver coin less. . . . Had I lost it ? No. You gave me the money that I might distribute it among the poor people, the poor children whom I meet on my walks. Money destined for alms I am not likely to lose. . . . Have I given it to somebody ? Of course, I have. To a beggar ? I do not know. Perhaps yes and perhaps no. But listen, you may perhaps understand it yourself.

" Yesterday the sunset was very beautiful—perhaps even more beautiful. . . . You have taught me how to look at things, and I am looking and seeing things which others of my age do not perceive. It is for this reason that I always prefer to take my walks alone. Yesterday I went to the outskirts of the town, to that spot on the river whence you can overlook the whole town. The houses rise higher and higher, one above the other, and those which stand farther away seem to be anxious to look over those in front of them so as to catch a glimpse of God's world. Therefore the farther they stand the higher they

rise.   And the setting sun looks down upon them, pouring
out its last rays upon them, bidding them farewell, kissing
them.

"And I see how the shadows are pursuing this last
sunray, how they are growing more dense, flowing and
penetrating wherever they can.   They are filling all the
empty spaces between the houses, all the vacant places
between the walls, lifting up and chasing the last reddish
light of the sun, driving it back to heaven whence it
came.   ' Go to rest, ye rays,' they seem to say, ' go to rest ;
it is our turn now.   Good-night.'

"And gradually it is growing darker and darker, and
the sky is becoming more sombre ; soon the stars will
begin to twinkle one after the other.   Watching all this,
I reached the cabinet-maker street, the last street in the
town which runs so steeply down to the river, not far from
the *Shuhl.*   And I came up quite close to the old Shuhl.
During the day the Shuhl looks terrible, so poor, so
ruined, so black with age.   Out of pity the spiders seem
to be anxious to cover the broken window panes with
their cobwebs.   And upon the hill opposite, at the other
end of the street, the slim Christian Church raises its
pointed tower and is laughing !

"But in the evening the old Shuhl has quite another
aspect.   For the first time I saw it yesterday in that light,
A lovely, dark-blue, light mist was shrouding the building,
and the windows without panes were not at all blind.
They were looking so seriously and thoughtfully into the
world.   The window-sills above seemed to live and almost
to move.   The painted lions seemed on the point of tearing
themselves away from the walls, and you might have
thought they were going to roar !

"You think this is my secret ? Oh no, Mummeshi.
All this I am seeing now as I am telling you.   I am
seeing it with my eyes of yesterday.   Ah, Mummeshi,
if I were only rich. . . . What would I do ? I would
repair and restore the old Shuhl.   I want to see the
Shuhl towering high up into the sky, it must be even
higher than the church, for it is standing so much lower

And a golden roof it shall have, and window-panes of crystal.

"Do you know, Mummeshi, what I think? After all, we can do without a Shuhl, for God is everywhere. Wherever a tear is dropped, God takes notice of it; whenever someone lifts up his eyes to Him, He sees him; wherever a sorrowing heart is sighing, he hears it. But if we are to build a Shuhl, then it should at least be a tall building, beautiful, shining, and dignified!

"Thus I thought yesterday. And suddenly I heard loud weeping. It was a soft and sad weeping, so sweet, so sad, and so soul-stirring. When you are playing on the piano I sometimes hear similar plaintive notes. And I believed, Mummeshi—to tell the truth, I wanted to believe it, and I purposely refrained from turning round so as to keep up my belief for a long time—I believed that the weeping and sobbing came from the old Shuhl.

"I imagined that yonder in the building sat the soul of the old Shuhl, wrapt up in a pale blue cloud; sat and wept. And methought that this soul was complaining of the sun which was not treating it fairly. Heaping whole sheaves of its light upon the roof of the church, it begrudged the Shuhl even one ray. In the most dazzling hour of noon the sun threw to the Shuhl, as if giving alms to a beggar, one pale ray. And this pale ray was stealthily gliding away over the building as if ashamed of itself.

"But it was not the Shuhl that was weeping. It was a little girl. She lay upon the sands, searching for something and weeping. When I turned round at first I saw only her worn-out dress—like some dark grey stain upon the golden sands—and a pair of worn-out shoes. And something else did I see. . . . Mummeshi, I am ashamed, I feel so warm. Imagine a wealth of red, fiery-red, golden hair—sparks seemed to be issuing from it.

" 'Why are you crying, little girl?' I asked. 'And what are you looking for in the sands?'

"Her mother, it seemed, had sent her out on an errand and given her a tenner. Someone had jostled her, and

she had lost the tenner ; that was why she was crying.
I would never cry, had I even lost no matter what.

"I asked her : ' Was it a big tenner—a copper coin, or
a white tenner—a silver coin ? '

"' It was a white one,' she said, never turning round to
look at me.

"' I will help you find it,' I said.

"Stooping down, I pretended to search for the lost coin
and found for her a white tenner.

"' Here it is ! '

"She jumped up full of joy, and with one shake of her
head threw back her wealth of hair, and then there
appeared, as if emerging from beneath a cloud, a small
alabaster white face. And there were eyes in it, Mummeshi,
eyes. . . . No, Mummeshi, I cannot describe those eyes.
There was so much joy shining in them. I have been
dreaming of these eyes, all night, all night.

"That is my whole secret, Mummeshi. You are
smiling ? You must not laugh, Mummeshi ! I will
never forget those eyes. Mummeshi !

"And may I go again for a walk in the cabinet-maker
street, to look once more . . . at the old Shuhl ? "

XXIII

THE STAGNANT POOL

———

THERE was once a stagnant pool. It stood apart, in a corner of the meadow where kine were taking pasture and young shepherds were throwing stones at each other. The pool was surrounded by tall-growing grass and prickly thorns, and a thin green screen, greasy and shining, separated the water from the air ; above it only once in a year the wind would tear asunder the green scum. In the stagnant pool, as is the order of the world, there dwelt only small worms, who devoured other worms, smaller than themselves. The stagnant pool was neither long nor wide ; it was not even deep. It was only on account of the thick slime, the water plants, and the rotten branches in it, that the little worms were unable either to fathom the depth of the stagnant pool or reach the banks.

The geography of the stagnant pool has still to be written. In return, however, pride had long ago opened its eyes in the stagnant water, and imagination was reigning supreme among those that dwelt therein. Both pride and imagination were very busy, spinning and weaving. And as time went on, the two had woven out some sort of a theory, supposed to have been handed down since time immemorial from ancient generations, a really wormy tradition.

The stagnant pool, it was maintained, was the vast ocean. Into this ocean all the four rivers issuing from the

Garden of Eden were discharging their waters. The waters of the *Hiddekel* brought with them gold—that was the slime wherein the worms found their sustenance ; the other three rivers brought flowers—which were the water plants where they were wont to play at hide and seek on holidays—pearls and corals—which were the rotten branches.

The green scum above, the soiled headgear of the stagnant pool, was the heaven above the great ocean, a particular heaven purposely created for the world of worms. Pieces of eggshell which had somehow found their way into the stagnant pool were supposed to be stars, and a rotten melon took the place of the sun. The stones which, thrown by the little shepherds, sometimes fell through the green scum, were, of course, nothing but meteors coming straight from heaven and hurled at the heads of the sinners. And when the sky sometimes opened and a few rays from the real world penetrated into the stagnant pool, burning up a wormy brain, then people felt and believed in hell.

But they lived happily in the stagnant pool, and how content everybody was with himself and with all the others ! Whoever dwells in that vast ocean must naturally be a fish, and so one worm called the other : pike or tench. Upon tombstones were engraved the words : crocodile, or Leviathan. To be called roach or smelt was the greatest possible insult, for which people did not forgive one another even on the Day of Atonement. And in the meantime astronomy, poetry, and philosophy blossomed like roses.

The pieces of eggshell, supposed to be stars, were counted until people came to the conclusion that they were too numerous and that it was therefore impossible to count them. In a thousand ways romanticists sang about the celestial family ; patriots were compared to stars, stars to ladies' eyes, and the ladies themselves to heaven itself, if not to hell. Philosophy transferred the souls of the pious deceased into the rotten melon.

In short, nothing was missing. Life had all the colours

of the rainbow.   As time went on, a code of laws with a hundred commentaries was elaborated, and thousands of customs arose.   And when a little worm suddenly had a fancy for some change, it was enough for him to think of what the world would say to this.   Immediately it would flush crimson, repent, and do penance.

But once a great misfortune happened.   A flock of pigs passed over the meadow.   Terrible feet tore the heaven, trod on the slime, crushed the corals and the flowers. They laid waste the whole little separate world.

Some of the worms who were asleep, buried deeply under the slime—and worms sleep long—were saved. When they awoke, the heaven above their heads was again patched up, and only the heaps of crushed, strangled, and trodden-down worms, lying scattered and unburied, bore witness to the terrible catastrophe.

" What has happened ? " asked the now awakened sleepers, and went out in search of some surviving worm who would perhaps be able to explain unto them the cause of the epidemic which had evidently occurred.   But it was not so easy to find a living being, because it is not so easy to survive the destruction of a heaven.   All those who had not been trodden down had died of fright, and all those who had escaped death on account of fright, had died of heartache.   The remainder had committed suicide, for to be without a heaven means to be without life. Only one worm had survived the catastrophe.   When, however, he told his fellow-worms that the heaven they were now witnessing was a brand-new heaven, that the old heaven had been destroyed by animals ; when he told them that a worm's heaven does not last eternally, that, maybe, only the general heaven is everlasting, the worms at once knew that he was insane.

With great pity they put him in chains and sent him to a lunatic asylum.

XXIV

VENUS AND THE SHULAMITE

In the *Beth-Hamidrash*, behind the big stove, sat two *Talmud*-students, Hayim and Selig. Hayim was reading aloud from a manuscript, whilst Selig was mending a shoe with an ordinary needle and thread.

" And beautiful was Hannah, like Venus——— "

" Tell me, Selig, I beg you, what do you mean by Venus ? " asked Hayim.

" Venus was a mythological goddess," answered Selig, stitching his shoe.

" What is mythology ? "

" Don't you know this either, Hayim ? You remember, last week, there came here a monstrous being, wearing a long apron and a red cap, selling liquorice and other sweet things cheaply ? "

" Aha ! "

" It was a Greek, and there is a whole nation of Greeks ! "

" And are they all selling liquorice ? "

" Go on, you fool ; they have their own country, Greece. The Greeks are an old people and are mentioned in Holy Scripture. Their country is called *Yavan* in the Bible, and their name is *Yavanim.*"

" What Yavan ? Is it the word from which *Ivan* is derived ? "

" Heaven forbid. *Yavanim* are only Greeks, the kingdom of *Yavan*. These Greeks were once a strong and learned nation. You have no doubt heard of Aristotle and Socrates, who are also mentioned by our own sages, such as Maimonides. Aristotle, for instance, believed in the pre-existence of the world. All these great men were Greeks, but although they were very learned and excelled in painting, sculpture, and other fine arts, they were idol-worshippers, serving idols."

" *Ou-vah* ! "

" You see ! And these stories, these tales about their idols, are known as mythology."

" Aha ! *Nu*, and what is Venus ? "

" In Greek mythology Venus is the goddess of beauty."

" What means goddess ? "

" You understand : among the Greeks every profession, trade, or art, had a particular god, just as we say among us that every nation has its particular guardian angel or patron-saint. Thus, for instance, sculpture, poetry, beauty, health, and strength—— "

" They all had their gods ? But what do you mean by goddess ?—a little god ? "

" No, god is a he, whilst goddess is a she."

" Ah ! Females ? They placed females in heaven ? "

" Why not, Hayim, why men and not women ? "

" That is true ; but I thought, Selig, that gods are always men and not women."

" You must know, Hayim, that the Greek gods are in every respect like mortal men. The only difference is that they live eternally. They beget children like mortal men, have wives and concubines, but they can never die. Thus, for instance, their supreme god, Jupiter, the greatest of them all, he who holds the thunderbolt in his hand, before whom all the other gods tremble and whom they fear, is himself a henpecked husband ; he is a mere nothing before his wife Juno ; he is afraid of her as if he had been some poor school-teacher, afraid of his missus. I have told you once about the philosopher Socrates and his wife Xantippé, the shrew. This lady, however, was nothing compared

with Juno. Now you can imagine what Jupiter had to
stand from his wife ; at least ten times a day did he wish
for death, but—alas—he cannot die."

" Well, in short, Venus—— "

" Well, Venus is the goddess of beauty, and I am going
to read you her biography."

Putting aside his half-mended shoe, Selig produced from
his pocket a soiled paper and began to read :

" Venus, Aphrodite, Apogenea, Pantagenea, Andia-
meta—— "

" Is that German ?   I don't understand a word of it,"
Hayim wondered.

" You silly boy, these are only names under which
Venus was known in various localities in Greece and
afterwards at Rome."

" Seems to me that the lady has more names than
Jethro, but what is the good of her names, you better
read to me her biography."

Selig continued to read :

" Under these various names Venus was worshipped in
different towns and cities as the goddess of love."

" Not beauty any more ? "

" It is all the same.   She was never born of woman,
but came out of the waves.   She is a wonderfully beautiful
woman, very fascinating—— "

" Fascinating ?   What is that ? "

" That means that she fascinated everybody, made the
blood course faster in the veins and so on."

" Aha, I see."

" She is represented entirely or half-naked."

" For shame ! "

" Her husband was Vulcan."

" What sort of animal is he ? "

" He was also a god, the god of fire, something like our
own Tubal Cain, mentioned in the book of *Genesis*.   He
invented the art of forging iron which is called in German,
Schmiedekunst ; you understand ? "

" A little."

" Venus had no children from Vulcan.   There exist

neither divorce nor marriage-ceremonies among the gods. For all that, however, she had many children from other gods and also from mortal men."

" What do you mean ? Just so, bastards ? "

" Don't be a fool, Hayim ! Since gods require neither marriage-licence nor divorce, there are neither adultery nor illegitimate children among them."

" Yes, of course, if you don't perform the ritual ablution of your hands before meals, you need not say grace *after* the meal. But did you not say that she bore children also from mortal men ? "

" *Nû*, what of it ? And what about our own ' sons of God ' who found the daughters of men fair, as mentioned in our book of *Genesis* ? "

" All right, proceed with your reading."

" From Mars she had two children."

" How did you say ? Merce or Marsena ? "

" It is neither Merce nor Marsena, but Mars—the god Mars, who is a warrior, the god of battle and warfare."

" Two children she bore unto Bacchus, who rules over wine and other drinks."

" A sort of Lot, I suppose, a great drunkard ? "

" Two children she had from Mercury."

" Who is he ? "

" Mercury is the god of thieves, merchants, business men, and messengers."

" Not at all a respectable match."

" She met a certain Anchises, an ordinary mortal man, on the bank of some river when she was walking about disguised as a shepherdess, and the result of their meeting was the birth of a boy. Once it happened that, being pursued by a band of robbers, she had to seek refuge in a cave, and then she called Hercules to her aid."

" Who is he ? "

" Hercules was a powerful god, that is to say, not a full-fledged god, but a semi-god ; alone and unaided he once cleaned out thirty-six stables in one day."

" Proceed, Selig, proceed ; by my life, I am beginning to feel sick of it all, believe me."

" Hercules hurried to the spot, he let the robbers walk into the cave singly, one after the other, and there killed them."

" Disgusting ! "

" Venus was of a very jealous and revengeful nature, wreaking terrible revenge on all those who dared to laugh at love. Once day she changed all the inhabitants of a certain town into oxen."

" I have had enough of it," cried Hayim, jumping up from his seat ; " it is simply sickening. Venus, a goddess —Ha, ha, ha ! She had a thousand husbands ; she slaughtered and killed ; nothing but fornication, adultery, and murder. It is a shame and a disgrace ! "

Hayim spat out, and Selig rose up from his seat, greatly annoyed.

" Look here," said Selig, full of indignation, " do you know what you are talking about and why you are spitting out ? You take a costly, beautiful garment and don it inside out, or take a cap and turn it inside out like some *Pourim* mummer. Venus is merely an allegory, a sort of an ideal, something like our own Shulamite in the *Song of Songs.*"

" Yes, of course, just the same. Ha, ha, ha ! You ought to be ashamed of yourself, Selig, to compare the two. The Shulamite in the *Song of Songs* is a healthy, fresh, buxom girl, iron strong ! Her brothers had made her keeper of their vineyards and she did not keep her own ; she is swarthy, her countenance is scorched by the sun, but she is not a gipsy lass for all that. Her neck is as white as alabaster, and her fragrance is more pleasant than that of all the meadows, woods, and vineyards together. She never lowers her eyes in her bashfulness, nor does she preen or puff herself up like a turkey-cock. She looks one straight in the face, for she has nothing to be ashamed of. Her eyes are sincere and kind like two lovely doves. And lips she has which are like unto two thin red threads, and she twists not her mouth nor does she make silly grimaces. She talks plainly, and honey flows from her lips. When you look at her, no evil thought will enter your head ; on the contrary, you simply lose the trend of your own thoughts.   She has only to look at you out of one of her eyes, and you will lower both your own like a thief.   Your heart within you begins to flutter and to struggle like a slaughtered cock.   She is simple, chaste, and pure like driven snow.   Now summer is in the land and new life begins to palpitate upon the meadows and in the vineyards ;   the turtle dove is cooing, the flowers are blossoming, the fig tree is in full bloom, and the grapes are sparkling.   Everything is coming to life, everything has woken up to new life, and a new feeling fills the heart of the Shulamite.   The feeling has come upon her suddenly and with all its terrible strength.   Her love is stronger than death, and deeper than hell is her jealousy.   Her love is everlasting, no rivers will submerge it nor will the sea itself extinguish its fire.   And her love is for one man only.   A young and handsome shepherd. She knows not that the shepherd is wearing a crown upon his head, that he is the most powerful king in the world. The Shulamite is modest, simple, frank, and honest. She plays not with love, has no followers ;   she is sorry that her beloved is not her brother, the son of her father, and that he had not sucked the breast of her mother that she might kiss him freely and frankly in the open square ! That, you see, is the Shulamite.   She is, as you see, the ideal of a truly Jewish daughter who can boast a real father and mother, not like your Venus, the wanton."

"But you are forgetting one thing," Selig interrupted his flow of words.   "You are forgetting that mythology only contains allegories, and that philosophical and religious thoughts are hidden in the mythological tales."

"Just the contrary—why should sublime thoughts and ideas be disguised and clothed in low allegories ?   How can one wrap up diamonds in a soiled and dirty rag ?   And again, is not the *Song of Songs* among us Jews also considered to be an allegory ?   Is not the Lord of the Universe Himself meant by King Solomon, He to whom peace belongs ?   Is not the house of Israel meant by the Shulamite ?   The pure though swarthy and blackened

house of Israel? But what is the good of all these
mysteries and allegories? The Shulamite remains after
all the Shulamite, whilst Venus, *lehavdil*, a thousand
times *lehavdil*, is a woman not worth talking about. You
hear me Selig? May her memory be wiped out! Omit
her name, cross it out from the book you are writing, and
put instead—let us see, what is the name of the girl you
are describing? Hannah, I think?"

"Yes, Hannah."

"Then write that she was as beautiful as . . . or rather
no, don't write at all. Do you hear, Selig? It would be
sheer insolence on your part to do so. Let your Hannah,
with her tiny feet, as small as pins' heads, be like anybody
you like, liken her to Miriam with her timbrel, to Abigail,
to Rahab, to Delilah, to whomever you like, even to Queen
Esther, but never dare to compare her to the Shulamite,
for no woman can be like her, none, do you hear me?

XXV

SHAMMAI RATMAN

———

Do you know Shammai Ratman? Of course, you do. Fancy it! Yesterday I met him in the street.

"Shammai," I call, but he does not hear me. I wave my hand, he does not see it. Like a log of wood, with open staring eyes, he stands there until I put my hand on his shoulder. "God be with you, Shammai!"

He awakes as from a profound sleep.

"A new idea," he smiles.

A wonderful thing, how new ideas are born. A man like other men, always worried, constantly hard up, requiring money for all sorts of expenses, for living, rent, schooling and such things; and such a man suddenly stands still in the middle of the street, like a log of wood, mouth agape, eyes wide open, and neither hears nor sees or feels. Why? In an obscure corner of his brain something is stirring; weaving a new idea. And the idea is being woven against his own will, without his knowledge, and mostly not for his own good. I knew plenty of people whose downfall had been brought about by ideas.

There was Reuben, who was always thinking, and he thought so long until he conceived some new idea and lost his own, and other people's money thereby. Then there was Shimeon, who grew pensive one day, and in this state abstracted something, and ever since he has been persecuted and harassed from all sides, and people throw stones at him when he is passing in the street.

Levi has gone out of his mind altogether. And had it not been for his wife who never lets him out of her sight, he would long ago have been hanging in some attic. Nobody touches Judah, and yet, since he has conceived some wonderful idea, he runs about in the street like one demented, always shouting "Help!" And Zebulun, too, you must know. Since he suffered in his head, he has taken a dislike to his wife and knows not his own children. He neither eats nor drinks, and walks about in rags. What is it that he wants? Go and ask him.

But in spite of all this I am rather fond of new ideas. Who knows but that among a heap of thrashed-out straw one might find sometimes a grain of wheat. Among the thousands of millions of new ideas there might be found one true idea. And whenever one discovers a new idea, who can fathom the harm or the good such an idea might bring in its wake? It may be only a flash of lightning, disappearing the next instant; a few dozen blind hens will never have noticed it and may even deny its ever having occurred, but it may also be a thunderbolt, and thunder is no joke. It may fall down upon the sands on the wild steppes and create no havoc; it may come down in the sea and be extinguished at once, but it may also strike a house and cause a conflagration. Before the fire brigade has had time to reach the spot, a whole town may have been destroyed and razed to the ground.

Great God! A new idea may contain an answer to all the bitter questions which are gnawing our brain; it may solve some of the riddles which are twirling and boring into our brain—who can tell!

And he, Ratman, is standing there before me, smiling and saying, "A new idea."

"Tell me!"

"Here in the street?"

I thank God that we are near a café. A few more sips of tea, and I know what it is all about. The world will not be turned topsy-turvy, nor will it be consumed by fire; there will not even be any whirlwind driving the dust into our eyes. Shammai Ratman simply wants to found a new society. After all, it is also something.

" Make me a member ! "

" What ? " he wonders. " You do not even know what it is all about."

" No matter," say I. " We want new societies, whether bad or good, foolish or wise, as long as there are societies, as long as there is activity and no lull. And now tell me what it is you want."

" I want to found a Society of Thinkers," says Ratman

" Thinkers ? "

" Yes ; simply thinkers."

" And what else ? "

" Listen, but I must first preface my explanation with a few remarks."

" Better and better. I love prefaces like my life, anyhow, more than the books themselves which they usually precede, because the preface usually contains something more out of the way."

" You are making fun of me," Ratman says, rather nettled.

" And are you afraid of being made fun of ? You, a man with new ideas. You ought to be prepared for everything, fists, fire, and water."

" All this," says Ratman, " I do not mind, because all the attacks are only so much yeast which causes the ideas to rise up, but to be made fun of, no ; the pricking with needles may frighten a man even if he be prepared to defy the stake."

" Well, then I won't make fun of you. Tell me."

And Ratman tells me. He had noticed that we loved everything except the process of thinking for ourselves.

" How do you mean ? "

" It is very simple. We are lazy, terribly lazy. We prefer to lie on the grass and chase the clouds in the sky."

" Or to sit and eat and drink," I interrupt him.

" Nonsense," says Ratman. " We are eating and drinking less and less. Sometimes we have to content ourselves with an apology for a meal, and pretend that we are as satisfied as if we had eaten and drunk. But there is no lack of clouds in the sky; everybody may look. And thus we are lying upon the grass and looking up to the sky. Some of us pretend to be studying astronomy and to be counting the stars : one, two, three, as far as each of us is able to go. When a storm happens to surprise us, we hastily jump up, ready to run away."

" Whither ? "

" Wherever you like, to the right or to the left, forwards or backwards, but on condition that someone shows us the way, is ready to be the first runner, the ram. We can walk, we are even able to run with swollen feet, no matter where ; but we require two things, first of all, there should be a leader, a ram running in front of us, and secondly this leader should never stop or turn round and ask us ' Whither ? ' We hate to think for ourselves ; thinking is simply poison to us.

" In every misfortune that befalls us, in every catastrophe we look around to see whether we could not discover a pillar, a pillar of fire or of cloud, as long as it is a pillar that will move along in front of us, showing us the way. A Moses comes along, and we leave the flesh-pots and the onions of Egypt behind us, following our leader into the desert. Midways we want to appoint another chief who will lead us back to Goshen. Moses delays upon Mount Sinai—our wives possess some jewellery, quick, hand it over and we will fashion a golden calf."

Another sip of tea and Ratman proceeds.

" They say that times are changing, but this is not true. We still hate the process of thinking, of searching, and reflecting, just as we did before. We are as lazy as of yore. We love falsehood not because its hair is combed, because it is decked out in finery and perfumed, but because it is safe and cocksure and promises everything as surely as if it had been there. An altar to God ? All right, we will sacrifice calves. An altar to Moloch ? It is better still ; there is no lack of children for burning. No matter what as long as we are told plainly what is required of us ; as long as there is no thinking to be done, and we are not commanded to think for ourselves.

" We could even stand truth, on condition, of course, that truth first cut its nails and did not tear our eyes out whilst talking ; on condition also that it did not run about naked and barefooted in the streets, did not hobnob with tailors' and cobblers' apprentices. Another thing, where are we living ? Under straw, wooden, and even stone roofs, but always in old, dry houses, and we want truth not to run about with a flaming torch in her hand. A tiny candle in a big lantern is much safer. Coloured panes are more beautiful and better. Whether the earth be rotating round the sun or vice versa is all the same to the pious minister and his wife ; the principal thing is to stick to what has once been said and not to think differently. Both the minister and the leaders of the community intensely dislike questions and riddles, to rack the head and cudgel the brain."

" Why are you so dead against the minister and the leaders of the community ? "

" Are they not supposed to be the best ? Every man, even the best and noblest, leaves some corner in his brain unoccupied. It is his Holy of Holies where no one, not even himself, is ever admitted. In this corner no plough-ing and no sowing is allowed ; the old thorn must not be disturbed, let it grow wild.

" These are bad times now. Women are emancipating themselves ; they are refusing to take off their earrings and hand them over to fashion golden calves out of them. The prophets have all died out one after the other ; angels are no longer revealing themselves. Since the automatic carpet-cleaner has expelled the broom from the house, witches have nothing to ride upon. To cast lots is out of fashion. It is good enough for the flapper to tear up a beautiful daisy and repeat : ' He loves me, loves me not,' or for a college boy to ask the same question whilst count-ing the buttons of his uniform. All this is good enough in love matters and for young folks ; it is not respectable where old people are concerned and social questions are at stake.

" Well, then what do we do ? We hate racking our brains, thinking for ourselves, and so we have invented a new sort of witchcraft, a new method of casting lots. We call it rules, mottoes, slogans, high-sounding words ; whatever you like if only we need not think. Every rule, every motto, every slogan, each high-sounding word is a magnet drawing the souls, as if they had been so much dust. The dust of the souls sticking to the magnet are the cliques, sets, groups, societies, parties.

" A motto is a good thing, and a high-sounding word is very useful. People have broken a window pane in your house, and the howling of wild wolves is penetrating into your room, disturbing your sleep ? All you have to do is to snatch up some ' ism '—some high-sound ' ism '— stop the hole with it, and continue to sleep undisturbed.

" A tiny worm with a brass snout has entered your ear, crept up to your brain and is boring—boring enough to drive you mad ? Snatch up a motto or a slogan and begin to shout, as for instance, ' The watch on the Rhine.' To sing is even better still. You need not be a German for it. Shout, sing, and the tiny worm will fall asleep.

" If you have not enough wool in your head to knit out an entire system or theory, no matter. Make big holes and fill them in with mottoes, with high-sounding words, and you will be a great philosopher. You will be supposed to understand heaven and earth, and certainly your own life."

" But what is it you want after all ? "

" What I want," said Ratman, " what I want is that people should not tear out their good eyes and put in their stead coloured and smoked glasses. I want people not to stuff their hearts and brains with high-sounding words. I want people to think for themselves."

" And wherein consists your new idea ? "

" My new idea is to found a society without any ' isms,' without coloured glasses ; a society whose members will not be ashamed to go about in the streets with a point of interrogation upon their foreheads. The members of the society will never try to persuade either themselves or others that they know everything and are able to heal every disease."

" And what will your society do ? "

" It will think and study, it will want to know everything, to get to the bottom of everything. When a member of the society hears a high-sounding word he will ask himself, and others, what this word really meant, what it promised, and if it did promise anything whether it was solvent and one could rely on its promise. When a member of the society hears some saying, he will ask himself and others to explain the real meaning of the saying, he will try to find out wherein lay its witchcraft, its attraction. And when he sees that it is only a fancy, an imagination, then he will prove that it is nothing but a lie."

Shammai Ratman grows enthusiastic :

" It will be the duty of every member of the society to fight against deceit, swindles, dreams, and empty words."

" And in the place of dreams and empty words ? "

" The society will give new ideas."

In a word, Shammai Ratman proposes to establish a factory of new ideas. This only God alone is able to do. A factory must have raw material, where will he take it ? And whilst listening to Ratman's words, methought that I saw a wonderful picture in the air.

I saw the storm-tossed waves of the ocean—a steamer in distress, one wave tossing it to the other, not far away are rocks against which the ship may be hurled and broken ; the sky is growing darker and darker, and the last stars are disappearing, the passengers see each other only during the flashes of lightning, and each flash is followed by a clap of thunder.

And not only the ship's crew, but all the passengers are anxious to save the ship, all are working hard. Small groups of frightened and nervous people are scattered all over the deck, in each group one man is commanding, giving instructions, and telling the others to *do* something, and all are working and exerting themselves. When the passengers grow tired, a few loud, high-sounding passionate words are uttered, and once more people become enthusiastic, gather new strength, and continue to exert themselves and to work hard.

One man suddenly leaves the groups, exclaiming aloud :

" We are working without intelligence, without knowledge, we are only obeying high-sounding words, ' isms ' and again ' isms.' We had better *think* ! "

And he walks away to a corner. Whilst the ship is in distress, is cracking and drowning, whilst the thunder is clapping—and the people are working with all their might —*he* is *thinking*.

THE END

GLOSSARY

Alshech, Moses, famous Rabbi who lived in the sixteenth century ; author of lectures on the Holy Scriptures.

Atj, word signifying indifference.

Ayn Yaakov, title of a work containing the Haggadic portions of the Talmud.

Baal-Akkeda, title of a Hebrew work, a commentary on the Pentateuch.

Baal Tekia, horn-blower in the synagogue on New Year's Day.

Baba Mezia, title of one of the tractates of the Talmud. It treats of man's responsibility with regard to the property of his fellow-men, property of which he is a trustee.

Batlen, a beggar student ; an idler, lazy bones, good for nothing.

Batlonim, pl. of *batlen*.

Beth-Hamidrash, synagogue, academy.

Cabbala, Jewish mysticism ; mystic philosophy of the Jewish religion.

Cantonist, Jewish boy taken as a soldier during the reign of Nicholas I, Tsar of Russia. The boys were called Cantonists until the age of 18, when they were incorporated in the regular army.

Cheder, schoolroom.

Dayan, an ecclesiastical judge ; an associate of a Rabbi.

Duties of the Heart, title of a famous ethical work by Bachya Ibn Pakuda who lived in Spain in the first half of the eleventh century.

Great Sabbath, the Sabbath preceding the Feast of the Passover.

Habdalah, benediction of the cup at the close of Sabbaths and holidays.

Halah, loaf of white bread baked for Sabbaths and holidays.

Hassidim, a Jewish religious sect formed in the eighteenth century by Israel Baal Shem Tob (Besht). This sect assigns the first place in religion not to dogma and ritual but to emotion of faith and sentiment.

Jeshibah, Rabbinical college.

Kaddish, prayer for the dead, recited daily during the first eleven months of the year of mourning.

Kamarinskaya, a Russian song.

Kav-Hayashar, title of a work.

Kiddush, benediction of the cup on Sabbaths and holidays.

Koiletsh, twisted oblong loaf of white bread, baked for festive occasions.

Korban Minha, title of a lady's prayer-book.

Kosher, proper for use, food prepared according to Jewish dietary laws.

Kuggel, Sabbath pudding.

Lehavdil, to distinguish between, I beg to distinguish; an expression used when inferiors are mentioned with superiors, e.g., the Rabbi and the yokel *lehavdil—si parva licet componere magnis*.

Leviathan, the big fish, which, according to Jewish tradition, will be served to the pious at the Messianic banquet.

Litvak, Lithuanian Jew; Polish Jews, as a rule, have a contempt for their Lithuanian co-religionists.

Lokshen, macaroni, vermicelli.

Love of Zion, title of a famous Hebrew novel by A. Mapu, written under the influence of the Romantic school.

Maharsha, a commentary to the Talmud.

Masoltov, or *Mazoltov*, good luck.

Megale Temirin, title of a mystical work.

Melamed, teacher, instructor; also used in the sense of someone who is anything but smart or a man of the world.

Mezouman, company of three to say grace after meals; grace said in the company of three is regarded as more solemn.

Midrash, Haggadic and homiletical work.

Mishnah, a portion of the Talmud.

Missnagdim, adversaries of Hassidism.

Mummeshi, mother dear.

Nebbich, poor thing!

Oko, a game of cards.

Ou-vah, Russian word, meaning *oh! how terrible!*

Passover-Haggada, the reading book for the first two Passover nights, relating the exodus from Egypt.

Pourim, or *Purim*, the Feast of Esther.

Rakia, sky.

Rashi, Solomon Yitzhaki's commentary to the Pentateuch and the Talmud. The letters are the initials of Rabbi Solomon Yitzhaki.

Rebbe, Rabbi.

Rebbetzin, the wife of a Rabbi or a teacher.

Reshit Hochmah, title of a devotional work.

Rosh-Jeshiba, principal of a Rabbinical college.

Samovar, tea-urn.

Shadhan, marriage broker.

Shadhanim, pl. of *shadhan*.

Shekhinah, Divine presence, majesty, or splendour of God.

Shlach-Manuth, Purim present making.

Shmah Yissroel, " Hear o Israel."

Shmoneh-Essreh, Eighteen benedictions, portion of daily prayers.

Shor-habor, the mythological bull which, according to tradition, will be served to the pious at the Messianic banquet.

Shtraymel, fur cap.

Shuhl, synagogue.

Talith, praying shawl.

Talith Katan, small talith, four-fringed garment of wool.

Talmud, the work containing the traditional and canonical laws of the Jews. It consists of two parts : the *Mishnah* and the *Gemara*.

Talmud-Torah, school of religious lore.

Torah, The Law, Holy Writ, doctrine.

Tosafot, commentary to the Talmud.

Trepak, a Russian song.

Trinenyou, diminutive of Trinah.

Trineshou, diminutive of Trinah.

Tseno-Urenoh, title of a work, a ladies' Pentateuch in Yudæo-German (Yiddish) translation.

Tsholent, food cooked in a covered oven, prepared on Friday for the Sabbath.

Unberufen, may Heaven help and preserve him or her.

Yosele, endearing term, diminutive of Yosel or Yossel.

Zohar, Cabbalistic work.

NOTES

Page 23.

1. During the week of mourning it is customary for the mourners to sit on low stools or even on the floor.

2. Immediately after the burial of the body, the soul is supposed to be still hovering in the death-chamber. Here it cleanses itself in the glass of water, afterwards drying itself with a towel or a rag placed at its disposal.

Page 24.

1. The man who performs the operation of circumcision usually lets grow a long and sharp finger-nail enabling him to perform the additional operation of *Periah,* or laying bare of the glans, which the Rabbis had instituted.

Page 26.

1. Orthodox Jews who only partake of food prepared in strict accordance with the Jewish dietary laws abstain from using the cooking utensils of the Gentiles and even of Jews who do not observe the dietary laws.

Page 28.

1. The finger-nails which, according to the Rabbis of the Talmud, are to be pared on Fridays must not be cut in the order of the fingers, otherwise certain misfortunes are supposed to follow. This is an old Persian superstition which spread among the Jews. Pious Jews never throw away these parings but either burn or bury them.

Page 30.

1. Euphemistic expression for " when we die." The speaker thus expresses the pious wish that either he himself or the person he is speaking about will reach the ripe age of 120 years, even as Moses did.

2. The souls of the very pious, before coming down to earth are supposed, according to tradition, to be dwelling beneath the Divine throne of glory.

Page 63.

1. The soup served to the bride and bridegroom in a separate room immediately after the religious ceremony. The bridal pair are expected to fast until after the marriage ceremony.

Page 64.

> 1. On the Sabbath preceding the day on which the marriage ceremony takes place it is customary to call up to the Law in the Synagogue not only the bridegroom but also other members of the two families.

Page 65.

> 1. Allusion to the words used by Jacob when he made his compact with Laban. Laban was a master in trickery, and Jacob suspected that he would deceive him. He therefore took care to state as clearly and explicitly as possible that he would serve him for " Rachel, his younger daughter," so as to leave to the Aramæan no loophole and excuse for breaking the compact. Hence the expression : " Rachel, your younger daughter," i.e., clearly and explicitly when dealing with individuals who are not particularly scrupulous or trustworthy.

Page 70.

> 1. It is an obligation for every pious Jew to eat three meals during the Sabbath day. The third meal is partaken of immediately after the afternoon prayers.

Page 89.

> 1. Orthodox Jewish women are not allowed to show their own hair once they are married. In former times the hair of the bride was shaved off on the day following the marriage ceremony.

Page 126.

> 1. A famous wonder-rabbi who, on account of his habit of using but few words, was known as the *Taciturn*.

Page 142.

> 1. It is customary among pious Jews to intercede on behalf of persons dangerously ill or dying, by reading in Synagogue the Psalms of David.

Page 159.

> 1. It was and still is customary in Poland and Russia for the townspeople to offer free meals to the student of a Rabbinical college. Each householder in turn invites the student to his house on a certain day of the week, and hence the guest was said to *eat days*.

Page 161.

> 1. Isaac Luria, the founder of modern Cabbala and of mysticism, who lived in the sixteenth century.

Page 169.

1. So called on account of the *Selihot* (pl. of *Silihah*) or penitential prayers recited at dawn during the week preceding the New Year and the days intervening between the New Year and the Day of Atonement.

2. The " awful days " or the " days of awe " begin with the New Year and end with the Day of Atonement. They are also called the ten penitential days. During these days the Lord is supposed to be seated on His throne judging His creatures, and Jews pray for mercy and repent of their sins.

Page 178.

1. Rabbi Elijah, the Gaon of Vilna, who lived in the eighteenth century. He was an antagonist of Hassidism.

Page 189.

1. There existed a superstitious belief among Jews in Russia and Poland that the meritorious deed of leading an orphan girl under the nuptial canopy within the precincts of the cemetery, had the power to stop an epidemic and to defy the angel of death.

Page 197.

1. According to tradition it is supposed to be proof manifest of a pious life for a man to die during the month of Nissan, the month in which the Feast of Passover takes place.

Page 203.

1. According to legend, Joshua, the son of Nun, who once stopped the sun in its course, is supposed to be the " man in the moon."

Page 206.

1. According to some of the Rabbis, Esther was not a peerless beauty, but rather pale of complexion, and hence it was really a miracle that the mighty ruler fell in love with her and preferred her to all the other beautiful women.